The Afterpains

Anna Julia Stainsby

RANDOM HOUSE CANADA

PUBLISHED BY RANDOM HOUSE CANADA

www.penguinrandomhouse.ca

This novel contains scenes and discussion of suicide, physical abuse, and infant death that may be sensitive to some readers.

LIBRARY AND ARCHIVES CANADA CATALOGUING IN PUBLICATION
Title: The afterpains / Anna Julia Stainsby.
Names: Stainsby, Anna Julia, author.
Identifiers: Canadiana (print) 20220485933 | Canadiana (ebook) 20220485976 |
ISBN 9781039006942 (hardcover) | ISBN 9781039006959 (EPUB)
Subjects: LCGFT: Novels.
Classification: LCC PS8637.T345 A69 2024 | DDC C813/.6—dc23

Text design: Lisa Jager
Jacket design: Lisa Jager
Image credits: painting by Kathrine Leigh Holley

Printed in Canada

2 4 6 8 9 7 5 3 1

Penguin
Random House
RANDOM HOUSE CANADA

For my daisy chain of women

VIVIAN

THIS IS WHAT HAPPENS when your family won't cut the cord.
You're left tethered, floating above them, watching their lives
unfold from a waiting room. Over time, you become a witness to
mundanity, bitterness, triumph, a legion of other states that follow
after they lose you. You watch them go through the motions. Living,
truly living, takes longer to relearn. You catch glimpses of it, rare
moments that suggest that, eventually, you will be able to rest. But
these come few and far between in some families. Mine included.

Right now, I am watching my mother, Rosy, tear up in a car
parked outside the supermarket. She is sitting beside a woman my
mother has only met once before, at a parent-teacher night years ago.
Her name is Isaura, and her daughter, Mivi, means just about everything to my brother. They're in the old Toyota where their children
lost their virginity to each other. Neither of the mothers knows this,
of course. I only know because I died nineteen years ago and have
seen just about everything ever since.

It's almost been two decades now, yet it's still too difficult for my mother to let go. Leading up to each anniversary of my death, my father and brother tense up, wondering how she'll handle it. It's the big question on everyone's mind come August. In our family at least. Everyone else seems concerned only with squeezing all the pulp out of summer. Most people seem happier that time of year, especially in Toronto, where heat is fleeting. But suffering isn't softened by warm weather in our house. If anything, it exacerbates it. Brings it to a boiling point.

We're months away from my anniversary, though. It's just begun to snow in Toronto. As I watch my mother, I count each flake collecting on the windshield, each second it takes for them to melt before the two women.

It's unlike my mother to get deep with anyone, especially someone she barely knows, but some maternal instinct led her into the car, sequestered her there with a woman she will now be forever yoked to. They idle for about half an hour, the windows foggy from conversation and Isaura's misty eyes.

When my mother opens the door to get out, Isaura reaches her hand across the console and holds on to my mother's. She thanks her. They both nod, an agreement to stay quiet, to keep the secret safe. My mother steps to the side and watches Isaura drive out of the lot, gazing at the warm gold of the blinker like it's a lighthouse.

As soon as the car's out of sight, my mother walks back into the grocery store to buy the bread she promised she'd bring home. The mantra that got her through that day she found out she was pregnant with me pops back into her head. It's the one she uses every time there's an unknown. *Gather the data first*, she thinks, *then make a plan.* She swipes the bread through the self-checkout scanner. Best to limit interactions when she's on the verge of a spiral.

When my mother gets in her car, she allows herself a few tears, stops before the point of no return, before her eyes get swollen and tender and there's no pretending. She thumbs the grey streak of makeup that's gathered in her laugh lines; she won't let it give her away. *Gather the data and then make a plan. It's time to make a plan.* For the first time in almost twenty years, she believes that she might actually be capable of changing, making things right for our family.

She sits there a while longer and writes a bullet-point plan on her phone. She's not instinctive like Isaura. She needs an outline, a to-do list. A structure with measurable steps like *See how much is left in the emergency fund* and *Get Eddie to Detroit*. Once she's done writing the list, she whispers it to me.

"All right, my girl," she says, a tinge of hope coating her words. "This. This is our new plan."

ROSY

I DON'T DREAD YOUR BIRTHDAY. On the first one without you, your father and I spent most of the day on the couch together like we did when you were alive. I wonder how much of it was muscle memory. Placing ourselves exactly where we'd been the last time we were all together, my belly almost as swollen as it had been then. On that first birthday, our neighbour Lorraine dropped off a cake in the morning. Some people might've found it strange, insensitive even, to bake a cake as garish as the one she'd made us. Angel food (how fitting), smothered in buttercream frosting, the borders piped, the top lush with marzipan roses. It was a cake that must've taken hours of meticulous work, pinching almond paste into coin-sized flowers, painting each petal until it blushed with realism.

Initially, the sight of your name in sugary, cursive lettering felt like an affront—I hadn't written your name in months, and there Lorraine was, adding hearts to the *is* like she'd been an old friend. Still, I could appreciate the hours she had dedicated to your memory.

As limited as my appetite was in those days of round-the-clock morning sickness, I savoured each sliver with that in mind.

I remember bringing the cake up to bed, setting it in the middle of the comforter, two forks stabbed into it. Crumbs littered the sheets, small dollops of icing, too. But we didn't really care about those things on your birthday. What mattered was honouring your life. Between bites, we talked about your navy eyes, sure that they'd just been that shade that newborns grow out of, wondering if you would have inherited your father's hazel eyes or my green ones. We recalled the feeling of your feathery hair, your padded feet, that gummy smile that you only treated us to once, milk drunk. We wondered whether the child I was carrying would look like you or not, unable to admit that either way would break our hearts.

Once our room got too hot, we made our way to the living room and pulled out your photo album. Your father had put it together around month ten. I can't remember whether he'd wanted to mark the occasion—your being gone longer than I'd carried you—or just thought it was time. He'd developed all 117 photographs of you and slid each one into the plastic sleeves of a photo album. Going through the book didn't make us cry. The photos were all so happy. But then we retrieved your box from the top of the storage closet.

From then on, each birthday that we summoned the courage to open the box would lead to an excavation. The careful removal of the onesies, which your father and I would pass between us, lifting each one up to our noses and making sure to set them back in the pile before any tears could alter the smell. We were stingy about every inhalation in an effort to prolong that bit of you. The sweet, powdery, milkiness of you. We'd paw through each scratch mitten, each pacifier, each pair of socks that we'd ever wrangled onto you, each burp blanket that we'd never had the time to wash. That was what would make us cry.

When there was nothing left, no more tears, no more memories, no more projections about what you might've grown into in the past year, we'd settle onto the couch that had moved with us from Detroit, where you were born, to Toronto, where we try to live without you. If hunger came, we'd order pizza like we had done in those first days with you. We'd eat it out of the box, in front of the TV, flipping through channels until we found something mind-numbing enough to distract us from missing you, if only for a few minutes. That was all we strove for back then.

It's different now.

We barely even talk about your birthday. Not since the bottle incident. On the birthday that followed what I did to Eddie, both he and your father stayed out all day. That has since become our tradition. Nobody mentions it, nobody risks "triggering" me—I think that's how your brother put it. It's funny, almost, to think that I could forget if they didn't remind me. But I let them stay quiet.

Today, like the last few birthdays, I stay home, alone, sipping coffee on the reading chair where no one ever sits, plucking through your album. On the arm of the chair, I've set my half-eaten piece of Black Forest cake, a layer of icing smeared against the thin plastic container. Every so often, I swipe my finger across it to scoop up some of the chocolate shavings. I let them melt on my tongue before reaching for more.

Your father and I still have cake for breakfast on your birthday. Eddie used to, until he understood the reason behind the tradition. That's when he started pushing away plates, asking us how we could stomach so much sugar first thing in the morning. I baked them every year after our move, but eventually I stopped to spare us your brother's disapproval. Now I just buy us each a single slice from the grocery store. Chocolate for me, red velvet for your father. He wakes up early on your birthday and we don't have our cake together anymore. I picture him eating his slice by the bay window this morning before going off to work, and keeping a bite or two to taste the sweetness again after lunch.

My ritual is simpler now that I spend your birthday alone. I eat my cake and go through your album, stroking the lilac embroidery on the cover that reads *BABY* in block letters. Slowly, I scan each photograph, to pace myself but also to see whether I find anything new. A clue, maybe, something I missed that might've saved you. For the most part, I just spot old clothing of mine I don't remember getting rid of.

Usually, people only print out their best or favourite photos, not the ones with blinking eyes and thumbed corners. But we wanted to keep them all. Each shot of you in the plastic bassinet at the hospital. The close-ups of the wristband inscribed with *Baby Girl Powell*. All the angles of your tiny body strapped into the car seat on the drive home. As I raise another forkful of cake to my mouth, I flip the pages. I go through all the firsts and lasts. Naps on the couch. Bath time. Pyjamas that hung too big on you, making you look like a tiny doll. Looking at the photos feels like taking a sip of water when you don't realize how thirsty you are. But I have to pace myself on your birthday. I can't drown in the memories. I can't open your box anymore. I haven't in years now. Mostly, because I'm afraid of the smell. That it's not there anymore. That no bit of you, even a particle, exists anymore.

So, instead, when I'm done with your album, I work. I spend the rest of the day in my home office, reconciling. I make things make sense. It helps to be sucked in by the cleanness of numbers, the reward of solving something that didn't add up before. A couple months after Eddie was born, I started working again. Ever since we'd lost you, I'd been diving in and out of lows so deep that not even your brother's arrival could pull me out. As strange as it might sound, numbers were the only thing, I felt, that could save me. Work wasn't exactly a cure, but it did feel like somewhat of a balm. I'd had my own accounting practice for a few years by then. Before Eddie was old enough to send to daycare, I had a sitter help out a few afternoons a week. Whenever she was here, whenever Eddie slept, whenever your father got home, I worked. On nights I couldn't manage to sleep, I could turn to numbers. Distract myself. Solve problems that weren't my own.

Before I open my computer to begin working, I plug my phone into the speakers by my desk and start the playlist I made for your father's fiftieth a couple years ago. It's a compilation of the musicians he and I used to watch in bars and clubs when we were young. The Gories, Big Chief, The Romantics. They're some of the only Detroit memories that I can stomach, probably because they feel so removed from you, from me as a mother. I was barely a woman when we'd danced to them. Since no one's home, I turn the volume nearly all the way up to drown out more thoughts of you. To try to move on from your photos and dive into my spreadsheets, fill my head with music and math. For at least the duration of fifty songs, I try to forget that you were born twenty years ago today and that I miss you just as fiercely as I did that first birthday.

In the afternoon, my eyes begin to sting from staring at the screen. Your father gave me a pair of blue-light glasses last Christmas, but I always forget to wear them. I run down to get the case from the kitchen, grab the remnants of the cake slice, and head back upstairs. As I collect icing on my spoon, the sugar making me swivel in my desk chair, I think about my plan, *our* plan, for this week. I think of Isaura, her last call, the one that changed things for me. I never reached out after that, even though I drafted what felt like hundreds of possible responses over the weeks that followed. My plan to mend things with my family got in the way.

I wonder what your father would make of it if he knew. I wonder if he'd think this plan is the best idea I've had in decades. If he'd go get us more cake to celebrate, sit on the couch by my desk, a plate balanced on his lap, and talk about everything. He'd believe me when I'd say I want things to be different. And just after I'd make my declaration, as if on cue, Eddie would knock on the door, and we'd get up and migrate to the kitchen to make a toast to you. We would not just ignore your birthday. We would celebrate it. And then we would live.

But things can't be that simple. That much I know. The image of the three of us dissolves, and I'm back to scooping warm icing into my mouth, alone.

By ten p.m., I've given up on working and returned to my bedroom. There's a book on my nightstand, a Mother's Day gift from Eddie, but I don't bother picking it up. My vision is blurred from twelve hours in front of spreadsheets, and regardless, I know I won't be able to focus. Instead, I just lie in bed and shut my eyes, desperately trying to fall asleep. I try not to check the clock while I toss around. It'd only infuriate me to know just how long it takes for my brain to surrender to my body's fatigue. I've kicked the sheets off the bed and wrapped half the duvet around my legs about a dozen times. It's muggy in our room. I could get up and open the window, but I don't know that it'd do much good. According to my weather app, it felt like thirty-four degrees earlier today. I can't imagine it'd be much cooler now. Plus, I'm afraid that much movement would be too stimulating. It'd just set me back in the process.

I push the covers off my torso and rest my hands on my stomach. There's a comfort in cupping the dough that never fully flattened after

Eddie. The roundness of it fits smoothly in my palms. Tonight, though, it feels emptier than usual. The thought of talking to your father later tonight filled me with nausea, and the only thing I managed to eat today was that slice of cake. In the early evening, I wrote down a short script like I sometimes do before a phone call. I don't think many wives do that before speaking with their husbands. It settled some nerves, but not enough that I could ingest anything other than tea.

Hours later, my hunger seems to have overpowered the nausea, and I can't seem to sleep without addressing it. I almost text your father to ask him to pick me up a burger on his way home, but I stop myself. I craved burgers when I was pregnant with you, especially in the middle of the night. It feels unfair to remind him of that today. So I continue to shift the duvet between my legs, convincing myself that it's too hot to eat anyway.

Eventually, a key turns in the front door. It's not until I hear footsteps climbing to the second floor that I know it's your father. Eddie must still be out with his friends.

Once your father undresses and slips into bed, I drag my fingers across his back, brushing away a few pearls of whisky-smelling sweat. He kisses my cheek, and I almost laugh. The liquor is practically seeping out of his pores.

"How was your day?" he asks.

"Okay," I reply. "Yours?"

"All right. Cake was good."

"Always the best part," I say, rolling over, away from him.

Even though it's dark, I can't bring myself to look at him. I focus on the sharp-edged numbers of the alarm clock. When I shut my eyes, a red *01:09* imprints itself on my lids. I wonder whether he will manage to remember what I'm about to say to him come morning. Perhaps he'll just think it was all a dream, a drunken half-memory. His breathing has already slowed. I'm not sure he's even still awake.

"I want to go back," I say, finally.

For a moment, I hear nothing. Not even the soft whistle that he normally emits when he's asleep. I roll back over to look at him and check. I can tell his eyes are open from the gloss shining in the darkness. He says nothing.

"I'll be good," I hear myself whispering, as though I'm a child. "It'll be different."

"Can we talk about this tomorrow?" he replies, telling me more than asking.

If I say no, I might ruin it all. If I cry, he will think I'm unwell again. I can't have that. I muster an "Mm-hmm," then squeeze his hand to let him know I'm fine. *See? Everything is fine. I am different already.*

I don't sleep. The week has just begun.

MIVI

MI VI—TOO PURE to be butchered, even by the most gringo of gringos. Two syllables, the first particularly worn, and the second, well, a rhyme. It's easier said than Yessenia, my real name, which was pretty much retired after it was written on my birth certificate. *Mi vi*—"my life"—came more naturally to Mami. It was a nickname that stuck, one I carried outside of our home when I wrote it with an upside-down *M* on my name tag on the first day of school.

No one stumbles through the pronunciation, but the novelty of it leaves a taste—one that people can't seem to identify, one that rolls around in their mouths and forces the question out: "Wait, what *are* you?"

Now I always laugh. I've tried out different responses: defensiveness makes people uncomfortable, sarcasm gets them all jumpy, neutrality feels sterile, so I go with light humour.

"Honduran. Little colonist blood, too, obviously."

It clears up the question of my appearance, the reason I'm lighter than my mami. It's better than how my abuela would explain my skin tone. Despite my pleas as a child, she'd refer to my father as "the splash of milk but nothing more," an analogy that was horrifically more graphic than she intended. I mean, she wasn't wrong—it's all he was. The reason I have a little less melanin. The reason people turn their heads and why every first exchange becomes a guessing game attempting to piece together furry brows, thick hair, light or dark skin (depending on who you ask). *Argentinian? Iranian? Moroccan? Indigenous?* No one ever gets it right. Full Honduran, even though my father could almost pass for a gringo. According to Mami at least.

Every so often, I'll hear my name called and think about how unusual it is for people to call you "their life" without even knowing it. Tonight, when Eddie yells it from across the streetcar tracks, I'm struck by that strangeness again. Maybe it's because I've never heard it that loud before, carrying like an echo in the empty street. Roncesvalles only ever gets this quiet a few times a year—during those dead days of winter, when the temperature drops below minus twenty, and when the August heat gets so oppressive that people flee the city for cottage country.

Eddie and I work on the same street, so once or twice a week, I'll get cut early at the restaurant and he'll be stocking the grocery store late, and we'll meet up before going out. Sometimes I get to take an open bottle of wine from the restaurant, and we'll drink it in the back of the streetcar while playing our games. The human names we choose for every dog on board get funnier with every sip, as do the backstories we make up for their owners. Recently, Eddie's been nabbing expiring produce—cherries at the end of May, peaches in July—to add to our streetcar indulgences. As he jumps over the tracks, his bags bouncing off his shoulders, I can see that he's tucked a carton of blueberries under his arm for us tonight.

"This is my contribution!" I shout, perking up from the bench

I've been waiting for him on. I wave my cigarette under the street light. His mouth widens into a smile as he squints at the gold filter.

The cigarettes, a pack of pink-and-gold Russian Sobranies, had been his gift to me after our falling-out. They were prettier and a lot more expensive than the ones we usually smoked together. I was sure he'd partly bought them for the aesthetic. On our first shoot since last summer, he got me to smoke one of them. I laughed when Eddie showed me the screen and I saw how much cooler the cigarettes made me seem in the photos. As he brought the viewfinder back up to his eye, he moaned over the fact that we could never be paid to advertise cigarettes. "Could've put you through med school," he said, the shutter sounding out. "The smoking doctor."

This morning, I found the pack in an old purse I hadn't touched since the spring. The cigarettes had gone stale, but I couldn't bring myself to throw them out. Beyond the sentimental value, they weren't easy to find. When Eddie had given them to me last November, he'd refused to tell me where he'd bought them. "The secrecy is part of the mystique," he'd whispered, before lighting one to share.

"God, those must taste like shit now," he says, joining me on the bench and taking a puff anyway. With his other hand, he sets his camera bag and the carton of berries between us. I reach across them to squeeze his knee. It's too hot for hugging, even at eleven thirty.

"Everyone's at Christie," I say.

"Again? This is getting a little predictable."

I shrug and take the cigarette back to put it out under the bench. "Streetcar's delayed by the way. Another five minutes."

While we wait, Eddie slides off his backpack and pulls out his Nalgene bottle. After taking the first sip, he passes it over to me. The spice of whisky wafts up to my nose.

"How was your shift?" I ask, before taking a swig. Brown liquor feels too hot in this weather, so I palm a handful of blueberries. I drop them on my tongue, thinking they'll be a refreshing chase, but instead, the berries gush, all hot and liquidy like they've just been fried. Eddie must've picked them from the stands outside the store. I take another sip to rid my mouth of the taste while he smirks at my revulsion.

"Better than Sunday's. That was a fucking brutal double to do hungover." Eddie grabs the bottle, takes a drink, then places it back in my hands as if it belongs to me. *Last sip*, I tell myself. "Oh, you'll like this: a guy came in today asking for artichoke. So I bring him to produce and he's just looking at me like he doesn't understand why I brought him there, so I point to the artichokes and he picks one up so gently like it's a fucking dragon egg or something and just goes, 'I thought artichoke was a fish.'"

I throw my head back and clap my hands over my mouth, half choking on whisky. The story wasn't even that funny, but it was the delivery, how deadpan Eddie can be. He can't hold the tone once I avert my gaze to avoid a spit take, though. Instead, he starts repeating, "Michael, Michael"—an inside joke from our dog-naming game that had me sent out of History for a breather in grade ten. The concept of a WWI dog named Michael wasn't technically funny, but when Eddie pointed to the grainy photo in our textbook and whispered, "Michael," with a straight face, I lost it. It's still just as funny to me.

When I met Eddie, the fact that we shared a sense of humour came as a surprise to me. He was the first boy I ever befriended. Before him, I hadn't considered that I could have anything in common with a boy—I already struggled enough with the girls. By the time I could speak enough English in New York to make my own friends, Mami and I were running away. Then, when I started elementary school in Toronto, some kids laughed at my accent. Others fixated on my inability to draw an *M*, calling me "Wivi" until the joke eventually fizzled out. At the beginning of grade two, Mami started bribing me with multicoloured marbles to get me to join games at recess instead of literally sitting on the sidelines. Everyone was collecting marbles then, and they were a big-enough incentive to convince me to try to make friends. That's how I met Maja and Zadie—an inseparable duo and the two fastest girls in our grade's daily game of red light, green light. They were the only kids who invited me to their homes, who made room for me. Once we found each other, three first-generation daughters who felt like home, I figured I was set.

And I was, really, until I met Eddie. We ended up subwaying home together on our first day of grade seven, and I remember thinking that not all boys were gross after all. That you could talk to some of them effortlessly, and that they could make you laugh so hard you missed your stop. For the rest of the year, we'd often go to the end of the green line and turn back around to prolong our time together, entertained by the games we made up.

Ever since then, we've played. We've laughed. We've stayed up late. Whenever his hand brushes up against mine, it feels as electric as it did the first time, when I blushed in the rush-hour crowd.

That last thought forces me to shut my eyes, swallow hard, like some punishment might help rewire my brain, avoid thoughts of Eddie in that way altogether. The whisky burns my throat and I cough.

"Let's go cool down," Eddie says with a laugh as he shuffles off the bench. The streetcar screeches up Roncesvalles. Everything brightens as it approaches us.

On days when the heat is so unbearable that it triggers a city-wide warning, the pools stay open until eleven. Those are the days we don't go to Christie Pits before midnight. We rarely go swimming during the day, partly because we're usually working, but mostly because it's much more fun to sneak in at night when we can have the pool all to ourselves.

It's just past twelve when Eddie and I get to the park. We push the pool's recycling bin against the fence and hoist ourselves up to the metal pickets. Standing on the bin, Eddie reaches up and grabs on to the thick branch of the maple tree that weeps over the fence, and he swings down to the deck. I hop up next, lower his camera bag down to him on the deck, and then climb over. Eddie's hands wrap around my waist as I let go of the branch. I try not to focus on how they feel against the silk of my dress, how it somehow feels more erotic than him touching my skin. To distract myself, I think about the last time I climbed over with Zadie, the time she lost her balance and tore her thigh on the metal. Her parents got mad at both of us when they saw the gash the next morning. "You girls can't just trespass on city property," her mom said while rummaging through their cupboards for a bottle of hydrogen peroxide. "And if you're going to get that drunk, have the common sense to not be *parkouring* over sharp objects," her dad added. Zadie apologized to me for her parents, then asked her dad how he knew about parkour anyway.

She didn't need to apologize. I never minded when her parents scolded us—not when we were nine, tracking in snow and salt and staining their new carpet; not when we were fourteen, cutting class, and running into them at the mall; not when we were eighteen after pool hopping. It sounds strange to say that I liked it, but I did. There's a comfort in having someone worry about you even when you're technically an adult. And although Mami always seemed to be fretting over me, work took her away so often. It's not like I had any other family around, someone to care about what happened to me when she was gone.

"Mi!" Zadie yells out, waving as though we wouldn't have spotted the only group bobbing around in the pool tonight. She, Maja, and James paddle toward us.

I wave back, then start unbuttoning my dress as Eddie and I head over to our friends. We shed our clothes at the edge of the deck and jump in. The water is bath-warm, and it makes latching on to the girls feel childlike. I worked three doubles in a row and haven't seen them in almost a week, which is a long stretch for us. Maja says I look like I've grown in my absence, and Zadie claims that my boobs look bigger. As bored as I'm starting to get of Christie, I'm struck by the feeling that this night will one day be a core memory. Swimming in our underwear, laughing under the neon lights.

Like the realization has just hit him, too, Eddie hops out to set up his camera and starts filming. It's best he starts shooting right away anyway in case we get kicked out. We've had trouble before, and once the speakers come out, residents on the street inevitably call the cops.

Eddie pans across the deck, and I allow myself a second to look at him—to see the shape of him as his underwear clings to his body. While he focuses his lens on the slide, I hoist my body up onto the deck to reach into his backpack and dig around. Now that I've cooled down, I pull out the whisky and take a swig. Then another. As I set the bottle back on the deck, I can feel Eddie's eyes on me, and I turn toward him to see half of his grin peering out from behind the camera. This time, I can't keep it in. Whisky sprays out of my mouth and onto the pavement, coating it in gold droplets.

"Got it," Eddie says with a wink before shutting off the camera and jumping back in the pool.

"Don't use that!" I say, splashing him. "Delete it."

As the water settles, I can see his hands inching toward my hips under the surface, that grin widening as he gets closer. Before he can reach me, a voice by the fence shouts out to us.

Andersen Beckett drops down from the fence and runs toward the pool, his braids bouncing against his cheekbones. He's a new friend we met in Kensington last summer, a twenty-year-old artist who consistently introduced himself with his full name, often adding that he was a sculptor in the same breath. It verged on pretentious, but he was too charismatic to write off. The first time Eddie and I talked to Andersen, after spotting him half a dozen times at our usual spots, we realized we had more in common with him than the same taste in bars. I drunkenly told him about my connection to New York, and he and Eddie bonded over their love of Italian cinema. We all went to Antonioni showings at the Revue that summer.

Andersen's a sculpture major at Parsons and has been spending his time between studios in Brooklyn and Toronto. We all follow his updates on Instagram. Eddie even subscribes to his newsletter. He was the one who told me that Andersen is going to be hosting his first show—a collection of eighty-five phalluses sculpted with chewing gum—in Bed-Stuy at the end of the month. To Eddie, Andersen is *it*. Living out the artist's dream, with only a year on us. Whenever the two of them talk about making art, Eddie gets this glimmer in his eye that makes me smile. But when they inevitably get lost in romanticizing New York, I want to shake Eddie out of the fantasy, talk him out of relying on a merciless city like that to forge success in.

On the deck, Andersen strips down to his boxers and launches himself into the pool. As he treads through his wake, he kisses the girls on their cheeks and slaps the boys' wet palms.

"It's been too long! Good thing I thought to text this one," Andersen says, hooking his arm around Maja. They slept together a few times last summer. We teased her about being his next muse, how excited we were to see her vagina rendered in sticky tack at his next show. I raise my eyebrows at Maja, who, back in June, took a vow of celibacy for the summer. An experiment to write about in her "Sex & Relationships" column in her school's magazine. *Good luck,*

I mouth to her, and she smirks before reaching over and shoving me underwater. Andersen laughs as I emerge, then asks how everyone has been.

"How are *you*, man? You're killing it in New York!" James follows the compliment with a dragged-out "Fuuuuck," just in case Andersen doesn't know how in awe everyone is.

I look over at Eddie, whose hands are no longer near me but instead stroking the water's surface back and forth around him while he listens to Andersen describe his upcoming show. His pace speeds with each name drop, each accolade, each New Yorkism that Andersen can't help but dole out.

As they continue to talk, I sink back down in the pool, my ears filling with water, muffling the sounds around me. I know where the conversation is going. *Let's go to New York, take photos, make money. You should come, Mi. Andersen says that agent's still talking about you.* No matter how many times I say I'm not interested, Eddie won't relent. Maybe because I lived there, maybe because it would be easy for me to move there as a citizen, maybe because ever since Eddie pictured us in New York together, he can't seem to let go of that image, of best friends taking a leap like that together. I don't want to have the same talk again, to have to poke holes in a fantasy I can't share.

So they talk, and I sink deeper, until eventually I push myself off the floor of the pool, kicking toward the surface.

Since I know Mami's asleep (deeply, after book club wine), I invite Eddie inside. He walked me home after the pool, even after I'd told him I'd be fine alone.

"It's not even a real detour, Mi," he'd insisted, even though it was. I'd rolled my eyes, then agreed, *to be safe.* The truth was, I was happy to extend my time with him, to pull the night like taffy before we resigned ourselves to separate beds. By that point, I'd drunk enough to subdue the voice inside that said it was a bad idea to sit in bed together and pass a joint between us.

"Did we bug you back there? At the pool?" Eddie asks, sitting on the edge of the bed, lit up by my bedside lamp. The yellow bulb makes him seem more tan, his skin dewy with summer.

I fixate on the way his cheekbone reflects the light until I suspect too much time is passing before I answer. My eyelids feel heavy from the staring and the weed and the bottle of wine I'd finished with the girls on the deck. The last thing I want to do right now is pick up the New York conversation.

"You know how I feel about it all," I sigh, my gaze wandering around his face in a way that might seem natural. I know it probably doesn't, but I hope that he's high enough not to notice my eyes bouncing from his cheekbone to his forehead to his lips and back, studying him. "My answer isn't going to change."

Eddie passes the joint, then untucks his legs and stretches out so that he's lying close to me. The narrow space between us on the mattress verges on too intimate, without exactly crossing a line. I guess that's how you could characterize our entire relationship after we replaced the habit of sleeping together with smoking.

"Look," I say with a pause, unsure how to verbalize the ache in my chest that tightens when I think of my time in that city. I decide not to try to explain it. "Who knows if Andersen's agent friend would work out anyway. But *even* if it did, I know I would just be another token dark*ish* girl for a few shoots and then be stuck sitting in casting rooms alongside fourteen-year-old Swedes with smaller bodies who'd actually book the jobs."

Eddie clicks his tongue, then pauses before he opens his mouth again.

"You have a great body, Mivi."

I shoot him another eye roll, even though I can feel myself flush. He hasn't talked about me like that in months.

"My ass got too big. Andersen doesn't know what he's talking about."

"It's a good one," Eddie says, his eyes peering so deep into mine I feel as though we are both naked, like things have not changed after all.

I put the joint to my lips and inhale. It hasn't been a seamless transition back to being just friends, but Eddie is only this earnest when he's high. *Flirting is fine*, I tell myself when the lines blur. When the smoke goes to my head and I can feel myself teetering.

"You liked it," I say, biting at the corner of my lip before I can stop myself.

"I do," he says.

After a few beats of silence, he reaches over to brush away my hair, the bits stuck to my neck by the humidity. His fingers move so gently, as though he's afraid of snapping the strands.

"Ed," I whisper, low and tired. The way no one wants their name to be whispered. *Stop. Please don't.*

"I'm sorry," he says. "Habit, I guess."

I take one more hit before handing the joint back to him like it might help soothe the burn. When I can no longer take the silence, I inch myself toward the edge of the bed to reach for the window, winding the handle until a breeze and the sound of sirens come in to relieve us. I shut my eyes, breathe in the air. I can hear him inhaling, the tip of the joint crackling, and then the shuffling of his body as he makes his way toward me. Behind me, he wraps an arm across my chest. I open my eyes. He hands me what's left of the joint.

"Good night, Mi," he says.

With my left hand, I cover his and hold it tightly against my collarbone before saying good night, too. I study our hands together, the hook of our pinkies that inevitably happens when they're near. The burn on Eddie's fingers looks more translucent today. For a moment, I wonder if the humidity makes his skin more sensitive, if I'm hurting him at all. If I am, he doesn't say anything.

When I let go, Eddie walks out quietly. I stand up, leaning against the windowpane to finish the joint. As I exhale, the cloud of smoke trails into the air, blowing toward where Eddie is headed. *It's like part of me is going with him*, I think for a second. Then I put the joint out on the ashtray. I'm too high. Way too high.

VIVIAN

A FEW YEARS AFTER I WAS BORN, my father had a pound of flesh cut out of his thigh. The scar was the size of a meat loaf, sunk deep into his leg, and whenever Eddie caught sight of it, the thought of what a speck of melanoma could induce made him feel faint. My father didn't look at his scar much. Sometimes, he would even forget that he was missing a piece of his leg. At night, he'd shuffle under the covers, finger the dip in the skin, and think, *Oh right, it's gone.*

At the beginning, that was how my mother used to refer to me—gone, missing, away. It's what I was to her. A missing piece of her own body. Sometimes, she would wake up clutching her chest for her phantom limb of a child.

Eddie wants to use our family's stories of loss for his film, but he can't. Almost two decades have passed, but so far, it's been too raw for him to knead into art. So he films other things: his friends, their nights out drinking "cold tea" past last call in Chinatown; the city at dawn; Mivi, of course. He pieces together footage that he says gives him "real-life stone to carve into." Although he'd never admit it to anyone, he has a sneaking suspicion that he might become the Michelangelo of cinema. This hunch he has about being creatively gifted is often followed with a wave of self-doubt, but he's heard that this is how all the big filmmakers felt at the start of their careers.

My brother looks like an artist, a cliché almost, especially right now, sitting mute in front of our father at the kitchen table, dressed in all black. His bed-head is pulled back into a bun of four-day-old grease and curls. He's barely looked up from his laptop all morning, too focused on reviewing footage from the night before, flagging the best clips to use for his film-school applications. My father can tell he's hungover—Eddie is generally moody, but it's particularly pronounced today. When my father takes a seat in front of him, his nostrils flare at the scent of weed wafting off my brother. He resists making a comment about the smell—he has to break the Detroit news to Eddie and doesn't want to set him off.

"Ed," my father says, "you remember it's coming up?"

My brother groans. He'd have given our father more attitude had the caffeine kicked in, but instead, the *How the hell could I forget?* just floats behind the pinkness in his eyes. Of course he knows.

"We're going to Detroit for it. All of us. It's important to your mother."

"Why does she want to go back?" Eddie asks, still scanning his screen. "I just—we've never gone. She's never been again. So why—"

"Why now?" my father says, as he lifts his brow and his forehead wrinkles. "It's been twenty years. Sort of warrants something big, doesn't it?"

"I guess."

"Look," my father says, resting his forearms against the table, slowly, like he's afraid that any sudden movement might make his son bolt. "She wants to see it."

"You really think this is the best thing for Mom?" Eddie looks up from his screen, no longer able to hold back the question that they both know the answer to. *We are enabling her*, my brother wants to say. My father knows it, too, and yet he also can't say it.

"She's never been back, Ed. She's never seen the grave. I think we should do it for her," my father says, his voice lacking the confidence he's trying to display. "We'll just go away for a bit. We haven't done a trip together in a very long time."

Eddie clenches his jaw, then starts typing, hard, on his keyboard, like it'll exorcise some of his frustration. *This is a joke*, he thinks. *A joke with a big painful punchline at the end.* My father leans across the table and pushes the screen down on my brother's knuckles. Eddie's left hand recoils first. The one with the paper-thin skin, the one that burned when he was three.

"Please don't pretend this is a vacation," Eddie says.

"Fine. Look, Eddie—"

"Please—" Eddie shakes his head and opens his mouth to say more but stops. Instead, he retreats, pushes the chair back from the table and walks away. My father does not follow him.

The whole thing is reminiscent of the bottle incident. Another fight brought on by August, by me, by my mother's needs eclipsing everyone else's. A reminder of the fracture I've caused in my family.

Five Augusts ago, when Eddie was thirteen, I watched them fall apart in this same kitchen. On my birthday, my parents were supposed to go to a retirement party for Ian, my father's boss, who had given our family an opportunity to start over with his offer to join Ford's Canadian ad agency. As Ian's right hand, my father had gotten close to him, had grown comfortable enough to share morsels of his grief, which were met with compassion and standing offers to take time off when he needed. His generosity was a salve to my father.

My mother hadn't wanted to go to the party. My father thought it would be a good distraction. That was how he often framed his attempts at getting her to meet his friends and colleagues—a distraction from me. He'd invite her to happy hours, try to connect her with the women from his office. But she couldn't pretend around them, the other mothers especially. They all seemed too perfect, too happy. All they ever complained about was not having enough time with their children now that they were back at work. My mother would ask about the latest campaigns they'd worked on or the TV shows they were watching, but the conversation always seemed to circle back to their family. She hated herself for it, but she couldn't stand being around mothers. That night, though, my father thought, was different. It wasn't just about a work commitment; it was about showing up for a man who had known about the baggage my father was carrying from Detroit and who didn't doubt his ability to thrive again in the right environment, distanced from the most painful memories of me.

In the afternoon, my father bought a bottle of Scotch to gift to Ian—a *Mad-Men*-inspired inside joke. When he got home, my mother was sitting at the dining-room table, still dressed in pyjamas. He set the bottle down beside her and placed his hand over hers.

"I don't think I can do it, Desmond."

My father launched into the Rolodex of responses he'd collected over the years. "We need to keep living. We need to celebrate. To see people and socialize. We need to not let it consume us every year. She wouldn't want us to stop living. Come, please. Let's just go for an hour. You might even enjoy yourself. Please."

Her face crumpled, and she covered it with her palms. When my father reached for her shoulders, she recoiled. "You won't change my mind."

Eddie looked over from the bay window, where he'd been sitting, scrolling aimlessly on his phone as he listened, hoping that our mother would concede. He had been planning on inviting some friends over while they were out.

"Mom," he said. She looked up. "You can't . . ."

"I can't what? Make my own decisions?"

She stood up, then placed her palms flat on the table, like the stance vested her with more authority.

"Eddie, this is between your father and me."

For a moment, Eddie said nothing. He just looked at our father from across the room. Then, through locked teeth, he managed to say it slowly. "You can't keep doing this."

"Doing what exactly?" she asked.

My father mouthed at my brother to stop, *now*.

"*This*, every single year, all the drama over Vivian," Eddie said, his voice trembling slightly. He'd started. There was no going back. "It's been fifteen years, Mom. You have to move on."

For a second, she didn't say anything. He'd never uttered anything like that to her.

"Excuse me?" She inched her hands back from the table, her head cocked as though she'd misheard. My father was shouting at both of them to stop.

"She's dead. She died fifteen fucking years ago. Move. On. Stop punishing the rest of us because you couldn't keep her alive."

And then she did it. Picked up the bottle of Scotch, made her way to the bay window, and swung it. But it didn't shatter. For a moment, the whole room filled with the sound of the bottle hitting Eddie's head. A round and full thwack. Glass thick enough to survive the initial blow, but not the impact against the tile when my mother dropped the bottle, the stinging smell of Scotch prickling their eyes. She waded through the liquor, her slippers crunching through the glass, to wrap herself around Eddie. "I'm sorry, I'm sorry," she cried, pulling him into her chest.

"Get off him!" my father yelled. He stepped through the glass to peel her off my brother, the shards cutting through his socks, turning the kitchen floor a bright red. It would oxidize, darken to a crimson in time. "Are you insane? Do you want another dead fucking child?"

My mother dropped to the floor, glass crunching around her knees. From the depths of her belly, she heaved. It was penance, this pain. My father cupped Eddie's face in his hands. He asked him again and again if he was okay, if he could talk. My brother said nothing. He would not say another word to my mother that August.

While my mother wept upstairs, my father took Eddie to the ER. He told the nurse that my brother had been playing baseball and had taken a flying bat to the head. The nurse sent Eddie to get a scan to rule out anything serious. Afterwards, as the blood and Scotch seeped into the tiles at home, my brother and father sat silently in the waiting room, my father gently nudging Eddie whenever he saw his lids flutter. He knew he was catastrophizing, but still, he couldn't help but think of leaving another hospital without his child.

Later, when a doctor confirmed that Eddie had a concussion but was okay to go home, my father sank into his chair. He wasn't sure why his body collapsed just then; he couldn't tell whether it was out of relief that his son would be going home with him, or if the wind had been knocked out of him when the injury his wife had inflicted had been named. She had done *that* to him.

The doctor informed them that after a few weeks of down time, Eddie would have to come back for another test—just to be safe.

"I'm so sorry, Eddie," my father said.

My brother shook his head, muttered that it wasn't his fault. The shock had worn off and he could form sentences again, not that he felt like saying much.

When they got back home, Eddie went to his room to lie down. My mother tried to follow him, but my father stopped her.

"You need help," he said. "Real help, from a hospital this time."

My mother didn't fight it. She understood the gravity of what she'd done. That technically, legally, she could lose her son over this. That regardless, she might lose her family if she didn't address her anger. If she could get a psychiatric diagnosis, she thought, to explain her behaviour, then maybe they would forgive her one day. They would understand it wasn't all her fault. And so she washed off the blood that had dried on her legs, and she asked my father to drive her to a clinic.

Over the next few days, all Eddie could do was lie in a dark room, thinking about nothing but our mother and her breakdown. Too much light made him nauseated, and he knew that if he just followed the doctor's orders, he'd recover faster. Besides, he didn't have it in him to fight it. He had no desire to get out of bed, let alone go out and socialize, see people, explain the bruise that had swelled from his temple to his brow bone, the redness in his eyes.

In the evenings, my father would sit at the foot of Eddie's bed, only leaving to pick up food down the street and set it on a dinner tray for them to eat upstairs. Perhaps it was my mother's absence that allowed them, for the first time, to speak about her honestly. Maybe it was just the darkness.

"It's like she hates me," my brother whispered one night. "In those moments, it's like all she wants is me gone and Vivian here instead."

"Your mother would die without you. She loves you, with that same fierceness that she loved Vivian."

"Loves," my brother corrected him. Then, pinching his nose as his head pounded, he asked my father how he could watch her use love as a defence for destruction. "Everyone's gotten hurt, but you won't stop it."

My father wrapped his hands around Eddie's feet the way he used to when he put him to bed as a child, holding on until he would fall asleep. He didn't know what to say. That Eddie was right? That some days he felt like he was caught in between it all? That he didn't know how to support his wife's grief while also protecting his son? It shouldn't have been so contradictory. But in our family, my father backing up my mother means justifying unjustifiable behaviour to the person he loves most.

"I'm sorry. I know it's hard to understand. And as much as I hope you will one day, I also hope you won't have to witness the person you love endure the kind of pain your mother has endured."

My father knew it was not a satisfactory response, not even close, but he could not explain himself further without somehow betraying my mother. He meant the vows he had taken, to stand by her for better or for worse. But still, as he walked away from his hurting child that night, he begged God to wake him up, to tell him that this was all just one horrible nightmare. That his wife didn't abuse their child, that he didn't have to intervene. That he had gotten up when I stirred, that he didn't have to spend a lifetime making up for it. For as much as he is unable to forgive my mother for the things she has done, he will never forgive himself either.

After a week of confinement, my father suggested that Eddie invite some friends over. By then, Eddie wasn't so swollen, and my father thought he should have some company. After they settled on a shareable version of the story behind his concussion, my brother sent out a couple texts to people he could bear to see. He knew that James and Mivi wouldn't make a fuss out of the yellowing bump on his head. Although he hid things about our family from them both, they were the people he felt most comfortable around. Eddie had been friends with James since kindergarten, and even though he'd only met Mivi a year before, he felt like he'd known her forever. It was a secret perhaps only to Mivi that Eddie had liked her from the start. He'd even confessed to it once—or rather, confessed to maybe liking her a bit—to James one of the first times they smoked together. Later, he took it back, blamed it on the weed. James, of course, knew the truth.

Up until that day, my brother had never had a girl in his bedroom. It was a big deal, made bigger by his feelings for Mivi. The thought of her there reframed everything about his room. It all seemed so childish. Stunted. The colour of the walls was a periwinkle that hadn't changed since it was chosen for his nursery. There were remnants of stickers on the ceiling, where my parents had once put up a galaxy of glow-in-the-dark stars to quell Eddie's nightmares. On the bookshelf, there were the embarrassing books about changing bodies and the complete series of *Bionicle Chronicles* that he knew by heart. And on the bottom shelf, there were books on grief and depression. On that day, even though the darkness helped conceal the bold lettering of the titles, they were the ones that stood out the most to him, the ones he couldn't stomach her seeing. He shoved the stack under his bed, his head pounding as he tried to make room for them, then carefully selected a vintage T-shirt that he hoped would not inspire any jokes about getting dressed in the dark. For good measure, he opened his blinds an inch and let a slice of light in.

When Mivi walked in, a little self-conscious herself, she admitted that she hadn't planned on coming alone. James was supposed to walk over with her but bailed at the last minute. It almost seemed like a set-up—a strange situation for a first date, but one that got right to intimacy. Eddie sat cross-legged at the head of the bed, while Mivi sat at the foot.

"What does it feel like?" she asked, almost immediately.

"Boring mostly. My head hurts a lot whenever I try to read or watch TV. And I weirdly feel like I'm gonna pass out or fall even when I'm lying down. Wouldn't recommend it."

"Yeah, I sort of feel like you're on your deathbed. Did you invite us to exchange some final words?" Mivi laughed, and my brother managed a little playful *tsk*.

"Well, I'm glad it amuses you. Give you a sense of *As I Lay Dying* or whatever before we have to read it this year."

"Well, hey, maybe you won't have to read it at all if your brain stays all swollen."

"Nah, Mr. Woodburn would make the class send tapes of you all reading it to me. Like note-takers but for the concussed."

They laughed, then sunk into silence for a minute.

"I *could* read it to you, if you'd like," Mivi said, breaking through the quiet. "Or anything, really. If that would be helpful."

"Oh God, now I really feel like I'm on my deathbed," he said, then pressed his thumb against his temple. "I mean, no. That's really nice, but just conversation is fine."

"Okay." She paused, fiddling with the hem of her blouse, allowing her head to dip and break eye contact for a moment. "So what happened anyway? James said it was something on your bike."

"Yeah," my brother said with a shrug, happy to be in the dark while he lied to her. "Um, you know over on College, by the Metro? I was just turning onto College, actually, from one of the side streets, and a car whipped past me out of nowhere and threw me off. Literally. Like a collision but without actually hitting each other. Just me and the sidewalk . . . I don't know. *It all happened so fast*," he said, emphasizing the cliché to make her smile.

"Did you hurt anything else? Scratch yourself up?" As she asked, she reached toward him, pulling his sleeves up a bit to inspect his body.

"I was wearing a jacket and jeans. Pretty thick, you know."

Mivi frowned, skeptical that he'd be that covered in August, but unsure as to why he would lie to her. Flushed, my brother steered the conversation away from his accident, and they began to slowly shift closer together on Eddie's bed, melting into a comfortable rhythm of repositioning without overthinking it. By turns, they lay on their stomachs or propped themselves up against the wall to stretch their legs.

The dark helped them feel comfortable, and all my brother wanted was to keep the conversation going. He felt the best he had in days. So he asked her lots of questions, to take the attention away from his concussion but also because he wanted her to stay. He asked about her summer. The volunteer program at the hospital. The internship at the clinic she planned on applying to one day that she thought might help her get into a fast-tracked med program. He asked her why she wanted to study medicine to begin with. Mivi talked about her abuela's pre-eclampsia, and about her desire to make her mami proud, to assure her that she'd one day be able to be completely self-reliant.

It was only when her stomach eventually grumbled that she realized she should head home for dinner, that her mami and Mrs. Saltzman, a family friend visiting from New York, would be waiting for her. Still, it took her a half-hour to peel herself off the bed, and then twenty more minutes leaning against Eddie's door frame as they threw one last things back and forth like a game of catch. After another stomach grumble, Mivi blushed, picked up her backpack, and said she'd better head out. She promised she'd be back soon to see him again, then stepped toward him to wrap her pinky around his.

"It's binding now," she said, unhooking her finger and readjusting the bag over her shoulder. "We'll just enjoy the last of summer

inside, in a dark, stuffy room. Really take advantage of the weather!"
My brother laughed, then winced a bit from the pain.

Even years later, he'd think of that moment with tenderness. It
was the day he began falling in love with her. And contrary to what
he's tried to make himself believe, he has never stopped.

While my father and brother argue in the kitchen about Detroit,
about her, my mother is awake upstairs. Despite the cues that she
should get up—the shooting pain in the small of her back, the numb-
ness of her coccyx, the aching of her limbs, yearning for a deep
stretch—the sound of her family clashing downstairs has frozen
her. She feels the same anxiety that initially set in a couple months
after they moved into this house, when my parents' marriage first
began to break down. A fog of unyielding grief, the depression that
weighed my mother down after Eddie was born, and later, the pressure my father put on my mother for another child, the fights about
whether my brother was being neglected, all contended for the
blame of their struggles.

My mother thinks of the arguments they had in the kitchen
while Eddie cried in the background. How, for months, my father
wouldn't drop the idea of fertility treatments, of counselling, of fix-
ing them with another baby, a girl to help them sort out their grief.
Even after they reached the conclusion that there'd be no more trying,
resentment burned white hot in both my parents. For months,
small disagreements would escalate into blowouts. My father would
yell; my mother would lock herself in their room. They wouldn't
speak until one of them eventually apologized, explained it as only
wanting the best for the family. The family they had. The family
they could be. She often thinks of that last one. The dreams of what
could be seem to be narrowing, especially with my brother wanting

so badly to leave now, to move. This is likely the last summer she'll have with Eddie at home.

My brother feels certain that things will be fine if he can get away. Not just out of the house, but out of the province, out of the country. He has done what my parents asked of him. One year of university in Toronto to study film theory, which he warned them would be a waste of money when he'd known out of high school that he wanted to go to a hands-on film school in New York. But that was the deal. One year. My parents had thought that would be enough time for Eddie to make friends in his program, maybe meet a girl. They'd hoped he'd reconsider leaving everyone behind. Because even though they've done a poor job of showing it, my parents hate the idea of not keeping their child close, especially after never having the chance with me. They're smart enough to know that if he leaves now, the way things are, he'll never come back.

As my mother tosses in bed, she can't help but ruminate over the possibility of her son miles and miles away, like the others. She tries to remind herself that it's still possible to prevent his departure. This morning, she is one day closer to closing the loop. As long as she can get her family to Detroit, they might be all right.

Eventually, everything quiets downstairs, but my mother waits for the front door to shut twice before getting up. She doesn't want to get involved today. Once she knows everyone's left and she's alone, she'll have her coffee and go for a walk to calm her nerves before she starts working. It's a ritual she only disrupts on my birthday. Every other day, her walk offers the promise of solace, time alone to try to centre herself. She doesn't think about being a wife or a mother or a daughter. She tries not to think at all.

As she makes her way down the stairs, she holds on to the railing. It's a habit now, one she's taken up to avoid touching the pictures that cover the opposite wall, particularly the baby photos that have historically stopped her in her tracks and pulled her toward them. Her favourite, a close-up of my father's palm cupping my head as I gaze up at my mother, still manages to make her cry. It's the only one of me that she took. Most of our family's life has been documented through my father's eyes. So that one is special. It's the sole proof of the tenderness with which I saw her.

No matter how emotional the photographs make her, she refuses to take any down. Once, standing on the stairs, she dragged her fingers across an image of my day-old face and brought two frames down with it—photos from Eddie's first day of school and my parents' wedding. Mine was the only one that broke. Now my mother tries to keep her focus on her hand holding the banister. When she's at the bottom of the stairs, she'll sometimes look up.

In the kitchen, she heads straight to the coffee maker. My father always prepares the pot at night and brews it in the morning. Five cups: one for him, two for Eddie, two for my mother. She'll drink one before her walk and one after, she's decided.

On the stove, my father has left out the small ceramic pot they use to froth milk. She pours a few splashes of rice milk into it and turns on the gas. Over the years, she's tried many milk alternatives before finding a favourite. Hemp milk. Oat milk. Cashew milk. Goat's milk. Flax milk. Almond milk. Coconut milk. Soy milk. Pistachio milk. A2 milk. It's not because she can't tolerate cow's milk. She's been chasing the newborn smell that she lost after Eddie was about six weeks old, the one she only got with me for a week. The pursuit is one she won't tell anyone about, not even my father. She knows it's a bit unhealthy. She hasn't managed to recreate my scent, of course, that newborn perfume, but rice milk is close, and close is good enough.

My mother pours the hot milk into a mug of coffee and sits in the bay window, riffling through the mail that my father brought in this morning. There's an open envelope, a fundraising letter from the cancer centre where he received treatment. Last week, they got a call from his oncologist—his yearly confirmation that his cancer has not returned some fifteen years after they cut out that lump of melanoma. She sets the letter aside. They donate every year. And although she knows there's no karmic connection between money and remission, she will send a donation after her walk, just in case.

There are two other letters in the pile: one from the University of Toronto for Eddie and one from the insurance company addressed to her, *Mrs. Rosy Powell.* My mother sighs. Her parents had it all wrong. Not just the spelling, but the fact that she wasn't even the slightest bit rosy anymore. For a second, she stops to wonder what they'd think of her now. Their Rosy, all grown up and out of Detroit, a sight they never got to see. It had been a quick death: car, utility pole. Both gone the week after their only daughter turned twenty, just as she was starting to understand her parents as people, and before she began to question whether she was destined to lose everyone she loved.

As she sips her coffee, my mother looks out the window, at the hydrangea bush in the yard that is beginning to yellow and the lawn that's beginning to thin, even though it's only mid-August. She pulls out her phone, opens her notes, and starts typing. *Fix sprinklers,* she writes above the plan that she'll execute once they're back in Detroit. A to-do list like that could only be my mother's. Household maintenance flanked by grand life plans. The pragmatic meeting the melodramatic. The modus operandi of her parenting.

MIVI

THE SOUND OF THE COFFEE grinder wakes me up a few hours after I fell asleep. Mami always jokes that she's the gallo of the house, that the whirring of a grinder older than me is her crow.

Before last winter, I could fall back asleep easily, but this year's different. If I'm lucky enough to get a nightmare-free night, I don't risk it for another hour of sleep. It's not worth waking up to fiery skin where I've scratched at invisible insects, or the panic of being swarmed still trapped in my chest. The narrative deviates slightly each time, but the setting—the hot mouth of my ancestors' jungle—is always the same.

Some mornings, I wonder whether the dreams would be as bad if Eddie was beside me. I picture his hand resting in mine as he sleeps, like he used to do. I wonder whether I'd feel like I had someone to pull me out of the traps I kept falling into in my dreams.

I miss sharing a bed with him. How sleepovers gave way to slow mornings whispering in bed, counting freckles on each other's bodies. Prolonging our togetherness by sneaking out the back door for cortados around the block. I miss sipping them with him on patios and people-watching behind sunglasses, laughing at the characters we'd turn them into.

We haven't done any of that since last August, since his mom had a breakdown and he'd asked to be alone once it was over. I often think of how I shouldn't have listened, shouldn't have run. I should've stayed and held his gaze. That morning was the last time he would look me in the eye for months. Afterwards, Eddie started retreating. He didn't go out as much. We stopped sleeping together, though we never discussed it. He would cancel plans last minute, leave my messages unanswered for days, especially the ones that mentioned her or what happened. I felt sick whenever I wrote about her, but it felt impossible to avoid. Eventually, Eddie just told me we'd talk more in person, that texting about his mom felt wrong somehow.

But each one-on-one plan fell through. In September, he cancelled the shoot we'd had planned, blamed it on school picking up. That's when I stopped trying. When he was ready, he would talk. After my last message to him, we didn't hang out for months. The only communication we had was the exchange of exactly seven memes and a couple sporadic texts.

Whenever I romanticize the notion of us being together, I force myself to remember how agonizing those months apart were. The thought of losing his friendship again is enough to deflate the fantasy. And even on days when I have my doubts about the other reason I'm afraid of being with Eddie, I remind myself of Mami's no-dating rule. I try to make myself believe that with two jobs and a tough school year ahead of me, there's no time for relationships.

If I'm going to be a good immigrant hija, I can't lose focus. I have to trade in a slice of youth for a fulfilling career. A busy life. Security. Mami isn't forcing me into anything. These are all things I want— things that will make my life full if I never have a partner or children. I know how that sounds, especially at eighteen, especially as a girl *in this day and age*. But I don't expect anyone to understand really, other than Mami. She's the only one who can actually relate, who knows what it's like to live with the fear of a curse cast over you like smog, who understands what it's like to split your heart in two to protect yourself.

Mami left for years to try to protect me. She still leaves often for her job, but whatever time she has in Toronto, she spends with me, trying to make up for her absence. Whenever anything good happens, no matter how small it is, Mami is the first to want to celebrate, to take us out for ice cream and sit on a bench with me and play our backstories game while chocolate drips down our wrists. She's the best at creating elaborate backstories for strangers, coming up with the right twists and punchlines, crediting her imagination to the soaps she watched in New York to learn English.

While she's the only one who will ever fully understand me, I'm lucky to have friends like Zadie, Maja, and Eddie, who do their best. I can be myself with them, mostly, and they love me enough that I can share my wins and losses without ever feeling like it's showing off or burdening. When I got that academic achievement award at the end of high school, Eddie invited our friends over to his basement and pulled out a three-litre bottle of champagne. Not the real stuff, but most of it got soaked up by the carpet when I popped it anyway. Later that night, he said he hoped I could see how proud all our friends were. I dipped my foot in the dark spot of the carpet and focused on the fibres frothing between my toes. It was all I could do to keep from kissing him in front of everyone.

I have to remind myself of the good sometimes—it's true that the question of the curse doesn't consume everything. I'm surrounded by great friends, my heart is mostly full, and my work schedule is busy enough to distract me from the empty bit. Most of the time.

Working at Le Duck isn't exactly part of the grand plan, but I need something that pays more than the internship at the clinic (a stipend each semester—four hundred whole dollars, taxable) to be able to keep working there and list it on my CV. Once I started serving, I realized that while it doesn't technically have anything to do with medicine, I could find a way to work it smoothly into my entrance interviews. Sometimes in the shower, I practise, talk about how working in a restaurant basically hones your bedside manner and teaches you triage.

The tips at Le Duck are good. Rich-people-who'll-pay-$120-for-magret-the-size-of-a-peach-pit-without-batting-an-eye good. I would happily stay there right up until the day I have Dr. in front of my name. Though in order to keep working there, I have to get into Toronto's med school. It's competitive, but I want to study at one of the best nephrology departments in the province.

"Que chistoso," Mami said when I told her that's what I'm interested in. "You who puts so much strain on your liver."

I fake laughed. "Mami, it's not liver, it's *kidneys*."

"Ah, the one that looks like a bean." She smiled. "Such a good catracha."

It had been my abuela's story that piqued my interest. After we left New York, I called her every week. Across the line, she would often complain about her pain, lingering issues she was sure were linked way back to her pregnancy with my mami. In a matter of months, her kidneys had been irreparably scarred, and her recovery was ongoing decades later—I was fascinated by just how much could go wrong when the kidneys were compromised.

After she died last year, I had a bean tattooed on my wrist. Sometimes, I try to feel the raise in the skin where the ink settled, follow the line, rub it back and forth. When I'm tired enough, it helps me fall asleep.

This morning, though, I don't lap the tattoo after the coffee grinder stops whirring. I don't try to fall back asleep. *My alarm will go off soon anyway*, I tell myself, as though that's the real reason. Today is my last shift at the clinic before it closes for a couple weeks to be renovated, and I have to get there early to finish filing patient folders in storage. Most of my work there is administrative, which is tedious, but whenever I'm hungover, I'm grateful that the worst mistake I could make would only affect workflow, not an actual human.

I drag myself into the shower, figure that with the extra time, I can rinse last night out of my hair. I cover the smell of smoke and Eddie with yucca and witch hazel, leave in a dollop of conditioner to help mitigate the damage from the chlorine.

After my shower, I section my damp hair into a sleek bun. My go-to when I don't have the patience to dry it properly. When I walk into the kitchen, Mami looks up from her book and raises her eyebrows at me. "Tired?" she asks. I shrug, which makes her laugh and then get up to pour me a cup of coffee. "I'll leave you some food for tonight, so you don't have to worry about cooking after work."

Babying me is a telltale sign that she's about to leave for a while. So is reading first thing in the morning, something she only does when she's hurrying to finish a book so she can exchange it at the library for a thicker "travel" one. Mami is a flight attendant, a "waitress in the sky" as she calls it. She always explains her trajectory as beginning on the ground, on her knees as a cleaner, and working her way up.

"That for your book club?" I point at the hardcover on the island, serving a raised eyebrow back at her. "Weren't you supposed to finish it for last night's meeting?"

"Don't judge me. I managed just fine last night without knowing the ending." She shoots back a playful sneer before continuing.

"I want to finish it before I leave tomorrow. Five days on, but I'll be back on your birthday."

Mami, who never turns down an overtime shift, has never missed my birthday. Not even when I was no longer a child, when I assured her it was fine, that I didn't really care about birthdays anyway. This was especially true after I turned fourteen, when she first told me about the curse that she was sure had been in our family for centuries.

"I can't believe it's your nineteenth, mi vi," she says, as she pushes the mug in front of me. "Your last teenage year. Almost fully cooked."

I pull my smile tight and hope that the strain of it reads as a byproduct of my hangover, rather than the truth. We both know what she's talking about. Almost twenty. That's the birthday she's been counting down to ever since she gave birth to a girl. To have her child clear of her teens without any babies of her own. I would be the first generation in my family not to have fallen for a man who left me alone with a child. Practically a genetic anomaly.

"Almost," I say, as I gulp down my coffee, holding in the burn.

ISAURA

PACKING ITSELF IS EASY. Mechanical by now. You roll up three sets of uniforms, a handful of underwear, two thick books that you slip into plastic covers so they don't get ruined during travel and you're not slapped with a library fine. At your age, the trips tire you out more than they used to, but you can still nap just about anywhere. You can still handle the time change and the too-soft hotel beds and the bad flyers, even the rude ones. The hardest part about travelling is the fact that you can't know what your teenage daughter is doing when you're gone. And you're gone a lot.

When you were a teenager, you didn't believe in the curse. Your mother hadn't raised you to. The word itself, *maldición*, was too storybook-like, too sensational. The punishment—pregnancy and the untimely death of the man who'd caused it—all just sounded like bad luck to you. Still, your abuela, whom you called Lita, was convinced that both she and your mami had been cursed, and she'd warned you about it since you were a child.

The curse would prey on teenage girls. More specifically (and this you hadn't read in any storybooks), teenage girls whose blood had been diluted by a Spaniard's a few generations back. One who'd coaxed the location of an ancestral city out of one of the mothers long ago. Lita called her Magdalena.

Magdalena was a sorter at the banana plantation that a Spanish military officer had just purchased in La Mosquitia. Sometimes, you were told that she'd impressed the Spaniard with her speed and dexterity—she could cut and sort hundreds of bananas blindfolded without ever slicing herself. Other times, you were told that it was her voice, the enchanting tune she carried as she worked, rippling across the tubs of water filled with bunches. Most often, though, you heard about her beauty. Doughy hips. Breasts the weight of cocos. The type of curls that can only be inherited, not achieved through any product. Pech hair that you have to cut four times a year so it doesn't grow past your waist.

The courting bit of the story was the part your abuela always skipped. She didn't want you to romanticize it. All you know is that he approached Magdalena and, despite her reticence to give any Spaniard a chance, despite the unspoken vow she felt she'd taken at birth to never let any of them get what they wanted, she fell in love. Within days of meeting the Spaniard, she lay with him in the rows of banana trees, exchanging sweat and dirt and, unbeknownst to either of them, planting the seed of a baby girl.

One day, he asked her about la Ciudad Blanca. Since he'd arrived, he'd heard stories about a legendary city in La Mosquitia, but it wasn't anywhere on the map. He wanted to know if it existed, if it was as lush and rich as he'd heard it was. She confirmed that it was real, the place of her ancestors. As a child, she'd carved drawings into the white limestone that surrounded the city.

The Spaniard asked her to take him there, promising he wouldn't touch a thing. She wanted to believe he wasn't like the others, that he just wanted to bear witness to her land, to understand its history. Understand hers. She made him promise. He shook his head, asking her why he would betray the woman he loved. And just like that, she set a machete in one hand and took his in the other.

It took hours of slicing through the rainforest and trudging past mangrove swamps to get inside the white walls of the city. On that initial trip, the Spaniard did nothing but observe as she told him about the history of la Ciudad Blanca. The city's mouth had opened to her ancestors like magical forests do—when refuge from evil is needed most. Nature was a protector of the innocent, she explained, and had been for her family, who had fled the conquistadors. In the walled city, they were left to start anew, shielded by the flora that they understood best.

Intruders who tried to enter the city often failed. They'd take the wrong path, be swallowed into the earth by snaky roots, tip off the spirits by the sound of their tread, the foreign smell of their blood. The mosquitos would target the outsiders and leave bites that would swell to the size of mangoes—they'd close eyes and airways, open welts that summoned more parasites. But even though the jungle surrounding the city was set up like a trap, some managed to fight their way in (or, in the case of the Spaniard, were assisted), and when they got to the heart of the city, they'd tear the riches out of the ground like weeds. Pocket nuggets of gold and buried treasure. Once they'd filled all the satchels they'd brought, weighed down by their spoils, they would leave and go home.

And then they would die.

Without exception, the spirits protecting la Ciudad Blanca made sure of it. The consequence of taking something from the city was always fatal. This, Magdalena knew. She'd even warned the Spaniard, trusting that he would understand the gravity of a violation like that. And besides, she told herself, he had promised, he loved her.

The next morning, after Magdalena went back to sorting plátanos, the Spaniard retraced their steps and did exactly as his forefathers had. He dug his fists into the soil until they were raw from pulling buried artifacts, his knuckles slick with blood. In his pockets, he stuffed stone carvings of the monkey king, spindle whorls, silver medallions embossed with symbols he'd never comprehend, marbled arrowheads, daggers with handles inlaid with mosaics of malachite and turquoise. The last item he found was a wooden doll of a woman, bloated with a child. His blood caked her face, dripped down to clot in the hole at the centre of her stomach. When the Spaniard could no longer carry any more loot, he stumbled his way out of the city, out of the jungle, swatting the air, the branches, with stinging hands, and returned to the plantation. He took Magdalena to his villa and made love to her, still clothed in the military uniform she'd met him in. Once he finished, he fell asleep beside her. The next morning, though, he didn't wake up. As she shook him, a single gold coin fell out of his jacket. Just then, her heart broke in two different places. Later, when she realized that she was carrying his child, she had no doubt about what was happening—she was being punished by the spirits.

Magdalena hoped that her child might be able to atone for her mistakes. But at thirteen, her daughter gave birth to a girl, too, the day before losing her first love. Some fifteen years later, that daughter split herself to deliver a child. Her lover was a man who hit her as often as he seduced her. She felt that forgiveness would save him. When he was still alive a year after their baby girl was born, she was sure she'd broken the curse. But, like all the others, it got to him, leaving her with a toddler and a couple of broken ribs that would never fully heal.

And so on. Mothers having daughters and losing the men they had loved. A curse that nobody had managed to break, one you weren't even sure existed until it struck you, too.

When you found out you were pregnant, you tried to blame it on the curse, the inevitable, but your mami wouldn't hear of it. She rolled her eyes at the word. She was the only one in the family to never call it a curse. She called it "what happens when you let men get what they want." Lita, at sixteen. Your mami, at fourteen. You, a late bloomer at seventeen, three months after you started going out with Antonio.

Once the pregnancy was confirmed, your mami kicked you out. You remember wondering what had happened to her empathy. If it had been severed after years of struggle. If she'd had to surrender it to get through the day. If not even the root of it had remained.

She had *been* you. In love with a boy who couldn't keep his hands off her. Kicked out by Lita because she couldn't afford to feed another mouth. Your mami was ill-equipped to handle a pregnancy. She'd left school after grade three to join Lita at work. She barely understood what sex was, let alone what it could do to her body. When she'd thrown up at the bakery where she'd worked since she was nine, her jefa told her what was happening. That was how she found out. You've never heard of anyone who can't stand the smell of fresh dough. Only your mami, when she was pregnant with you. "Es el colmo!" she would say. The greatest irony for a baker, to retch at the smell of bread.

It got better before it got worse. Even though your papi had slammed her head against the side of Lita's house when he found out, she moved in with him. Married him, too, because his parents were making her sleep on the couch in their living room until they were wed. And also because she was pregnant, and to her, the good moments still outweighed the bad, and because it was just what you did. Nothing changed after the wedding, but at least she could sleep in his room. And even though they weren't exactly honeymooners, it was better than waking up to his mother banging pots around, and having to throw up in a bucket in the living room when the bathroom was occupied. Your mami's new husband had his very own ensuite she could use, and she'd always maintain that that was the highlight of her time there.

A few weeks later, though, she traded the morning sickness for pre-eclampsia that landed her in the hospital and, according to your mami, prevented her calves from returning to their original shape. Her vision was affected. So were her kidneys. She was given medication that didn't seem to do much.

When she began losing blood, her husband had to ask the neighbours to donate theirs. He went door to door because they didn't have blood banks back home. They just relied on people answering their doors, hoped they had the right blood type. Your mami was hooked up to bags for a couple days before she ripped herself off to go to work. There was no use in bringing a baby into the world without a job to pay for it. She went back to the bakery with a dishtowel in her underwear. It was the Honduran way. Whenever you feel weak, you remind yourself where you came from: a place where mothers can't wallow. They just plug their wounds with boiled cotton and drink infusiónes for their rotting organs. It's not like they have any other option.

When you were born, the size of a doll, with light hair all over your body, they called you Pelucha—"stuffed animal." For your mami, for many of the women you saw shunned in your town, the wedge caused by pregnancy was dislodged by the arrival of a baby. It was nearly impossible to direct anger toward something so small, so innocent. When your papi died the night of your baptism, your mami and you moved home. Within weeks, you weaned so that your mami could go back to the bakery to help Lita.

Seventeen years later, you followed your mami's orders and moved in with Antonio. There was barely any time to argue with her anyway. She left for New York a couple weeks after you found out you were pregnant. She'd be joining women she'd befriended at church, working as a cleaner, sending money home. You'd begged her not to leave you when you needed her most, and she'd scoffed. "Why do you think I'm going? You need money, not someone to hold your hand."

Lita was under strict orders to not let you come home. If you were going to raise a child, you would do it under his roof, your mami had said. She knew she couldn't afford to take care of you both. Lita had already been burdened once—your mami wouldn't let it happen again.

You wanted to ask her what you'd do when he inevitably died, but there was no point. She'd blamed your papi's death on drunk driving, not vengeful spirits. If anyone else was to blame, it was the priest at your baptism, the one who brought out tequila for the family after sprinkling holy water on you. You held on to a kernel of hope that she might've been right, prayed the thought like a rosary bead. Each night before you fell asleep, you begged for a son to break the curse.

If Antonio's mother had been alive, you thought, you'd be on the street. Your own mami couldn't stand the thought of a teenage mother under her roof; you couldn't imagine a woman you didn't know taking you in. But Antonio's mother had died when he was a child, which made his father an anomaly. There are plenty of single mothers in Pespire, but single fathers are rare. Un unicornio, he called himself. He was good to you. Cooked well and, when you were pregnant, would actually ask you if you were craving anything. "Plátanos," you'd reply every time. You could've had them for every meal, and some days, you actually did. Though you didn't have a sweet tooth back then, some nights were so hot that you craved paletas, mostly coconut, sometimes lemon, and he would make his son run to the pulperia to get you one. Antonio wouldn't go of his own volition.

You wondered if his father had been this kind before his wife died or if that loss had changed him. Maybe he wanted to care for you because he missed her and welcomed another female presence in their home. Or maybe he just saw you as a wounded animal in need of nurturing. In any case, you felt guilty for it, but you were grateful that she'd died.

Your relationship with Antonio got worse throughout the pregnancy. You'd only been dating for a few months when you moved in. You hadn't had the chance to find out who he was until it was too late. Pregnant, simmering with hormones, confined to a home that was not yours, you found out that as much as you loved him, you really did not like him.

Everything he did made you mad. The space he took up in that twin-size bed. How late he would get home from school. How unserious he was about his school work. They had kicked you out. You didn't get to study anymore. Instead, you helped with the housework and the meals, and when there were no chores left, you read everything on their bookshelves, slipping away from your real life for hours at a time. You were aware that those moments of solitude would soon be limited. For a little while longer, you could pretend that you weren't in Pespire, collecting purple stripes on your belly like claw marks. You thought you were lucky because at least you weren't living in a time of cholera. That you weren't a Maya sacrificed to the gods. They had worse fates than you. You could sequester yourself with a book and forget that a world existed outside of the one in your hands. In its pages, you could experience passion and unconditional love. You could pass the hours with a romance that seemed so real that a single sentence could double your heart rate. Sometimes, you'd wonder how you would handle everything if you could no longer break free in that same way, if the baby would keep you from it, constantly interrupting your attempts.

Then you'd wonder how terrible it was to already be planning an escape from the life you would make with your child.

When the nurse placed her in your arms, you felt like throwing up. It was all too much. Fear and attachment and fascination at the fact that you had unwittingly grown this little person. Ten fingers, ten toes. A full head of hair matted down by your blood and guts. Swollen lips that knew exactly how to nurse and that, somehow, would turn your nipples to open sores in a matter of days. You hadn't realized how gruesome motherhood would be.

Holding her made you feel less alone. A little more important, too. Like you mattered, like you hadn't just been a mistake your mother made when she was a teen, like you had a purpose now. But that, too, was terrifying.

After they'd taken her away to the nursery, your mami called. Broke almost an entire gestation's worth of silence. Through the receiver at the hospital, you could hear sirens and the buzzing of voices, American ones it seemed, swarming around your mami's. She asked you how the birth went. You told her it was horrible. "Mmm, por su puesto." You told her it was a girl. "Por su puesto," she said again, though that time, the words seemed more coated in defeat. That was the end of the conversation.

Yes, of course she was a girl. You spent that night sobbing in your cot. You must've looked like such a child. Lying on your side because your stomach was still just as bloated as it had been with your daughter inside, your head buried under a pillow, crying. The next morning, when the nurse set her back in your arms to feed again, your girl looked at you for the first time. Her eyes, two shiny black beads, the roundest things you'd ever seen, fixed on yours, and you decided that there was no point in lamenting her life so early. It was unfair to

ANNA JULIA STAINSBY

50

assume that the two of you couldn't break the curse together. You tried not to wonder how many mothers had had the same thought.

When Antonio arrived at the hospital, he'd wanted to name her after himself: Antonia. But you had another name in mind, one that had come from a book you read. He'd never laid a hand on you until that night. You couldn't believe he had hit you. You were still in the hospital, wearing one of those mesh diapers that you would continue to bleed into for the next six weeks. There were nurses around. The slap wasn't that hard, you thought, nothing like the pain of the thirty-two-hour labour you'd just endured. It was a bad unit to mea-sure violence against, you came to realize later, but in the haze of postpartum, it was the only logic you could cling to. You could handle pain. You didn't have a choice. Still, you pushed back. You could not name her after someone like him. He relented once you started raising your voice and your daughter started crying, though he didn't stick around to ask what you wanted to name her instead. As you signed the paperwork alone, you wondered whether there was enough love between the two of you for him to be taken by the curse. Part of you hoped so.

Back at your new home, the days blended into fuzzy, milky blurs. You cried a lot. Sucked on the inside of your cheek as you breastfed, trying to distract yourself from the pain of it. Between feedings, you kissed your daughter more than you'd ever kissed in seventeen years. Things with Antonio got a bit better. He wasn't a natural with your daughter, but he was entranced by her. He'd hold her stiffly and study her little mouth twisting as she dreamt. He was sweet to you for a while. Told you he'd marry you, the strong girl who had given him a tiny perfect one.

But, eventually, the illusion of safety, the picture of the three of you as a happy family drifted away. Antonio only started treating you worse. Yelling louder, hitting you harder. He stopped caring that your shouting matches woke the baby. Later, you wondered how different things might've been if you'd had a boy. Not just for the curse. You wondered if Antonio would've treated you any better. If there might've been more respect, more gratitude. If you would still be in Pespire, if you would've had more children with him before he died, a life full of noise and hair to braid. It's strange to admit, but you are glad it got so bad that you had to stuff your things into a bag in the middle of the night and fly away.

You've packed hundreds of bags since that one at Antonio's, boarded hundreds of flights, left your daughter behind more times than you can stomach. And yet you haven't outgrown the fear that your first departure instilled in you. The one that says you cannot protect her from afar. Maybe you cannot protect her at all.

VIVIAN

EDDIE HAS BEEN PICTURING my grave all day. He knows that going to Detroit means seeing it in person—a first for him and my mother—and his insides churn when he thinks of how my mother will react. There's no scenario in his mind that ends well, that doesn't leave her either paralyzed or frenzied by grief. His anxiety is compounded by the fact that Mivi's birthday falls a day after my death day. He missed her party last summer. The thought of not spending her birthday together this year fills him with guilt.

Still, Eddie doesn't want to tell Mivi about Detroit. She knows too much already. He doesn't want to reveal yet another layer of dysfunction in his life. He feels that if she were to unpeel all the layers of our family history, the ones kept hidden for decades now, there would be no way she could ever truly love him. He's sure she'd be disgusted by all the rot underneath. And so he has to be withholding in order to keep that door from shutting completely.

Last summer, Mivi witnessed my mother's rage. Her screams woke them up that morning, unwittingly confined the two of them to my brother's room as she smashed all the plates in the cupboard. My father tried to stop her, dodging the ceramic shrapnel as he apologized. He had, for the first time, shared the story of my mother's suicide attempt with his former boss, who'd told his wife. She'd meant well by texting my mother the day before my anniversary to offer a safe space to talk yet my mother had never felt so betrayed. Enraged with my father, she yelled that she wished her attempt over seventeen years ago had worked.

Eddie almost threw up from shame. Anger came soon after, when that shame mutated into something even more toxic. He'd seen our mother's scars, but he hadn't known when they were from. He'd thought that maybe she used to cut in periods of depression, not that she'd tried to end her life. But now he knew. She had tried to kill herself when she was pregnant with him. In his eyes, she had tried to kill him. He knew from the pity he saw on Mivi's face that morning that she understood it, too. Eddie had never felt so exposed.

Soon after she stopped screaming, my mother climbed upstairs to her bedroom and undressed for a shower that my father had convinced her to take. He knew that things always felt more surmountable after a shower. Before she turned on the water, she heard the back door slam shut. *Eddie*, my mother thought. *Fuck, Eddie.* The potency of her anger had made her forget that her son was home.

She ran to the bathroom window and saw Mivi scampering away in the yard, looking back at the door she knew she'd closed too loudly. My mother had thought she was out of tears, but the sight of Mivi fleeing and the thought of Eddie hearing his mother admit to trying to kill herself, and trying to rid herself of him, broke her anew. Before she could attempt to make things right, she stepped into the shower, some part of her still hoping for death in the steam and water. A rebirth on the other side, a chance to be a person who would not ruin another summer. She turned the handle of the faucet and scalded herself as though the pain might be at all redemptive.

As her tears washed off her face, she thought of what to do. She thought that maybe she would ask Eddie for Mivi's number. She could reach out, apologize, explain her behaviour somehow, anything to save face for her son.

While my mother didn't know Mivi well, she felt desperate for her understanding, for her not to think badly of her. This was partly for Eddie's sake, but also because of who Mivi's mom was. They'd only spoken once before, but Isaura had left a strong impression on her.

They'd met at parent-teacher night, sitting outside the classroom in hard plastic chairs rife with gum older than their children. My mother, who normally came to these nights with my father, did not usually make small talk with other parents. She'd always been standoffish with them, the mothers especially, ever since preschool drop-offs when they would ask if Eddie had siblings, whether she was planning on giving him any, if she hoped for a girl, to have one of each. Later, when their children were in middle school, those same mothers would tell Rosy how lucky she was to only have a boy, that their girls were driving them crazy, that they stole their clothes and shrank them, that she was fortunate to not have to deal with all the hormones and bloody sheets. They would inevitably punctuate each complaint with *but*s. "I can never stay mad too long." "She's still my best friend." "I'm so blessed." None of them were willing to end on anything other than love and no regrets. My mother hated that.

By high school, most mothers knew she was not someone to chat up in the hallway, especially when her safety blanket of a husband wasn't with her. Isaura knew none of this. The night they met was her first time attending and meeting other parents at the school. As she took a seat beside my mother in the quiet hallway, she broke the silence.

"I love your shoes. They're very chic," Isaura said. "I could see a French girl wearing them."

My mother looked down at her derbies and blushed. Her style hadn't evolved much since her college years, where she'd discovered that monochrome clothing and leather shoes made for an easy uniform. She'd never been complimented for how she dressed before. My mother smiled meekly, yearning for my father, who was home with the flu. She was convinced that he could hold a better conversation mid-fever with another mother than she could in perfect health.

"Thank you. I love yours, too," my mother responded, feeling a little juvenile for parroting her so obviously, until Isaura's mouth split into a wide grin and she clicked her ankles together.

"I have to say I'm pretty proud that they've held up this well," Isaura said, her face still beaming. "They survived half a decade in New York."

My mother let a beat of silence pass before asking if she'd worked in fashion there.

Isaura laughed. "Close. I was a cleaner. One of my clients worked for Condé Nast, so she got lots of freebies. Guess she didn't love these shoes, because they were my Christmas bonus one year. I would've preferred cash, but I guess no matter how big the bonus was, I would've never spent it on designer shoes."

As my mother smiled, her wrinkles softening her angular face, it dawned on Isaura that my mother was probably the same age as her own. She hadn't spent much time with mothers since she'd left New York, and the realization felt confronting. For years, pain had built up inside her, waiting to be purged, to be shared with someone who understood.

Hopeful that my mother might, Isaura began by telling her how she became a cleaner. She told her about getting pregnant at seventeen and not wanting to risk an illegal abortion in Honduras. How when her daughter was only a few months old, she had to move to the U.S. to make money and support her. When my mother asked how they reunited, Isaura shared the logistics of it all, but also about how difficult it was. She shared how much she'd wanted to send her back to Honduras, how she'd wished her grandmother could've raised her daughter instead. My mother was stunned by Isaura's display of maternal ambivalence. She had never before heard a mom speak so candidly about parenthood without adding a *But she's the best thing that ever happened to me*, like she had to repent for the truth.

As my mother carefully doled out questions, Isaura told her about her mom, who had gotten her the job in New York and who was still there, begging them to visit over the holidays. Isaura wanted to go, but money was tight.

"Yessenia would rather go to Honduras, and saving for that is hard enough. I don't know. It'd be nice to go home, the three of us, once my mom is done with New York. But until then, I'm trying to get her an iPhone so that I can at least see her face when we talk."

Although my mother felt compassion for Isaura's predicament, a knot of envy twisted inside her as she listened to what sounded like a normal mother-child bond. To have a mother who wanted, would even beg, to have her child close. To have a child who wanted to see their mother's face. She didn't have that.

Growing up, her family had loved each other in a quiet way—no professions of adoration, few moments of affection. My grandmother showed her love by hand-knitting wool sweaters in my mother's favourite colours and by brushing her daughter's hair gently, never pulling on the knots. To my grandparents, love was keeping their child healthy, bathed, clothed. The night they died, my mother had turned down their invitation to go out for dinner downtown. There had been no pleas to join them, no guilt tripping. Just an "All right, we'll see you later then."

She'd lived more of her life without parents than with them. And while she had mostly become resigned to being parentless, comfortable even, she found herself pained by the thought of Eddie ever feeling content without his. Yet she could not imagine herself and her son in Isaura's situation. Her asking him to visit. Him yearning to see her face. She was jealous of Isaura, and ashamed of herself as a mother. But Isaura's honesty was disarming. She had been trusting enough to share things with my mother that the perfect mothers with all their right feelings about their children never had. For the first time, it made her feel like she was not alone in her motherhood. Her shame was there, but it didn't make her want to curl up alone with it. And in the rush of it all, my mother tried something she'd never done. She let a stranger in.

"I . . . I lost my mother when I was young," she said. "Too young, really. I was barely twenty. Try to go see her if you can. It'd make her so happy."

"Ay, I'm sorry," Isaura said. "That is young. Do you still miss her?"

My mother paused. She seldom allowed herself to think of my grandmother. Their relationship had been cleaved before it could fully flourish, before my mother had a chance to become an adult, to really figure out who she was. She pretended that Isaura had asked about me instead.

"Yes. I think about her every day. I wonder what she would think of me now. What her relationship would be like with my son. I miss looking at her and seeing myself. I think I lost a lot of myself in her."

"That makes sense. Of course. Of course. I'm so sorry . . ."

"Rosy," my mother said with a smile, the moment punctuated with a touch of humour. How funny, to have shared so much with a woman whose name she did not know.

"Isaura."

For a few more minutes, they continued to talk. About their mothers. About their children, who they eventually realized were friends, when my mother said Eddie's name. About the fact that they were both only and already teenagers. How quickly time passes.

When the math teacher called Isaura into his classroom, my mother wished her good luck and said she hoped she could manage to make it to New York for Christmas.

After that night, my mother thought a lot about Isaura, though she never pulled her email from the PTA's list to ask her to go for a coffee, never asked Eddie for help arranging anything. But she would often find herself wondering if Isaura had made it home for that visit, if her mother was still alive.

The night after she smashed the plates, she sent herself Mivi's contact information from Eddie's phone while he was showering. His password was the same as his PIN, the one she'd suggested he use instead of his birthday when they'd set it up at the bank.

As she typed her message to Mivi, she thought of that parent-teacher night. She wondered whether Mivi would be as receptive to her vulnerability as Isaura had been. Mivi was much younger, but still, she hoped that compassion might be an inherited trait. She hoped Mivi would understand that she hadn't meant what she'd said, that she shouldn't let her outburst come between her and Eddie, that he deserved love more than anyone. But in the end, my mother could never gather the nerve to hit send.

My brother decides he won't tell Mivi. He feels it'll be easiest that way. He'll go to Detroit, make it back in time for her birthday, and he won't have to see that pity on her face again, won't have to feel broken by it.

As Eddie cycles to the grocery store, he practises asking for some time off. Not that he needs to worry about being shot down. His manager likes him, mostly because he is always on time and never high, traits hard to come by in the business, apparently. In his head, Eddie mulls over his phrasing of "a cottage weekend with friends" until he pulls up to the staff entrance. In the back room, he shoves his backpack in the banana boxes that serve as lockers for the part-timers before heading to the floor. He decides he'll ask his manager once his shift is over.

My brother has been working at the store since he was fifteen. He got the job soon after photography became his new obsession and he realized his monthly allowance of twenty dollars would only stretch so far. Eddie had discovered my father's abandoned cameras in the basement and quickly blew through the expired film he found.

When my father was younger, cameras were basically an extension of his body. He'd been the first in his family to own one, spending most of the money he'd made lifeguarding one summer on a Canon Demi. He found profound satisfaction in figuring out how to manipulate the light, how to engineer a striking image out of the simplest subjects. He captured oddities in Detroit that seemed to go unnoticed. The hairline fracture in the brick of his high school where moss seeped out like leaking yolk. The plastic, peach-coloured muscle men that someone had scattered throughout his neighbourhood, in places like mailboxes and windowsills. He photographed them in a way that made them look like giants.

When he met my mother, the shots became more focused on sentiment and less concerned about technique. He wanted to capture the moment; style became secondary. As his family grew, he took fewer shots of buildings and light play, and more of my mother and me, and later, Eddie, before he lost all his baby fat. When my brother found the cameras and expired film, he asked my father to teach him how to use them. They spent hours together, logging apertures, playing with lenses, watching how-to videos when my father couldn't remember how to use specific features.

After Eddie got his first shots developed, sunset-hued and striped with age, he sat going through them for hours, looking at the grain and the detail that the camera had pulled from the scenes he had set with his friends. He began to look at everything as if it had the potential to become an iconic shot. He experimented whenever he had the chance, often photographing his friends at school, sitting on the front steps, lighting cigarettes, backs against the metal railing, fingers wrapped around not-quite-aesthetically-pleasing coffee cups from Tim Hortons. When he got a little better, Eddie asked to shoot Mivi so he could practise portraits and editorials.

They'd been friends for a few years at that point, good ones, too, but that first shoot was the first time they got to be creative together outside of their games. That afternoon, they went to High Park and ate up two rolls in under an hour, capturing Mivi in a long floral dress that was once her mother's, one of the many hand-me-downs Isaura had inherited from her clients in New York. They were both surprised that they'd shot so many frames so quickly, but also by their desire to keep going, to extend their time together. When they finished the shoot, they climbed their way out of the weeds where Mivi had posed and walked toward the water, where they smoked. They talked until the sun fell and the reflection in the lake looked like Eddie's first shots—orange and glimmering.

Although they were only in grade ten, they mused about plans after high school. The future was what they always talked about when they weren't playing their games. Mivi spoke about her longing for independence, for a career that mattered, one that might make break-throughs in women's health. Eddie shared his desire to leave Toronto, maybe go to New York. Mivi told him what she remembered of living in New York. The landlord who looked the other way when, at one point, six women lived in his one-bedroom apartment. The expense of it all, her mami running all over working, collecting coupons from flyers strewn in their mailroom, bringing home expired foods her clients asked her to toss. Mivi wasn't as discouraging about New York in this conversation as she would be later, once they'd gotten closer and she could share the other reasons she'd hated the city so much. The memories of her mami picking her up at school with a black eye. That apartment she would cry herself to sleep in after her stepfather came home drunk and seething with baseless jealousy.

But that day, they kept things lighter. They talked about how fun it would be to plan a group trip to celebrate graduation in two years, if not to New York, then maybe to a resort in the Caribbean. Honduras maybe, Mivi joked before shaking her head. She hadn't been to either New York or Honduras since childhood. It would be strange, wrong even, to go back to Honduras and just get drunk with their friends in a resort. She couldn't imagine her first interaction with another Honduran outside of her family being at a swim-up bar. What would they think of her anyway? Probably nothing, she figured. How would they know that she was one of them? She didn't look like it. If she opened her mouth, her accent wouldn't help. Maybe instead, they could just go camping for the weekend, Mivi suggested, take shrooms and sleep under the stars.

It wasn't lost on Mivi and Eddie that they were sinking into rom-com-level corniness, talking about leaving the city as the sun slowly tucked itself away, making it even easier to talk. They joked about it. Embraced it when their friends found out and teased them about their "sunset date." It was easier to joke that, yes, it was the night they realized they were soulmates than to deny it altogether.

Eddie noticed quickly how easy things were with Mivi. So easy that he thought of asking her out that night, but they were already out, so it seemed stupid. Instead, they just kept shooting.

After that night, they would pick out a new location once a month or so and shoot all day. Each one felt like a play date they never wanted to go home from. When Eddie bought himself a Super 8, he and Mivi went to Sugar Beach at sunrise to film her snaking through the candy-pink umbrellas. Later that year, he filmed her at the CNE, capturing her howling as the Pharaoh's Fury swung them back and forth. He had never found her more beautiful. It was after that that they kissed for the first time, their cheeks tight from laughing, eyes sparkling under the neon lights.

For a couple years, neither of them worked up the courage to take things further. Even though she knew she was bending the rules, Mivi didn't want to fully betray the promise she'd half-heartedly made to her mami. Eddie followed her lead. Their relationship wasn't uncomplicated, but it suited them at fifteen and sixteen. They'd alternate between nervous, jokey flirtation and secretly kissing at parties when alcohol fuelled them with enough confidence to act on their desires.

It wasn't until their last year of high school that they had sex. A heatwave that September drove them out of the city to shoot somewhere breezier. Sober but blanketed by the seclusion of a leafy pasture miles away from Toronto, they pushed down the seats of Isaura's car. Neither of them could recall exactly how it happened, only that Mivi leaned in for a kiss as Eddie fiddled with the keys in the trunk, and the rest just followed. They sank into each other, laughing softly as they rolled over seat belts and old Tupperware, hands clasped. That's how it started. Naturally, like it was just part of the process.

They'd create new work every month or so, adding only the best shots to Eddie's website. Eddie had documented seventy-four rolls and twenty-nine hours of tape of her, though he thought he could have filmed hundreds. Whenever he looked through the lens, he would think, *It's too soon. We're too young. We have too much to do apart.* It's always been too soon with Mivi, and that's why he has to capture so much of her.

ROSY

I DON'T KNOW HOW to get your brother to participate without caveats. When we sit down for dinner, he asks when we're leaving. Your father tells him, "Soon," and is met with Eddie's pursed lips that I know are just barely holding in his stipulations.

As I await Eddie's pushback, we eat mostly in silence, spinning corn on the communal pat of butter, passing the salad bowl until only sunflower seeds and green onions are stuck to the bottom. When your father and I get up to clear the table, Eddie breaks the silence to warn us that he can't be away for too long.

"If I'm going to get all my footage by September, I can't take much time off. All my subjects will be gone in a few weeks for school."

I lean over the sink to compose myself. He won't go easily. I'm mad at him for acting like the teenager he is, at myself for hoping he'll be different. *They're your friends, not your subjects*, I want to say. *That makes you sound like a scientist or a dictator.* I inhale, steady my voice. If I even accidentally drop the wet, buttery plate, they might think I'm losing it again. *This year has to be different*, I'd told myself back in the winter.

"We won't be gone long. Just a few days," I say.

"Then I'll bring the camera. There's a cool sculpture gallery in Hamtramck I want to get some footage of. I can get some videos of the city or the cem—"

"Eddie. You can't think I'm going to let you capitalize on this."

"If I can't use this for my work, then what's the point?"

I turn around to face him and wipe my hands on my pants. My palms are pink from gripping the edge of the sink too hard. Before I can answer, Eddie stands up, raising his shoulders with the disbelief of an eighteen-year-old artist who's been stifled.

For a moment, I stare at your father, who is not oblivious to the tension, just unwilling to intervene. He continues to load the dishwasher in silence. I can always feel him cowering in August. He gets quiet, reverting back to the child of a former military surgeon, one who learned that it was best to keep quiet in times of conflict. He allows Eddie his meltdowns. Indulges mine.

Your father could raise his voice and tell Eddie he'll never understand what we've gone through, what August feels like to us, what it's like to lose everything you have ever wanted, over and over and over again. He could hike up his shorts, show Eddie the scar he has to carry, the one that I know isn't just from the sun or uncontrollable cells; it's from loss. From bottled grief. Not a day goes by that we do not think of death. Yours. Your father's. He could ask Eddie how you just get over that. He could grab his son, for extra impact, shove him against the wall and ask him if he understands. He could let his own battle wounds steer his parenting.

But he won't.

"Art can be healing, Mom," he allows Eddie to say without interruption.

It's the arrogance with which he says it, as though it's a ground-breaking thought, something I could never understand without him explaining it. Me, who has done art therapy, who has drawn and drawn and cried over your distorted face. It's the deluded thought that he might be able to heal me, the fact that he believes it could be true, too, that pushes me to lash out.

"What you are doing, Eddie, is not art," I manage to say out of a clenched jaw. "It's probably best that you hear that now."

"How would you even know?" your brother replies, calmly. At first, I'm proud of him, of this quiet confidence that I rarely see in him. But then it's his turn to strike back. "It's not like you've ever asked to see any of it."

As the words come out of his mouth, the same feeling of regret that took over after the smashed bottle and the broken plates floods me. The one that makes me want to lurch toward him as though my arms can collect the bits I've broken. As though a hug could some-how fix things. Except this time, he runs away before I can move toward him. Your father follows him to his room. And then I'm alone in the kitchen, in the middle of another mess I'm incapable of picking up.

As I finish washing up, I hear the front door slam shut. Your father's left to cool down. It's what he does sometimes before we fight. It's been a while since I've heard that door slam. We haven't had many reasons to fight lately; perhaps we're due. Maybe it's his fault for not backing me up, mine for blowing up. If grief has taught us anything, it's that we need to be teammates.

When you died, Lorraine told me to look after my marriage. She warned me that most don't survive the death of a child. Your father and I did our best, and I think we did well overall. Initially, loss didn't fissure our relationship; it soldered us. It made a lifeboat of our marriage. But when we had Eddie, when our heartache was supposed to have been remedied by our new baby, it felt like we were beating against a relentless current.

A few months after Eddie was born, your father saw that I was struggling. He could tell I wasn't being myself, that I had withdrawn. I blamed my behaviour on fatigue, even though, really, your brother was a good sleeper. It was as though he knew to go easy on us.

Your father didn't buy my excuses. He didn't understand why I wasn't completely taken, head over heels in love with our miracle. "I do love him," I'd spit back. "I just . . ." Sometimes, I'd complete the sentence by saying I was overwhelmed, hormonal, tired, grieving. I'd say that maybe I wasn't a good mother to a baby or even a toddler, that sometimes these things come with time, that some mothers don't know how to handle their kids until they're teens. I'd tell him it was different when one was both the stay-at-home parent and self-employed, when one's office shared a wall with the nursery.

We got into fights about how I parented Eddie. Whether I should've breastfed him, whether I should do more skin-to-skin to connect with him. The insinuations that I did not love him the right way filled me with vitriol. I'd kept him healthy, fed, alive. I couldn't help that Eddie would reach for your father over me when he was around. In the evenings, your father would insist I join bath time, and whenever I declined, he would sulk. I'd go into defence mode, lamenting all the laundry that needed to be done, the pile of dishes to be cleaned. The truth was, I was happier to do that than spend more time with my child. Your father knew that. He couldn't understand it.

We took turns sleeping on the couch. We spent so much time arguing about how to just be a unit, the three of us. I thought about what Lorraine had told me, wondering how we'd taken such good care of our love when we were in the deepest pits of grief and how we could barely handle the stress of a child who, for the most part, was not a particularly demanding one. As our tug-of-war continued year after year, I wondered if our marriage was not meant to survive.

And then, not long before Eddie's third birthday, I found the mole.

Your father was convinced that it had always been there, but I knew he was wrong. The next week, we all went to the doctor, Eddie restless in my lap, my desire to yell at him to *Just. Sit. Still*, curbed by fears I couldn't even give words to. Your father, who could read me, offered to take him, but I shook my head. I knew I had to reassure him. I could handle our son. I could be a good mother. I could do it.

The next few weeks were a haze of blood work and biopsies and scans. Each time we left the clinic, your father said, with a relieved sigh, "Well, at least this is happening in Canada." In the midst of it all, your father insisted we still throw Eddie a birthday party, so we did. Two days before they sliced into his leg, he was holding your brother up as he swung a baseball bat at a piñata in the living room. Eddie's preschool friends squealed as your father lifted each one up for a turn.

At the hospital, they cut out the tumour and a rectangle of flesh around it "to err on the side of caution." After the surgery, he had a few weeks of recovery before radiation began. The month of treatment that followed was long, but at least I felt a sense of purpose, taking care of Eddie while your father couldn't. I drove us to the hospital, packed snacks, bought booklets of stickers and dollar store toys to distract your brother when he got antsy. One quiet afternoon in the hospital, I pushed Eddie down a long, empty hall in a wheelchair. He howled as I ran as fast as I possibly could, like if we were fast enough, we could save your father. It wasn't logical. But it was the most fun I'd been as a mother, and it was all for him, for your father. I wanted him to step out of the radiation therapy room and see us dashing down the hall, hear his son laugh harder than he ever had with me, see his head slumped on my shoulder when he was tuckered out from too much play.

We had to wait a while to find out if the treatment had worked. Your father was on leave from work, and while he was home, I made it my mission to prove to him (to myself, too) that I could carry us no matter what happened. Every day, I woke up at five to work for a few hours before anyone got up. I froze batches of the boys' favourite meals. I took on the evening duties your father always did. After dinner, I'd take Eddie to the skating rink to get us both out of the house. I'd breathe in the cold air and watch your brother improve night after night, and only then did I feel alive. My cheeks and lungs burning, my toddler a reminder that life did not stop for tragedies.

When we'd get home, I'd bathe him, then let him pick something to read from his bookcase. If your father was still awake, he would sit at the end of the bed, squeezing his son's tiny feet the way Eddie liked, watching him doze off in the crook of my arm. I did my best to push away the cloud that set over me when I felt drained and couldn't stomach the thought of taking care of anyone but myself. Sometimes, after your father fell asleep beside me, I would sneak downstairs to watch the Shopping Channel. I never bought anything, but that wasn't the point. For an hour or two, I could anaesthetize my brain into picturing a life where I would have a reason to buy a tennis necklace or a pasta maker to show off at dinner parties. As vapid as I found some of the hosts, I also envied them so much that I fantasized about being the women they played, attending brunches and weddings and girls' nights in new dresses and "life-changing" makeup. I would fall asleep thinking of their powdery faces, switching their features out with mine as I dozed off.

The night before we found out that his CT scan was clear, neither of us could sleep. We spooned on the couch, his thigh wrapped around me. He placed my hand, gently, in his scar. I thumbed the tissue, the skin that rippled in the crevasse. He winced, and the thought of not feeling his scar fully healed rose like a mushroom cloud. I tried to rid myself of it by picturing us old. The softness of our muscles, the sharpness of our bones. In that moment, as I moved my hand from his leg to his face, I wasn't afraid of aging.

When I'd noticed my first wrinkle, your father told me he couldn't wait to see more. He couldn't wait to love them. I'd rolled my eyes. I was twenty-seven. Almost a decade later, all I wanted was for him to be around to trace each one, to follow them with his thumb, to see our lives on my face. You, your brother, the homes we grew out of, the ones we built. On that couch beside him, I prayed that I would get to see it all on his face one day.

"If I die, I need to know you two will be all right," he whispered into my neck.

We won't be, I wanted to say. *How could we be?* But I didn't. I cleared my throat of the lump that had been swelling, then whispered back, "Don't worry."

After the sun has set, your father comes home. He is damp with sweat, his shirt too thick to have been worn outside an air-conditioned home. I sit up at the kitchen table, where I have been for the past hour, sipping tea, mulling over an apology to him and Eddie. Before I can say anything, he rolls up his sleeves.

"Don't you ever speak to him like that again," he says, his lip trembling. "That is the last thing he needs to hear from his own mother."

I inhale, bow my head as he catches his breath. I realize I was wrong, there will be no fight. There's nothing to defend. I recoil at the table as your father holds on to the back of the chair like it's keeping him from lunging toward me. He asks me why I even think of hurting our son. He says he knows I didn't mean it, that he's not sure if that makes it better or worse.

"Worse, I think," I admit, but I can't explain why. Did I want to hurt him? Do I need everyone around me to be as miserable as I am? It can't be so simple. "I'm so sorry, Desmond. I just . . . I will fix it with Eddie. And I will be better. I promise I will be better this year."

"You promised that already. I don't need to hear that anymore. I need to know how."

I don't know how to respond. I'm not ready to tell him the plan, the *how* yet. He lets go of the chair and steps away.

"It's been twenty years for me, too, you know," he says, finally. "I'm not taking it out on her brother. I'm not doing that to her memory."

I can't look up at him. He's right.

As I listen to him walk up to our bedroom, I imagine you picking up your baby brother as he weeps, him settling at the sound of his big sister's voice. I say I'm sorry, out loud, to you. To him.

"I'm sorry," I say again and again until I start laughing at how ridiculous I sound, whispering apologies alone at the kitchen table. As I throw my head back, I catch my reflection in the window above the sink and laugh some more. I can't believe it's been twenty years. The number, the fact that I'm still acting this way, the scolding I just got from your father all make me laugh harder, the shame morphing into this thing I have to expel from my belly in a fit of laughter. I go on until I can't look at the person staring back at me in the window, her crazed eyes, her streaked face. I wipe my face and then go up to bed.

MIVI

ONCE I'VE SHOWERED OFF the buttery smell of Le Duck, I crawl into bed and text the girls to let them know I'm not going to meet them tonight. They'd stopped by the restaurant for a drink before going to a house party, and I'd considered rallying after we closed. Now that I'm home, though, the exhaustion in my body is hard to ignore. My muscles feel as though they've been bruised, my forearms tender to the touch.

It doesn't help that I worked a double shift on only a few hours' sleep. Not that the routine is unusual for me, this summer especially, but after months of bad sleeps, my body seems to now be demanding rest. I open Netflix on my laptop and spend a few minutes scrolling through shows to fall asleep to, but I don't have the energy to commit to anything. The voice in my head berates me for missing out on the end of the summer, but as I shut my laptop and melt into my mattress, I try to focus on how good it feels to not do anything. I could try to catch up on some sleep and maybe have enough energy to make plans with the girls tomorrow. For at least one night, though, I know I won't run into him, won't be risking anything, won't be tempting fate, won't be crossing lines. I repeat this like I'm counting excuses to fall asleep.

But almost an hour later, I am still awake, my brain hazy from repetition.

If Mami was here, I would climb into her bed. Migrating to her room isn't exactly a regular occurrence, though it has been happening more often since the dreams started. There's something about being near her that makes me feel protected, and in more than a regular mother-daughter way. It's almost like, if I fall asleep beside her, the smell of her blood, of her essence, might protect me. The spirits might see me as more Honduran if I'm curled up next to her.

On bad nights, I open her door, poke my head in, and say I want a sleepover. Mami just smiles and pats the bed, says "Ven, mi niña." She hasn't questioned why this keeps happening lately. I don't think she wants to—she likes having me back with her, like the early days. Before falling asleep, we watch TV or swap service-industry horror stories. Sometimes, though, she shares too much about the men who flirt with her at work, or she pries into the girls' relationships or mine in a way that no white mom would. I know it's just her way of being close to me, but too much of it irritates me and makes me revert to acting like a child. When we verge closer to being sisters than mother and daughter, I either run away or manipulate her into babying me, having her recount the stories she used to tell me at bedtime when I was little.

As a kid, I'd always ask Mami for stories of back home. I pretended to remember. Really, other than a few hazy images of Lita's house, I couldn't recall much. I'd been too young to even hold on to most New York memories, save for the ones tinged in Mami's pain. Pespire might as well have been a place out of the fantasy books I used to read. But it made Mami light up when I said, "Sí, lo recuerdo," so I did.

Everything I knew about Pespire was through Mami and her stories. I'd asked her endless questions. If the ground looked like ours. If they lived in apartments or houses. If they needed to clean up leaves in the fall. Most of the time, she told me stories of her childhood. Growing up in her abuela's home. Not having shoes until she was eight. Never knowing her father, like me.

She'd tell me that when it rained back home, it didn't smell like worms like it does here. On hot, rainy days, the leaves released a perfume like toasted wood.

"You can get that smell in the rainforest at the Science Centre. Smells funny to you, right? A little weird?" she said. I would always shake my head, as though admitting that I held my breath whenever we walked through would prove I was a traitor.

When thunder would shake the windows and wake me, she would soothe me with lore from back home.

"You know, we loved nights like these back home," she would say to me as I laid my head on her belly. She would tuck a piece of hair behind my ear and scratch the bone like I was a cat. Mami said the rain was like a gift. She and the other kids would run in it like it was a giant warm shower. "Que rico fue." It was the only time they had warm water to bathe in.

"But in La Unión, a few hours away from Pespire, they really, really love thunderstorms. At the end of the spring, when they need the rain the most, and when the biggest downpour comes to relieve them, it rains fish, silver *fish*."

I would picture them like sardines, shiny things that looked like raindrops from afar but would appear bigger and bigger as they got closer, falling to the ground.

"The people there say it comes straight from the hand of God. It happens at night. In the morning, once all the fish have fallen, the town gets together and they have a feast. Your abuela even told me that they have a pageant with the girls. One of them becomes the Senorita Lluvia de Peces, and she gets to dress up like a fish or a mermaid, o algo así, and she gets paraded around town."

In the most ominous voice she could muster, she would profess that no one had *ever* seen the fish fall from the sky. People stayed in to avoid being struck by them. Since no one witnessed the event, the fish seemed to just appear, like a blessing. When I asked if anyone ever sold them, she told me that to sell a divine offering is sacrilegious. The fish were eaten only by the community, their bones kept as memorabilia. Tiny, sharp talismans of hope stowed in safe boxes or displayed on altars.

If the story didn't put me to sleep, or if I just wanted to hear more despite my heavy eyelids, I'd beg for sólo una más. She'd then tell stories of the animals that hung around their porch, like the three-legged stray dog who was so tiny and sweet that they'd ironically dubbed him Danger (pronounced dahn-jeir). When I was younger, she would tell me about la Ciudad Blanca without mentioning the curse.

"It was the umbilical cord of our people, where we came out of the earth," Mami would say. She'd set it up as a shrouded gem, just like the fish from the sky. Nature tucked all her secrets away, she said. The bigger they were, the better she hid them. La Ciudad Blanca was some of her best work, hidden away below the jungle's lowest plains, enveloped in thick pine savanna. It was a well-thought-out shell, practically impenetrable to the Spanish invaders its creators were escaping. Some parts around La Mosquitia are protected by the military, but la Ciudad Blanca itself is protected by ancient deities. Deities who don't like intruders or the people who aid them.

I remember feeling so excited when we started studying Latin America in middle school and my teacher opened the unit with the

Mayas. At some point, I raised my hand to talk about our Honduran ruins, how somewhere—nobody really knew where—there was a whole city surrounded by a white stone wall, and it was full of treasures that couldn't be unearthed without certain death. Some of my classmates asked for sources. Others were confused as to how no one was able to find it for centuries, not even NASA or Google Earth. One boy said it just sounded like a legend, basically "a cross between a fairy tale and a Bible story." Someone else said that la Ciudad Blanca, the White City, sounded like it was a place full of white people; it might as well have been in the suburbs. The class erupted in laughter. I remember crying when I got home.

There were lots of stories that Mami told me about my father. I found out later that most of them were lies, invented tales she conjured when I wouldn't stop pressing her for information. She'd made him seem kind, just not ready to be a father. Besides that, she'd said he was unable to get a visa to come to the States, or later Canada, even for a visit.

When I was a kid, I used to lie in bed after hearing stories of him and wonder if he thought of me at night the way I thought of him. If we were ever both up at the same time, the same slice of moon on our cheeks, thinking of one another, wondering where exactly the other was and how they were. Some nights, I tried to see if I could unlock some telepathic powers within me. I thought that the bond between a father and a daughter should be strong enough to not be obstructed by distance. I would try to send messages. I started small, with numbers (my age, the date, the temperature), colours (my favourites, ranked), snapshots (pictures I drew, our meals, Mami's face). I'd try to feel for his messages in return. Professions of love. Images of his house, of him. I didn't know what he looked like. Maybe one night, he'd return my minus twenty-two degrees with a plus thirty-two degrees, just to tease me. Or send back a shot of tamales, his hands unwrapping the plantain leaf to let the masa cool down. I thought I might almost be able to smell the dough and the meat inside if I tried hard enough.

But my father never sent anything back. Night after night, I kept everything on alert, sensors open like suction cups. Eventually, I gave up on my telepathic attempts and figured that he wasn't ready, like Mami had said, that I couldn't contact him in any way.

When I turned fourteen, she told me the truth. All that she'd lied about. Why she'd left, who my father was, what had really happened to him. In a single breath, she shattered not only my history but my future. According to her, according to a curse I tried so badly to disprove through statistics and logic, my adolescence would be governed by this superstition, an irrational thing that loomed over us. I was not to date or fall in love or have sex with a man until I was twenty. Mami wanted me on the pill anyway, just in case anything happened or I was anything like her as a teen, unwilling to believe in the curse.

For the first time in my life, I yelled at my mami. For believing in myths, and worse, for letting them dictate what we could or could not do, for letting something so obviously designed to manipulate and shame the women in our family control me, too. I called her uneducated. Stupid. *Of course* she got pregnant when she didn't use protection. It wasn't a curse.

"If you listen to me, mi vi, even if you don't believe it, just indulge me," she said. "You can break it. You can be the one to end this if you don't let a man get what he wants. If you don't get pregnant before twenty, it will all be done. You won't have to have a child before you're ready. No one else has to die."

I promised her that I would not be another statistic. I told her that teen pregnancy was not a genetic predisposition.

"I never said it was scientific, mi vi." She shook her head. "Not a predisposition—a maldición."

"Mami, I'm an American who lives in Canada," I told her. "Even if it is all real, do you seriously even think that I'm Honduran enough?"

Until then, she'd held a straight face. But that last bit made my mami cry. I think about that moment a lot these days, especially at night, shuffling around, looking for cool spots in my bed. I find myself wondering whether I jinxed it with those words, brought the curse on with my arrogance. Or was it beyond words, beyond science? Was it bound to happen no matter what? I can't find the answers, only more questions. I count them like sheep for the rest of the night.

ISAURA

IN THOSE EARLY MONTHS, you didn't know that newborns need to be fed upwards of ten times a day. That every few hours, the tears and the screams would be from hunger. That her weight was supposed to increase at the beginning, that she wasn't supposed to be so small for so long. You fed your daughter three times a day, after your own meals. Rocked her and checked her diaper and cried alongside her when she wouldn't relent. No one told you.

You found out later when you joined your mami in New York. "Mija, why did you think she was crying all that time? Why did you think she was so flaca?" You said you didn't know. You said she wasn't there to tell you.

She hadn't known about the beatings until Antonio's father called. When you could no longer disguise the bruises, he intervened. He reached out to a connection at the embassy and got you a rushed visa to join your mami in the U.S. With his permission to make a long-distance call, you picked up the phone to talk to her. You weren't sure it was all realistic, this image of you and your daughter and your mami all together in New York. When she picked up, she told you she'd gotten you work as a cleaner with her. You would make decent money, three times what you could ever make at home. You would live with her, share her bed. But you could not take your daughter. Not without Antonio's consent, and there was no way you would ever get that. You could lose your daughter altogether if you tried to leave the country with her. It was too big a risk. The only way to provide for her, to one day get her back, was to leave her. To make money in New York and send it back to Honduras. You cried over the line as the image of the three of you evaporated. Leaving your daughter felt impossible, but your mami assured you it was not. It was what mothers in our country had been doing for decades. "Besides," she said, "you'll be no good to her when he beats you to death. Get out, and then get her out." You knew she was right.

At two in the morning, you stuffed all that you could in a bag. Underwear. Shirts. A single book. The visa you'd been given. You wanted so badly to put Yessenia in that bag. You couldn't even kiss her one last time. You'd spent that last evening inhaling her, but still, it felt torturous that you couldn't even approach her crib, see her lashes flutter as she dreamt. The fear of waking her and, in turn, Antonio was too big a threat. That night, you put your fingers to your lips and hoped that some of you might hang in the air and reach her after you sent that final kiss toward her.

The next morning, Antonio's father would tell him what he'd done, and Antonio would never speak to him again. Meanwhile, you cried your way through Newark airport, shivering from the cold and the heartache that had spread through your entire body. Your body did not feel like yours without her close by. But in order to get her back one day, you had to keep moving.

On one of the first nights you spent in that Brooklyn apartment, your mami told you how wrong you'd been about the feedings. You thought you might die of guilt. Before you understood what trauma was, you had to live with what felt like a blade twisting inside your chest, because you had starved your child, because you hadn't known how to mother. Only after time, when the pain had eased, could you begin to understand why your body had reacted like that, all those years away from hers. What it still does to you sometimes when you lie awake at night, remembering how little you knew, how little you still know.

You called Lita from New York every Sunday, when she went to church and could receive calls in the rectory after the service. Neither of you had a phone at home. You'd go into Manhattan to get to this one booth where, if you placed a quarter just right, you could bypass the long-distance charges. There was always a lineup, but the chatter in Spanish made it tolerable. That, and knowing that you would soon be able to get an update about your daughter. When he'd moved out of his dad's, Antonio had dropped Yessenia off at your abuela's. He couldn't handle her alone, especially not after he got a job at the garage in town. Sometimes after work, he'd stop by your abuela's to see your daughter. Maybe once every couple of months, like it was a checkup. He'd leave handprints on Yessenia's clothes, black and sticky from the cars he spent the day sweating under. The only real proof of her father was a black thumbprint on her first pair of shoes.

Sometimes, Lita would put your daughter on the phone, but all she could do was coo or cry, and her tears only reminded you of how terrible a mother you were. How you didn't take care of her properly when you were home, and how you could barely help from afar. All you could do was send money. Whenever you heard oil crackling in the background—women from the church frying pupusas—you wanted to weep. You missed your home. The way it smelled of fried masa and laundry detergent and gasoline.

As much as you hated Antonio and wished the curse had taken him before he'd escalated the beatings from slaps to punches, you sort of missed him, too. Time and distance blurred the memory of violence and sharpened the good things he'd once made you feel. Wanted. Beautiful. Loved. You hadn't ever felt safety or certainty about him, and yet you often fell asleep wondering if things could've been different, if they still could be if you went home with money. Maybe you could start over. Be a family.

You saved as much as possible. What you could spare from your pay went to your abuela at the end of the month. The rest went to rent and food, which you split with your mami and the other women in your apartment. But each holiday bonus and the money from every extra shift you covered you stashed in a sock under your pillow. Seeing it grow gave you hope that you might be able to see your daughter before she forgot you completely. You'd save enough to go back and forth for a few years, then move back to Pespire when you'd made enough to buy a small home for you and her. And him, maybe, too.

When you almost had enough for a plane ticket to go visit, you called Lita to tell her the news. You thought she'd be elated. But she was silent.

"Isaura," she said, "he died last week. He's gone."

You didn't have to ask who. Your body knew before your brain did—your knees buckled, and you had to hold onto the phone booth to steady yourself. Your body knew exactly what had happened.

"Keep saving money for her, mija," she said. "Bring her to the U.S. Give her a chance to escape all of this."

———

A year passed after that call. Then two. None of it got easier; you just got more used to living with the gash of longing. For your daughter, for your home, for the family you could've had with the man you inadvertently killed. Whenever the ache threatened to debilitate you, to prevent you from doing what you'd come to this country to do, you reminded yourself that he might've killed you, too, if you hadn't left.

Sometime during your second summer in the city, you met someone, an American twelve years older than you who worked at the bagel shop around the corner from your apartment. It was where you went when you wanted to treat yourself. Back then, they charged fifty cents to add lox to a bagel, but for you, he'd ribbon slices of fish free of charge. You would sit at the counter and practise your English with him, and he'd be patient when you struggled. When you would take a while to remember a word, he would pick a caper off your plate and sneak it into his mouth. He called it incentivizing you to learn the language. You laughed, then cursed him in Spanish.

He proposed only three months after that first bagel, a week after he butchered the pronunciation of *Te quiero*, and you probably did the same to *I love you*. He knelt down in the middle of Fort Greene Park, which was where he'd taken you on your only date outside of the bagel shop. The leaves had gone from green to gold in that time, and you couldn't believe how quickly everything changed. With your hand in his, he promised to take care of you in a way that nobody from home could, which was another way of saying, *I can make you American*. You couldn't have asked for anything more. You married him after a short engagement, with his co-worker as your witness because your mami couldn't do it without ID. She'd been skeptical about it anyway, but you convinced her when you said it wasn't just for love (that was a bonus), but for security, for Yessenia. At city hall, you wore a short white dress with the tag tucked inside, scratching your back. You'd return it the next day, before moving into his place.

———

The apartment was bare-boned and beige—the walls, the couch, the bedsheets, all one shade of oatmeal—but to you, it was big, a one-bedroom on the other side of Brooklyn. When you had more time, more money, you would add some colour to it and make it your own. But in the beginning, it didn't matter. Even though you did sometimes miss living with your mami, living in your new colour-less apartment was infinitely better than sharing a bathroom and a kitchen with five other women. Though you never spent that much time at home anyway. Mostly, you were in other people's, cleaning them, making them look new again. Your constant exhaustion almost felt worth it when your clients came home and lit up at the sight of their apartments, all tidy and pristine. Like maybe you were doing something right after all.

At night, you and your husband would collapse on the couch, your bones aching from being on your feet all day. You'd play with each other's hands and talk, leafing through the Spanish-English dictionary you kept on hand in case you got stuck on a word. He'd ask about Yessenia and your mami and your abuela, talk about bringing your daughter over, raising her with you. A few nights a month, he'd go visit his "brother" in Jersey, and at the beginning, you really did think that's who he was spending time with. You thought he was a family man, that he'd make a good father for your child. You might've kept on believing that he was the best thing that had happened to you had you not found out about the other women. You confronted him about them, and that's when he started hitting you, some six months into your marriage.

That's when you realized how little you knew him, really. In the three months you dated, you'd only fought once, about you "flirting" with the cashier at the bagel shop, and he'd apologized with a bouquet of roses so big you thought the size was a reflection of how bad he felt, how good he actually was. He hadn't laid a hand on you or given you any indication that he might. Before he was violent, his moments of jealousy made you feel special, not threatened. It took you years to realize how wrong that was. He had been on a power trip the whole time, only offering things you couldn't possibly refuse. To corner you. To pin you down. Later, you found out he'd been engaged before, at least twice, to other immigrant women who ended up leaving him before the wedding. It was too late for you.

Somehow you found yourself in the same relationship you'd fled your home to escape. You would not admit this to yourself for years. Instead, you reminded yourself of how profusely he apologized after he hurt you. How different it was because this man could admit that he was intimidated by you (you, a nineteen-year-old), that he was afraid of losing you, that the girls you found out about meant nothing. It was not the same as Antonio, because there were other new factors to blame: alcohol, his parents, an Irish-Catholic upbringing, your cultural divide, the system (whatever that meant). Half of you truly believed that he was sorry after he hit you, that he would do better, and that he did love you. The other half knew you didn't have a choice either way. He'd already petitioned to bring Yessenia over. You'd gotten a green card and so would she. In a few years, you'd be citizens.

When you called to tell your abuela that you could finally bring your daughter over to the U.S., you barely managed to get the words out without crying. It almost seemed fake. That's how lucky you felt back then. Sure, you had to put the phone to your left ear to avoid pressing the bruise on the right side of your face, but it didn't matter. You were getting your daughter back thanks to him.

Once all the paperwork had gone through and you had sorted out her travel arrangements, she landed at LaGuardia, sleeping in the arms of an escort holding a sign with your name on it. Strangely, the memories of the wait are foggy to you. You can't recall what it felt like to count down to her arrival. Not even the night before. Perhaps you tried not to think about it. Too afraid that something would prevent her from coming, from reuniting three years after you'd snuck out in the night.

When you scooped her up out of the escort's arms, she smelled of home. The humidity of the rainy season in her hair. The chemicals her dress was laundered in. You placed her head on your shoulder and breathed in deeply. It would be the last time you would ever smell Honduras on her. When you brought her home, your mami came over to meet her and slept on the couch. It was like you were given a second newborn bubble, complete with your own mother and a husband this time. Seeing your mami hold your child felt like witnessing some sort of miracle. Not just because you were all there, together in the United States, but because Yessenia was an extension of her, too, the vessel that would launch farther than either of you could go. But until then, you would both hold on, orbiting around her ceaselessly.

You tried so hard to make up for lost time. To soothe her when she cried out for your abuela, to keep her warm in weather she hadn't even known existed. You wondered whether your separation had stunted your maternal instinct. You had to figure out how to become her mother again. To get to know her and adjust to belonging to her, as much as she belonged to you. Once the rush of your reunion had passed, you doubted your ability. On bad days, you wondered how you were supposed to raise a child when you still felt like one yourself. She would go on incomprehensible hunger strikes and throw tantrums that you couldn't make sense of, so you couldn't appease her. Some days, she would refuse to walk, forcing you to drag her writhing body on your way to work. You would brush her hair while she slept, because she rejected your touch while she was awake. On really bad days, you wondered if, how, you could send her back to your abuela. You hated to admit it, but she knew Yessenia far better than you did. She knew what to do. You told yourself that Lita probably missed her, that you'd be doing them both a favour, that Lita had raised two generations already, so what was one more?

But when you had good days with your daughter, it gave you faith that you might not screw her up completely. Slowly, she began to trust you enough to let you brush her hair. She started to listen to you. You'll never forget the first time she climbed up on the couch to rest her head on your lap. It was like being given a second chance. In time, you got so attached to having her close to you that you couldn't bear to leave her with anyone else for fear you'd lose her again. It wasn't logical, but whenever you were apart from her, worry spread across your body like hives. The guilt of ever wanting to send her back to Honduras seeped into your bones. The desire to repent for your separation, for the years you spent learning, failing, to be her mother, heightened everything. You still catch yourself now, almost two decades in, afraid that those crucial years apart left you with an unstable base.

Back then, you were just putting one foot in front of the other. Figuring out how to parent for one more day. Getting her dressed, clipping her nails, washing her. In retrospect, it was those little tasks that gave you the confidence to feel like you might be able to do it, to really be a mother. Things as simple as getting her hair into a clean braid made you feel so accomplished.

Your husband didn't go out of his way to help with her, but he could be sweet to her; he always ruffled her curls when he walked by her, made sure to kiss her good night. In some ways, things were okay.

He wouldn't hit you in front of her, so you tried your best to keep her close. But his jealousy got worse. Ironically, he would accuse you of cheating. He would question you when you ran a few minutes late, when your schedule changed unexpectedly because of work or your child, and then he'd leave the city with no explanation the next day. The constant meetings with lawyers to get your immigration papers in order only exacerbated the stress. Every so often, you would have an argument that would either send you and your daughter running home to your mami's or have him locking both of you out. Yessenia got used to sleeping on your chest, even when she was too big for it.

Until she started school at age five, you brought your daughter to your jobs, set her on the couch to nap or watch TV as you swept and dusted. Most of your clients were at work when you came by anyway. The only one who really got to know your daughter was Mrs. Saltzman, a woman in her seventies who'd stopped leaving her apartment in the winter after she'd broken both hips in a fall.

Mrs. Saltzman loved Yessenia. Once she'd met your daughter, she began asking you to come twice a week. She'd have you wash clothes you were almost certain were clean and press them even though you doubted she'd wear them. If Yessenia was sleeping when you got there, Mrs. Saltzman would hold her. You'd offer to set her down, but she refused. "Do you know how good it feels to hold a sleeping child?" she asked, and you laughed. Yes, of course you did.

If Yessenia was awake, you would have her sit on the living room floor with a stack of stickers and a pad of legal paper. Mrs. Saltzman would recline in her reading chair and talk to her, ask her where she would place the next star or which colour she liked best. Yessenia's eyes would shoot between Mrs. Saltzman and her sheet of stickers, her tiny fingers trying so hard to perfect their pinch to pull each sticker off the sheet. It amazed you how quickly they began to understand each other. That was how she first learned English. As your daughter grew older,

Mrs. Saltzman upgraded her craft box from stickers to pastels and watercolours. When you both became citizens (you first, then Yessenia once you had your paperwork), she bought her a Lego set of the Statue of Liberty that they spent hours working on. And when Yessenia started kindergarten, Mrs. Saltzman insisted on buying her school supplies. You had never seen your daughter as excited as she was on her first day of school, her new Disney backpack slung over her tiny shoulders.

Whenever you think back on that time, you are still overwhelmed by her generosity. The tips and bonuses that allowed you to help your abuela when she was sick. The love Mrs. Saltzman doled out to your child, to you. How long she had known about the abuse, you'd never find out. You thought you'd always been thorough about covering up your bruises, and the one time you went into work with a black eye, you said you'd been mugged. You'd even conceived of a backstory so detailed (a pocket knife, your stolen Walkman, luckily not your wallet because you hadn't had it on you) that you really thought she'd bought it. But when she got you a job in Canada, it became clear that what she was proposing was an escape. Her late husband's airline was expanding their Toronto team. They would sponsor you and Yessenia.

"I have a life here, a husband," you said.

"Precisely," was all she replied.

As you looked at your child diligently practising her handwriting at the table, her small six-year-old body drowning in your husband's old T-shirt because she'd grown out of her clothes seemingly overnight, you shook your head. Mrs. Saltzman pulled you into the kitchen, her bony hand stronger than you'd imagined. She assured you that if you were worried about him coming after you, she would handle it. Her attorney could get in touch to file a restraining order and help you arrange a divorce. She would see to it.

"I can't," you said. "I should get to work."

But Mrs. Saltzman dismissed you before you could clean. As you walked out, you remember thinking you'd disappointed her. Maybe you weren't as strong as she thought you were, maybe she would fire you to teach you a lesson. You wondered how you would make enough money this week without your shifts there. But when you reached into your pocket for your MetroCard, you realized she'd still slipped your pay in your jacket without you noticing. Yessenia asked you, in English—the only language she spoke around you since school started—why you were crying when you saw the cash. You didn't know how to explain it.

The two of you got off at your mami's stop. You had to talk to her. The thought of leaving a man who had done so much for you, whom you loved as much as you feared, curdled your stomach. Leaving him felt inconceivable. The thought of having failed another relationship made you sick. In her apartment, you sat Yessenia in front of the TV and told your mami everything. What your marriage had become, what options you'd been given. She grabbed your hands.

"What are you going to do about it?"

"I don't know."

"Yes, you do. You will do what's best for your daughter."

"She'll lose everything she knows again. Her home. Him. He loves us. He's never laid a finger on her."

"She won't miss him one day," she said. "You have to think about that. You have to make tough decisions. You think I wanted to come here? To start over all alone? No. But mothers don't think about what they want. They think about what their babies need."

Her grasp tightened as she spoke, the fervour of her pain bruising your skin.

"Okay," you said.

Only when you got up to head to the pay phone to call Mrs. Saltzman did your mami let go of you. Across the line, you could sense Mrs. Saltzman's relief, too. She promised that she would call her attorney, that they could meet with you whenever it was safe for you. "The hardest part is almost over," she assured you before hanging up.

You met with the lawyer later that week, after one of your shifts in Manhattan. He'd drawn up the papers, would keep them until you landed in Toronto. As you dragged the pen across each page marked with an X, your throat tightened. You knew it was what you had to do, and yet it was crushing. Signing out your life in New York with your husband's last name. Gambling on a new one that you could only hope would be better for your child. You'd leave the next time your husband left the city to visit his "brother."

The day before you left, you picked up your daughter from school and brought her back to your mami's one last time. You would sleep there for the night. After Yessenia dozed off between you, you talked about bringing your mami over to Canada, too, but she didn't want to leave. She had her women here, a community she'd grown to love. She didn't want to have to start over again. That final sleepover would be the last time you ever felt her so close.

In the morning, you went back to your apartment, packed up your things in a single duffle bag. To Yessenia's disappointment, you didn't drop her off at school. You remember her crying about missing her friend's birthday. There was supposed to be a party in the classroom, cupcakes. She'd never used the word *friend* before. Her classmates had teased her about her English, made it impossible to get close to any of them until now. As she dragged her feet behind you, you knew you didn't have time to let guilt in. You promised her there would be other birthdays, other schools, other friends. You didn't wipe away her tears that day. All you could think about was getting to Mrs. Saltzman's. You were terrified your husband might come home early and notice the missing clothing and passports.

At Mrs. Saltzman's, she handed you two envelopes, one fat with cash and the other holding the details of your new life. Two plane tickets. A map of Toronto. Instructions to guide a taxi driver to your new place. The number to call when you arrived at the apartment, along with the name of the landlord, who was an old friend of the Saltzmans. You remember breaking down in her living room, asking why she was doing all of this.

"I don't have children, dear. And I can't take it all to my grave," she said, as she reached her arms out for Yessenia, and your daughter settled in them one last time. "She deserves more. So do you."

The three of you held each other until you saw the cab pull up outside the window. You didn't know it then, but you would get to hug her again, when she came to visit you both in Toronto for a week almost every summer until she died. Ever since that first flight from JFK to Pearson, at every takeoff and every landing, you clutch the cross around your neck and mumble a prayer to Mrs. Saltzman.

A week after you arrived, Mrs. Saltzman called. She was checking in to see how you were adjusting to Toronto. You managed to chat for about ten minutes before Yessenia started pulling at your skirt. But before Mrs. Saltzman would let you go, she admitted that she had called to share some news, too. Information that the attorney had passed on to her after he'd arranged the papers. Your husband had been found in the courtyard of your old apartment. Broken spine, no pulse, gin for blood, basically. The police ruled it a suicide.

You remember holding your daughter as you dropped the phone. Mrs. Saltzman's voice was drowned out by the sound of your wailing and Yessenia's "Mami, it's okay. Mami, Mami, my Mami." It was just the two of you, alone in a new country, grieving another man, another father figure. In that moment, you wondered just how you would tell her what she'd been born into.

VIVIAN

MY FATHER KNEW YESTERDAY. He could tell from her demeanour. The slow sips. The stony way in which she moved around the kitchen. She started shutting herself down in preparation for my anniversary, hardening her shell to endure it. Just before bed, my father asked outright when she wanted to go to Detroit. "Tomorrow," she said.

That was it. No more warning, certainly not for Eddie, who was out that night until four. The only heads up he got was when my father barged into his room this morning to announce their imminent departure as a simple fact.

"Wake up, Ed. We're leaving right after we eat."

Eddie groaned under his covers.

"Pack a bag with enough for a few days. Essentials."

"Today? Right now, this second? It's not even—"

"After breakfast, I said."

My father shut the door, leaving Eddie muttering on the other side. He did it. Told him what was happening, ripped it off like a Band-Aid so that my mother wouldn't have to.

Now, as my father leans against the wall in the hallway, guilt begins to build in his chest. He knows that this is a tough week for Eddie, too. Tougher in some ways, because he always has to put my mother first. Most parents put their children first, my father thinks.

My brother swings his bedroom door open and my father flinches.

"Wait, Dad—when are we coming back?"

"I'm not sure. Your mother and I will decide once we're there."

Eddie groans. He wasn't prepared to leave today. My anniversary is still two days away.

"You really don't think this has gone on too long?" Eddie asks, with sleep in his voice. He clears his throat before continuing. "Every year I think this August might be different. She might not—"

My father pushes Eddie back into his room to prevent my mother from hearing any more. He shuts the door behind him, even though he suspects the sound will still seep out.

"How could you think that she could ever forget?" he spits out as quietly as he can.

"I'm not saying forget, just find a way to cope! It has literally been two decades, and she has not held it together one August. Not one! I didn't think I had to remind you of the shit she's done in the past."

My father wants to cover Eddie's mouth so that my mother doesn't hear, and also so he doesn't say something he can't take back. But my father also wants to hug him. He kicks himself for not sitting at the foot of Eddie's bed and palming his feet to wake him up. For not approaching this conversation with his son in a gentler way, with the sort of careful compassion he almost always offers his wife. He should've given him a hug.

"I'm sorry, Eddie. This time, it won't be the same. This is big for her. We're going back."

"My time off starts tomorrow. I have work today, in two hours."

"No, you don't. Called the store already. Family emergency. You're off for the week."

Eddie's mouth hangs open, but nothing comes out. My father reaches for his hand, and my brother pulls it away.

An hour into the drive to Detroit, my mother turns around to watch Eddie sleep. It's been years since she's done that. He's got his head against the window, and there's a patch of fog on the glass by his mouth. He seems more childlike asleep in the back seat, tuckered out from fighting our parents, resigned to acceptance and rest.

The cruel things she said to Eddie in the kitchen play back in her mind as she watches him. She imagines how he felt after she told him she didn't mean any of it, that she lashed out without thinking. How he must not have believed that she doesn't hate him. My brother stayed quiet while she leaned against his bookcase. He listened but never rewarded our mother with an acceptance of her apology. She should've written something to read from instead of relying on memory and not saying the right things. Forgetting the most important bits. It's too late now, but she opens her Notes app and tries anyway.

Tell him you're sorry you didn't want to let him bring his camera. Promise him you'll watch his film, even if it's pain-ful. Maybe he was right, anyway. It could be cathartic. And maybe making it would help him make more sense of why we have to make this trip.

She tells herself she'll try to pull him aside in Detroit and do over her apology. After she rereads what she's written enough to feel slightly hopeful again, she scrolls through her other notes and pauses on the one she wrote after she sat with Isaura in the car last winter. Her plans for this August. Her theories on why each anniversary has devolved into catastrophe. She had to think about this August as logically as possible.

In tallying her failures with my brother, she realized that the way she'd hurt him most was by not being there. By not watching over him, by leaving him, by running away. Not only in August, but consistently. He was right: she didn't know much about his art, or his goals, or his relationships. She'd never told him she knew Mivi was there that morning she humiliated him. She hadn't even checked in with him after her initial apology. She didn't ask why Mivi wasn't coming around anymore. It was easier not to hear tough answers.

When Isaura made that revelation about Eddie in the car, my mother realized just how disconnected she was from her son. She'd had to learn the news by piecing information together from a woman she barely knew. And so she told herself that it was time. This anniversary, she would be there for him, *really* be there. She would use this milestone to create a new one. To start over.

When looking at the screen makes her too nauseated, she turns around again to look at her son's face and the rising chest that she used to stare at over his crib for hours. It's been years since she's felt like she might be able to make up for what she lost by giving another child her all. Twenty years later, though, she's starting to believe that it's possible. It may seem arbitrary, two decades—what does it really mean? But she felt it in the car with Isaura. That she had to go back. That for the first time, she might be able to face her baby without breaking.

Eddie sleeps through the entire drive to Detroit. At the border, the officer doesn't even ask my parents to wake him up. They probably seem somewhat wholesome—a family returning to the city they're from, to visit old friends. The officer welcomes them back.

As they weave their way into the city, my parents' eyes strain to stop tears from falling. They focus on the road as they speed past sights like the gutted train station, now surrounded by heavy machinery. When they reach downtown, the smell of smoke and meat seeps into the car as they pass a street festival that neither of them acknowledges.

To get emotional about buildings and neighbourhoods almost seems childish to them. Of course things have changed. But my parents are not here to mourn Detroit or turn over the stones of the city. That's for sightseers and historians. They are neither. They are excavators with a single task.

"We need a room with two beds, please," my mother says as she leans on the hotel's counter. It's a chain hotel, sanitized and nondescript. A couple of plaques hang behind reception, boasting regional excellence and a high Tripadvisor score back in 2011.

The clerk at reception struggles with the system for a moment, jiggling the mouse. My mother taps her fingernails against the laminate counter as the screen loads.

"How long will you be staying?"

"Do you have any rooms free for the week?" my mother asks.

"We won't be here for the whole week," Eddie says as he turns to my mother like a child, looking at her as if to say, *Right?* He's still got the mark from the car window imprinted on his forehead, but it's his selfishness that stands out most to my mother.

"We do have one vacancy. It's a room with two queen beds, and it's going to be $250 a night."

"That's perfect," my mother says to the clerk.

"And how many nights would you like me to put down? Did you say the full week?"

The clerk looks at my mother, his shoulders tense, hands floating just above the keyboard. He needs an answer. So does my brother. Eddie turns around, hoping to see my father walk through the entrance and weigh in, but he's still out parking the car when my mother decides.

"Three nights. Put us down for three, and after that, we'll see."

ROSY

AFTER UNPACKING, I DECIDE to walk alone. Your father takes Eddie to a diner for a late lunch, but I'm not hungry. Besides, it's best to keep myself away until I feel calm again. The nausea that crept in during the car ride hasn't passed just yet, so I return to the remedy that has gotten me through many Augusts: aimless, quiet walks.

I head in the opposite direction of our old neighbourhood. Your father and I decided that we'd save that visit for your anniversary. I don't want anything to set me off this early. For now, I'll just walk down Woodward, my tense muscles, from my jaw to my thighs, loosening slowly as I move through a street I once knew each crack of.

I'm surprised that the smells have not changed when so much else has. I can barely remember what the Starbucks and the Lululemon used to be, but the blend of exhaust pipe fumes and yeast from the distillery brings me back, and I can remember what it was like to walk around here at fifteen, at twenty. It's funny to think that, in time, you can take comfort in things you once despised, all because they're familiar.

When I reach the CVS before the big intersection, I inhale deeply and steady my gaze on the glass doors. My feet move toward the doors before I realize my body is on autopilot. I step back before they slide open, and suddenly it occurs to me that there must be an archive of my life inside that CVS. Prescriptions for penicillin and birth control pills and Tylenol 3 and diphenhydramine and fluoxetine and Lexapro and Zoloft and antihistamines. A constellation of medication doled out through the years. An insight into the path I took, connected by drugs and a body that could not seem to function without them after I lost my parents.

I think of what else Detroit has of mine. City Hall has every kind of licence and certificate. Marriage, stillbirth, birth, death. Each landmark of our lives stamped and signed. It has all the other paperwork that came in between—all the documents about the home we owned, my business registration, and permits. The public library has a record of all the books we took out. The hospital, a file of all visits. The soil has my babies. With the first one we lost, your first brother, we scattered the ashes across our old lawn so that he'd be home, close to us. And the other, you, we put in a tiny wooden casket in the middle of Mt. Elliott Cemetery. When we left Detroit, I felt like I was abandoning my children. Leaving them alone in another country. I resented every inch of that drive to Toronto, throwing up into a plastic bag, Eddie kicking me inside as waves of sickness overtook me, as though he, too, was punishing me for taking him away from his siblings.

As I walk on, heat rising from the baked asphalt, I can't help but feel on edge. I am more present, more vulnerable than I was in the car. I am not just passing through, I am participating. I am back, my head swinging between buildings, glaring at everyone walking toward me on the sidewalk. Until this moment, I hadn't thought about running into anyone I used to know. I hadn't realized how much I feared recognition.

We don't have any family left in the city. Your father's parents died a few years after mine did, and I don't know what happened to our neighbours, to our old friends. Some, I know, have moved out of Detroit. Others, I've had no contact with for ages, not even a passive connection on Facebook.

It's not like I hadn't wanted to come back. I hadn't wanted to leave, either, but we didn't have a choice. It was too painful to keep living with all the reminders of what we'd lost. The house might as well have been wallpapered with your face. We'd planned to wait out the year that everyone insisted we let pass before making any big decisions. A few months short of your anniversary, though, I found out I was pregnant. Although we stayed for your one year, as my due date approached, neither one of us wanted to bring another child back to the home you died in. Your father, especially, wanted to move from the home he almost lost me in, too. He started putting out feelers for new jobs that summer, so when the job offer from Ford's Toronto ad agency came in late September, we took it, and put the house on the market the next day. I should have been more stressed—I was moving to another country in my third trimester—but it was a relief to leave that house and the memories there. A fresh start was what we both needed. For a while, I wondered how callous our friends and neighbours thought we were for packing up and leaving. Never returning to show off Eddie; never celebrating friends' weddings with them; never again visiting the graves of our parents, something your father and I had occasionally done together, bonding over becoming adult orphans too soon.

Later, I wondered if anyone back home thought of us at all. We hadn't kept up with any of our relationships, really. Your death had exposed the fragility of our friendships. My friends from childhood just didn't seem to fit in my life anymore. Initially, they wrote, a couple dropped by, but I think my grief was too challenging for them. Most weren't ready to accompany me through more suffering after I'd lost my parents. I realized that the foundation of a lot of those friendships was based not on connection but on how long we'd known each other. It wasn't solid enough to weather your storm. My college friends were all mothers at that point, and I couldn't stand to think of them, let alone be around them. What they had and what I lost made it impossible to maintain any kind of relationship. I knew I couldn't hear them talk about their children, about how their second or third pregnancies were going, about the sleep regressions and clogged milk ducts and all the other things you should be able to vent to other mothers about. I also knew that I couldn't vent to them, either, tell them what was always on my mind. I knew the last thing these new mothers wanted to hear about was babies dying out of the blue.

Lorraine tried to reach out after she heard about you. I remember rolling out garbage bins to the curb one morning, early September maybe, and Lorraine running out to me. She pulled me into her arms, and I stiffened at her touch. There's nothing worse than a hug when you already feel fragile. It'll push you over the edge, snap you.

Although, maybe what's worse is someone trying to relate to something they haven't experienced. Particularly when, to you, their experience pales in comparison. She'd meant well, trying to connect, sharing her own experience with a miscarriage, and offering up advice about grieving them.

I never told her, but I'd had a miscarriage. And a stillbirth. I'd had both before you. In part, that was why it came as such a shock when I found out I was pregnant with your brother, that he'd somehow withstood my lack of effort to keep either of us alive. I wasn't taking care of myself before or after I got pregnant with him. I never thought he'd be the one to stick.

My first pregnancy didn't last long. Eight weeks. Not viable. A stream of blood followed by three weeks' more. The pain of that loss seemed to lessen as I evacuated the last trace of it. I remember the doctor telling me that many women miscarry that early without even realizing it. That brought me some solace. I had known. I had been in tune with my body, with my baby, even if they hadn't survived. The doctor didn't offer a reason, just a statistic. If one in five pregnancies ended in miscarriage, I figured I'd gotten mine over with. And because it happened so early, it passed easily. I felt fortunate about that.

The second made it past the first trimester. I didn't tell anyone other than your father; my height worked to my advantage to conceal the bump. Your father and I joked that the baby was standing upright already, like a tiny diver in my torso. We kept waiting to tell others, getting more creative sartorially to keep it hidden. Three months. Four. We figured we'd announce at five. By that point, we thought, it would be safe, and regardless, I wouldn't be able to hide the pregnancy any longer.

But we didn't get the chance. The doctor went over the possible causes once the bleeding started. I can barely recall any of them. I was too focused on the pain of it, of bleeding out. I knew what was happening. There was no use in slapping a diagnosis on something when the damage was already done, when he was already gone. Your father and I just cried. Desperately, he asked if this was definitely a miscarriage or if the baby might still survive in the NICU. I remember the doctor correcting him, using the word *stillbirth*, not *miscarriage*. Then he put his hand on your father's shoulder and said he was sorry.

In the middle of the night, they cut him out. We held him and marvelled at the translucence of his body. Nothing looked wrong with him. He was undercooked, tiny, but that was all normal for twenty weeks. I couldn't help but feel that the issue was with me.

That I hadn't provided my child with a safe-enough home. I'd feel that with all my children, though with Eddie the most.

Things were hard for a while. But looking back on it, I handled it well. Not many people knew, and that was a blessing, I thought. No questions to answer or having to relive that day by talking to other people about it. I had your father. I reminded him that the loss was just as much his as it was mine when I saw the way he looked at me as I peeled off another blood-soaked pad a couple of weeks after we lost him. We took on that grief together, taking turns shouldering the weight when the other couldn't. When the finality of it all hit your father and he could not muster the strength to get out of bed, I brought up soups to him, read him the sports section of the newspaper, and moved the TV to the bedroom so we could watch old comedies as we fell asleep. When I would suddenly start crying in the car while running errands, he would have me pull over so he could drive. The cooking and the cleaning were started by one of us and finished by the other, each act of support leading us back to each other.

Our marriage became stronger, for a time. We never raised our voices, never placed blame. I'm not sure how we knew not to do that. As crippling as some days were, I thought of our first loss, how we'd managed through that one. I figured that someday, sooner than we realized, we would be fine once again.

I was right. It took time. Even though the doctor had told me that none of it had been my fault, I had to quiet the guilt, replace it with facts. There was no reason to believe that my body was culpable. Life went on, work carried me through each wave of sadness. Eventually, we started trying again. It took ten months to get pregnant with you, and when it happened, I was terrified. Your father was not. Either he could sense that you were strong or he knew that I just needed someone to be. He would sometimes joke, "The third time's the charm!" and I would just look at him, wondering how I'd managed to get so lucky.

Your brother doesn't know about the others. We don't talk about them. We never even gave them names. For a long time, this made me feel like a bad mother. After you died, I felt I was not fit for parenthood at all—I suspected I was missing some maternal instinct that was necessary to keep a child alive.

After the doctor had pulled your sibling out, I held him for what felt like hours, but eventually, I handed him to a nurse. I gave him away. I let them cremate his tiny body. When you died, I couldn't do it again. Your father was the one to give you away. I'd felt too weighed down by the grief I had for the others. That grief, that love caught in amber, was the last bit of you all that I had; I couldn't let go. Instead, I clung to it. I thought that if I held on to it, no matter what happened, I would still feel tethered to you, I would still be your mother for as long as I felt the weight of you inside.

As I walk through Detroit, I think about what being a mother to someone who is no longer alive really means. I think of my mother and wonder whether she might have had any answers, whether she'd ever lost children, whether I had siblings whose dust had settled somewhere in this city. When she was alive, she never confided much in me, but I wonder if motherhood could've bonded us. I'd always suspected that I'd been unplanned. Maybe she could've admitted that she'd never wanted me and then imparted a lesson about accidents. Told me that God laughs when we make plans, that there's no use in fighting what happens.

I think of Isaura. Neither of us had planned our children. I wonder if I could call her before your anniversary, ask if she has any advice for me. But what if she doesn't understand? What if I misread her? What if she realizes that I have no idea what I'm doing, that I may have pretended in that car, but that even twenty years after what happened to you, I'm still not sure what it means to be a mother? That she should never have listened to my advice. That I am not someone she should be friends with. I pull my phone out, thumb the thread between us for anything that might prove me wrong. A sign that shows she understands me, that we have a real connection, that I might have a chance, and that she might pick up, and she might know what to do now. She's a mother, she's a real mother, I know it; I could see it in the way she cried for her child in the car. But just then, a call from your father lights up the screen, and I answer it.

"Where are you? How are you doing?" he asks.

I tell him I'm coming back, then hang up and put my phone back in my pocket.

MIVI

TWO GIN AND TONICS DEEP, and with half a head of hair curled, I'm finally starting to wake up. Even though I'm not feeling particularly enthusiastic about the prospect of going out dancing after the restless night I just had, I want to see the girls. Between sips, I ribbon up sections of my hair with a ceramic wand, watch as steam rises and fills the bathroom. My hair didn't always need so much help with volume or curl. But when I was younger, I resented my thick curls, and every other day, I fried it into submission, straightening each strand until it sizzled and required balms to soothe the breakages. It was my mami's hair, and I loved my mami's hair, still shining like hard candy—a black wheel of licorice that she'd unspool at the end of the day. But that was on *her*. On a woman whose entire being was made up of sweet Honduran dough, whose complexion softened the transition of black curls to brown skin, whose dark freckles picked up on her black mane as though they were from the same paint swatch. Mami treated her hair gently, like she did all things she loved. She practised patience as she combed through her hair, slowly in order to not break the knots but work through them instead. At night, she'd weave her fingers through like she was stitching the strands into safety, securing them in place, then lay her head on a silk pillow she never travelled without.

I knew it hurt her that I fought my own hair so much. She'd beg me to let her apply treatments to heal the damage I'd done, buy me leave-in conditioners that promised to make my curls full and glossy, try to teach me how to work with what she'd given me. I didn't relent until a full clump of it fell out in the shower and left me with a bald spot the size of a peach pit.

Since then, I've tried to repent with masks and leave-ins. But until the texture is restored, I use curling irons on nights I want to be a bit extra. Since this is going to be one of my last nights out in a while, I'll go big.

Once school starts up again, I'll trade in my socializing for studying in the library. I'll limit distractions so that nothing can impact my GPA. Last year, I had a blip in the fall semester. Mami tried to convince me it was just the adjustment to university, but I knew I'd been distracted by Eddie. The lack thereof. All that was unsaid, by both of us, during those months apart. In lectures, I would mull over our texts, regretting each mention of his mother, worrying that my attempts at normalcy had been insensitive, composing and deleting paragraphs in which I tried to verbalize the tension that had gnawed at me since that morning at his house. Whenever I'd see him across campus, I'd avert my gaze, and then be unable to shake my cowardice all day. The few times he'd send a message, the words would be printed on my lids for hours, analyzed even as I wrote my mid-terms.

Stop, I think as I dab more eyeshadow into the crease of my lid. *Just stop thinking about him. There's no way it could possibly end well.* A single flake of blue glitter falls into my drink, but I take a sip anyway. I wonder what it would look like in my stomach, if the fleck will be digested or stick to my insides.

Leaning over the sink, I drag a doe foot around my lips until they are covered in a berry shine. I pout, study my face in the mirror, then swipe on a bit more gloss. My reflection frustrates me. How stupid to look good and only think of the person I can't be with, playing over our conversations again and again. Wondering whether he might join us later tonight, what we'd do after. How many drinks I could have without slipping up. *No.* Slipping up isn't even on the table. I pick up my glass and down the rest of my gin.

As much as I dread Eddie moving to New York, a part of me hopes he'll leave. That would be the easiest way to keep us apart. So that I can't just turn to him when I'm drunk and craving his comfort. We could still be friends, but the distance would make it impossible to be more. Eventually, we would replace each other with work and school and new people. Maybe I would find a boyfriend to tell our story to one day, and we would laugh at how Eddie and I once were, our puppy love.

If he gets into that program in Manhattan, school will start next August. I wonder if that's part of his motivation to go to the U.S.—a guaranteed escape from his sister's anniversary. He told me that if he could, he would go earlier, in July, to settle in a bit, get to know the city, maybe even find a job assisting at a studio.

If he moves, I'll visit. Once. I'll take it as an opportunity to close two circles—the one with Eddie and the one with New York. Even though I don't want him to go, I have a feeling that seeing him in the city might reframe some of New York for me. Technically, it couldn't all be bad if Eddie was a part of it.

I'll go for a weekend in the fall, maybe.

I imagine him showing me around his new neighbourhood like he's a local. We'll get coffee in those blue-and-white paper cups from a bodega, which he'll call a bo-day-gah and I'll pronounce properly just to tease him. He'll probably film me. Capture my hair, which I'll have in one long braid bouncing against my leather jacket. It'll be that perfect weather you dream that New York is in the fall. A hint of coolness with a full, fat sun beating down. My ankles will be out. Eddie always laughs when I say it, but I think exposed ankles are so sexy. *You're so fucking Victorian,* he'll say when I balance my weight on one leg and wiggle my other ankle at him like a tease. He might film it just to make me smile. And then he might just realize that I'm right.

He'll ask if I remember any of it. I'll say not like this. No feminist bookstores or nine-dollar turmeric lattes. We'll walk by the building where my abuela lived, and I'll tell him that this was where we'd sometimes come for fried fish and sleepovers. I'll share stories about her, my strong abuela, who loved us so much. Not too far from our old stomping grounds, Eddie and I will go vintage shopping, and he'll convince me to get a silver flapper dress for New Year's. It might make me sad for a moment to think that he won't be there for it. But it will also give me hope. Maybe by then I'll have someone else to dance with, someone else to shed sequins onto at the end of the night.

Afterwards, we'll get coffee and sit on a bench. Eddie will ask if I want a cigarette. I'll say I quit, because by then, I will have. He'll smile. *Look at you,* he'll say. We'll walk some more, stop by a gallery, contemplate what a wall made up of shattered glass and parking tickets means. Eddie will guess communist ideology. I'll say it's clearly about menstruation. We'll laugh. I'll ask him to please not make any art like that.

Maybe later, we'll meet up with some of his new Brooklyn friends. They'll have strange names and be ethnically ambiguous, and maybe that'll be all I'll have in common with them. There'll be cans of LaCroix on a milk-crate coffee table and an ashtray in the centre. I'll want to smoke, but I'll just shake my head when offered.

When it comes time to go, I'll realize the agony of leaving your heart in another country. I'll think of my mami. How she did that with me. How had she done it? I won't know how it could feel any worse, but I'll know it had to have been for her. On the train to the airport, I will cry. People will barely look.

And then it'll be over. It'll be too painful to leave again, so I'll just never go back. After getting my final hit, I'll be able to quit him, too.

VIVIAN

AFTER LUNCH, MY BROTHER and father joined my mother in her wanderings. My parents pointed out all their old spots, how different they all looked now. The Whole Foods that had replaced their favourite coffee shop, the one that made those pillowy pretzel sandwiches my mother brought home when they were too lazy to cook. The *For Lease* sign in the bar where my parents met and where my father proposed, buzzing off a single rum and coke. The bulldozers parked in front of my mother's first accounting office, ready to transform it into a new condominium. When they approached the hospital where I was born, and where they took me after I died, my mother put her sunglasses on. As she tried to conceal her tears, she wished that my brother had brought his camera on their walk. She wanted to capture the landmark in case it was ever torn down like everything else. But she knew that if she snapped a picture with her phone, she'd never stop turning to it, like a vice. She doesn't have any photos of me or Detroit on her phone. It'd be like keeping a blade in her pocket.

Maybe Eddie could take one on his phone, she thought. Maybe if she asked him to, he would believe that she had faith in him. He'd understand how great the task would be, how much she trusted him to capture something so important. But she couldn't get out the words before the building and the moment were behind them.

My brother was too focused on her to fully take in the sights of our parents' lives. He couldn't peel his gaze away from my mother's sunglasses, the gradient plastic giving away pooling eyes that he could only view as menacing. Our father squeezing her hand just bolstered Eddie's suspicions that she was on the brink. Eddie knew our father was trying to soothe her before she fell apart. *It's only a matter of time before she does*, he thought. As he looked at our parents, he realized that if this were a movie, he would be out of frame. An extra following the leads. The camera would pan right past him to them, the tension of the muscles in their palms, the way in which they seemed to never need to speak to understand each other. He continued to walk behind them a while, wondering if they would even notice if he disappeared.

Although it's after midnight now, it's still early for Eddie. He wants to stay up but doesn't want to wake our parents, so he takes his phone to the bathroom in the hotel room to camp out on the floor, like he's a cat. The yellow light makes a frame of the door, but it won't bother my parents. They aren't used to sleeping in complete darkness. In those months when everything still felt raw and making it upstairs was a feat, they would often fall asleep on the couch with the lights on, holding on to each other.

Eddie scrolls through his text messages and opens his thread with Mivi. If he could write to her, get a sentence out, he thinks, he might be able to leave the bathroom, fall asleep, endure the trip. He wants to hear from her, to hear her say that everything is going to be all right, that he won't be hurt the way he has been before. He knows that she has no control over what will happen, but still, he's sure that hearing from her would give him what he needs to get through the next few days.

Just then, a water bottle falls off a nightstand. Through the bathroom door, Eddie hears the metal clang against the baseboard. His chest tightens. He's sure that this is it, the inevitable meltdown after a day of exposure therapy. My brother imagines the scene erupting on the other side of the door, my mother thrashing around the hotel room, unable to keep it all inside. He presses his ear against the door, his heart rate speeding up as he listens. But the room has gone quiet again. All Eddie can hear is the sound of my father's whistling breath. He has always been a deep sleeper, but my brother wonders how he's not more alert today.

Eddie doesn't hear my mother make a sound. From the bed, she eyes the bottle on the floor that she accidentally knocked over when she turned on her side. She considers getting up, grabbing it, but she's nearing sleep and decides not to move.

When he realizes there won't be a breakdown yet, my brother returns to his phone. He attempts to write to Mivi but doesn't know where to begin. She doesn't even know he's in Detroit. He keeps drafting new messages and deleting them.

Hey, can you talk?

Hi, a bit of a long story but

Mi, I didn't tell you that I left yesterday. My parents

So, I'm in a hotel in Detroit. May or may not be haunted. Probably not, I think it was built in like 2007, but I'm feeling weird here.

Mivi, I need

He gives up on texting before deciding to just call her. "Fuck it," he says under his breath. He needs to hear her voice. The speaker vibrates in Eddie's ear, and he can feel his lungs ballooning as the ringing drags on. His mouth is dry from the forced air.

"Hi, you've reached Mi—"

Eddie presses down on the screen and tries one more time. He stands up, puffs his chest out in front of the mirror as though seeing himself act strong will help him keep his cool across the line. The ringing starts up again, but it seems louder now, and he begins to think he shouldn't be calling. It's too loud. My brother looks in the mirror again and quickly flicks the light switch off. In the mirror, he saw something in his eyes that he can only describe as a yearning. He can't bear to witness himself looking so desperate.

In the dark, he oscillates between two prayers—*pick up, don't pick up*—the words corroding in his brain as he repeats them until they start to lose meaning. He breathes feverishly into the phone.

MIVI

WE LEFT JUST BEFORE LAST CALL. Zadie had put a hole in her shoe from dancing, and the fatigue I'd pushed through for the better part of the night crept back in when we went to order a third round of shots. Maja stuck her finger in my mouth as I yawned at the bar, waiting to order some tequila. When I barely reacted, she laughed. "Time to go, I think," she said as she shook her head at the bartender.

The three of us sit on the curb by the bus stop, sweaty heads on each other's shoulders. Since she's already broken her celibacy vow once, Maja orders an Uber to Andersen's. "He's only here for like another week, so I might as well," she says.

"Should we do dinner on your birthday?" Zadie asks. "Like a little thing with the three of us before we all go out?"

"Doesn't have to be a birthday thing," I say, before I cut myself off with another yawn. "But I'd be down."

"It'll be a birthday thing," Maja says, squeezing my knee. I roll my eyes. "Hey, you deserve to celebrate this year."

"That it's finally over?"

"Well, partly, maybe. If that's what you'd like to focus on."

Maja transitions from squeezing my knee to stroking the cap. It feels too soon to celebrate anything. Like if I do, I'll remind the curse that I have more time. None of us says it, but we all know this is the real reason I'm not into my birthday this year.

"We can also celebrate the fact that you'll finally be able to retire your fake ID. No more bouncers threatening to cut it up," Zadie says, winking. She's trying to make me smile, and I do. The blue lights of the night bus appear in the distance. "Just come to mine on Tuesday. No more arguing."

"Good timing," Maja says, as a car pulls up to the curb. She kisses the tops of our heads before running over to her Uber.

On the bus, Zadie and I sit by an open window near the back. She shuts her eyes and leans against the glass. The air is still heavy, but the speed of the bus in a trafficless lane pulls in the air. A treat after four hours in a hot bar. Across from us, a couple is leaning against the doors, their tongues barely contained in each other's mouths. I reach for my phone and my earbuds in an attempt to block out their wet sounds. First, I notice the 6 percent charge, then the four missed calls, all from Eddie. I didn't check my phone once at the bar. I turn to Zadie to see if she saw my screen. She might think I lied about not sleeping with him anymore if she saw that he called four times in the middle of the night. But her eyes are still shut. I quickly text Eddie: *Low battery. You okay?*

I put my earphones in. Distraction, loud, focused distraction. I'll be home soon. If he doesn't answer, I'll call back. My battery is draining quickly, but I can't help but click the home button every few minutes, checking to see if a text came through that I missed.

——

As soon as I get home, I plug my phone in and put it to my ear. He doesn't let it ring before picking up, but the line is silent.

"Eddie?"

He whispers back, "Hi," and the knot in my chest comes undone ever so slightly.

"I can't do this," he says feebly. "We just drove down and . . ."

I sink down against the kitchen counter, the skin of my belly absorbing the coolness of the stone, counteracting the rush of heat that set in with Eddie's words. He doesn't even need to tell me. It's almost Vivian's anniversary. I know where he is. Why he's calling.

"I didn't know you'd gone. Left. I—"

"We did. This morning." He exhales. "Yesterday, I guess. We're at a hotel."

He never told me he left.

"I need to see you, I think," he says.

"You *think*?"

"Mivi."

I shut my eyes.

"What is it that you want, Eddie?"

"I just . . ." His voice breaks a bit and, with a whisper, disappears. "Need to see you."

"I'll call you in the morning. Go get some sleep." I cross my arm over my chest and sink my nails into the other. "Okay? You'll be okay."

Eddie's breath quickens. I press harder, my nails digging deeper. *Hang up. Hang up now.* I wish it silently until eventually he whispers, "Okay." When the line disconnects, I set the phone down. I count the tiny crescents I dug into myself. A wave of nausea passes through me, and I think of the fleck of glitter churning in my belly.

———

I only ever allow myself to indulge in the memory of that last night with Eddie when I drink, but I've turned to it so many times over the last nine months that the reconstruction of it has grown detailed and lush.

I had friends over one weekend in November while Mami was travelling. A beer staff in the making, a roll of duct tape under the couch. The kitchen table covered in a plastic cloth from the dollar store. I'd almost felt like Lita, whose furniture was always kept under vinyl coverings like she was in a museum. But by ten that night, the blend of beer and moscato pooled in the wrinkles of the tablecloth made me feel less geriatric and more like a responsible teenager.

James and Eddie walked in just as the Solo cups were being rearranged on the table. Someone was asking around for cards, but I couldn't respond and point to the drawer where we kept them. Heat was rising inside me, flustering me. I hadn't invited him—after weeks of silence, I hadn't thought he would come.

As he waded into the apartment, the girls poured me a shot. "It's only weird if you make it weird," Maja said as she handed me the glass. "We don't know what's been up with him anyway, but it probably has nothing to do with you." In a sense, she was right. Eddie hadn't been out much since August, though most of our friends assumed it was because university had taken over. After we swallowed our shots, I wished I could tell them what had really been up with him. With us. He hadn't asked me not to, but I couldn't betray Eddie's trust like that. Instead, I asked Zadie to continue the story she'd started when the boys had walked in. Old sexist tweets written by her Psych TA had surfaced, and he had been fired earlier that week. She waved the screenshots in front of my face, distracting me from tracking Eddie as he moved through the crowd.

It took him a while to make his way to me. A lot of people wanted to catch up with him, hear what he'd been up to, how school was going. I couldn't help but try to listen to what he said as he updated friends, as though it might be the only way I could hear about his life. Even after replaying that night over and over in my head, I can't say whether it took him a few minutes or an hour to get to me. All I know is that eventually I was slicing limes when I felt a hand on my shoulder, and I turned around to face him. Before either of us even said a word, he pulled me into his chest. I could smell his pomander deodorant on him, mixed with a faint trace of tobacco. My eyes pricked at how familiar he smelled, like Christmas morning all year.

"I'm sorry," he whispered.

"Hi," I said back. "Hi. I'm sorry I'm getting lime juice on your sweater." I laughed as I rubbed my hands across his back.

Eddie's head shook. "No. I'm sorry. I mean it."

I held on to him for a few more seconds, staring at the pilling wool of his sweater, afraid that looking him in the eye would make me break. I stepped back so I wouldn't draw more attention to us. As I wiped my sticky palms on my pants, I told him I couldn't talk about it now, that I was too many drinks in. Really, I just didn't want to cry at my own party. Eddie picked up a lime wedge, poured himself some tequila, and assured me that we would have a fun night and talk another time.

"Enough making up, then," he said, before downing the shot and biting into the lime. "Time for games."

Eddie pulled out a deck of cards from the junk drawer, and it was exactly what I'd wanted. Laughter, stupid drinking games.

After rounds of King's Cup and when the beer staff reached the ceiling, people started trickling out to catch the last train. A few stayed later, languorous on the couch, eventually calling Ubers when yawns started spreading like a virus. When James offered to split one with Eddie, he declined. He said he wanted to walk. He didn't, of course. Once everyone was gone, he reached into his backpack and gave me the pack of Sobranies, wrapped up in a silver ribbon.

"I feel like most people apologize with flowers or something," he said. "But I thought that you'd prefer these. They're sorry cigarettes. And a belated birthday gift, too."

That's when I kissed him, and he stayed.

Even all these months later, my stomach lurches at the thought of that night. Not at the thought of the sex itself. That was good. That felt like running to each other at the airport. But after so many mornings spent on the floor by the toilet, it's hard to think about that night without acidity prickling under my tongue.

He woke me up the next morning. His hand on my shoulder, shaking me gently as he sat up against the headboard.

"I missed you" was the first thing he said. "Every day I didn't talk to you, I missed you so fucking much, Mi."

I sat up and just held on to him, his balmy skin pressed against mine, his scarred hand brushing my cheek. That semester, I'd learned that sick babies who were held healed faster, that skin-to-skin contact was a powerful thing. I thought of that in that moment. Just being there, feeling that closeness was enough. Neither of us said anything else about the time we were apart. It felt a bit strange not to hear a proper explanation from Eddie, but in that moment, I was just glad to have him back. To hold him and to soak each other in. Then to have sex one more time.

Eddie came over again a couple days later. Mami was back from her work trip, so we went out for a walk after he'd said hello to her. As we walked, he told me about Vivian. It seemed to come out easier when he could just look ahead. With his hands in his pockets, Eddie spoke of how his sister had died, how his parents clung to her still. He told me how ashamed he was that I'd heard what his mother had said. That he'd been afraid I would question ever being with someone like him, so burdened by the baggage of his family. That was why he'd been avoiding me since August. He'd wanted to run before I did. As snow came down, I snuck my hand in his coat pocket and thanked him for being honest. He clenched my pinky before continuing.

"I know it sounds stupid, but when James told me you were having people over, it made me fucking sad that I found out through him," he said. "I got it. I got why you wouldn't want to invite someone who hadn't made any effort to see you or talk to you in months. But it just kind of hit me that if I didn't go and see you in person, we'd drift further and further. And right when I saw you the other night, I remembered how much better everything is with you. You always get everyone dancing at parties. You get people to open up. The games are better, the conversations are better . . ."

"The sex is better?" I said, unhooking my hand and setting it back in my own coat. A stupid attempt to deflate the sincerity of the moment. It saddened me to think that he'd avoided me to beat me to the punch of breaking his heart. More than that, it broke mine to think that I might end up doing just that.

"Of course." He laughed. "You're my best friend, really. And I should have had more faith in you. I should have known you wouldn't judge me for my family."

I assured him I could never judge him, and Eddie promised he'd never run away again. Our pace slowed to a syrupy stroll as the snow started coming down faster. We pulled up our hoods, and Eddie reached over to tuck my scarf in my coat and zip it in. As he fiddled with the metal tab, we allowed ourselves a few more seconds of indulgence, our eyes fixed on each other's. His struck me as darker, an olive turned more bottle green, and the thought of misremembering the colour of his eyes after only a few months apart rattled me.

Eddie wrapped his arm around my shoulder. Before he could say anything, I told him that as great as the sex was, I thought we should take it slow.

"Do you mean like . . ." He couldn't get the word *date* out, but I shook my head before he could try.

"No. I mean, just back to being friends."

We wouldn't risk anything that way. He wouldn't sabotage us if shame got the better of him. I assured him once more that thinking we should keep things platonic had nothing to do with his family—it was just the right thing to do. My heart, my grades, my everything wouldn't take a hit if I lost him altogether. I would rather have him in my life as my best friend than as an ex. And even though my heart ached as I rejected him, I told myself it would heal. One day, it would not be as excruciating. Neither of us said anything as we walked down Bloor and let the wind and snow fill the silence. Eddie didn't move his arm.

"We'd probably just fuck it up anyway," he said eventually.

I nodded, biting my lip to keep from crying as he thumbed my shoulder slowly, refusing to give in to the awkwardness of him holding on to me as I shattered the prospect of us.

It's that last bit that I can't bear to think of sober. I know I can't regret what I said, and yet, if I were to think about it too much, I know it would consume me altogether, paralyze me to the point where I wouldn't be able to even go through the motions. When I'm drunk, at least I can allow myself to cry, knowing that I will soon fall asleep and, when I wake up, I will have another chance to move on.

ISAURA

WHENEVER YOU DO the Scandinavian circuit, you think of your time in New York. Of the city's wind tunnels that prepared you for all those chilly Nordic countries, and, of course, for Canada.

It's funny to think that you ended up working in such cold countries and planting your roots in one of the coldest. You were from a small city known for the heat—Pespire. On cold and dark mornings, you try to wrap yourself in the memory of your pueblo; the baked clay houses and the cat naps you took on top of fish crates.

You spent most of your childhood outside, on Lita's porch. It's where you dunked rosquillas in your café con leche every morning, and then again after school. When no one was looking, you'd draw on the planks of wood in pencil and, when you were done, scrub it off with rainwater from the bucket. You'd learned to read sitting right there, on Lita's lap, slowly inching your way through the gauzy pages of the Bible, instilling in you a love for story, for escapism, for the magic that is picturing entire lifetimes in the palm of your hands. Lita's porch was a landing strip for family and neighbours who'd walk by the house. In the evenings, when everyone was home, you would all sit outside to talk and have an evening coffee and sometimes pupusas when Lita had enough cheese in the icebox.

Things were slow then. Most things, you'd find out, you were late to. You learned some basics at home (cooking, storytelling) but other things (basic lettering, arithmetic, things you couldn't believe Yessenia was being taught in her kindergarten class) weren't introduced to you until you were eight and started school. Shoes were another thing that came late. You'd never needed any up until that point. Your feet were thick, the soles and heels like cured meat.

Here, people call lateness "CP time." You didn't have a word for it at home. There was no rush. No reason to. It was why New York was hard on you at first. Back then, you never would've believed you'd one day settle in its Canadian counterpart, "a manageable New York" people called Toronto sometimes. New York was fast. The heat wasn't like it was in Pespire. It was a smoggy, humid casa de fieras of tourists and cars and annoyed New Yorkers yelling at both. The heat wasn't enjoyed; it was suffered through. It was to be escaped when possible. Most of your clients had air conditioning. People who could afford a cleaning lady could afford not to sweat all summer. You took refuge in the artificial coolness. When you first discovered it in a bodega in Brooklyn, the feeling shocked you. The piercing harshness. You felt you understood why everyone was always sick in the U.S.

But, of course, you acclimated. You took those workdays in cool apartments as respite from the heat of the city. From the C train, whose windows would pearl up with condensation. From the blazing one-bedroom apartment. It was almost impossible to sleep during the summer in a room filled with the body heat of five other grown women. Sometimes, you rolled off the bed you shared with your mami and onto the floor. It wasn't easier to sleep there, but at least it was a little cooler.

It's not like you were used to much sleep in those early days in New York. But even two years after you left home, thinking of her at night still felt tender. Urgent. All-consuming. She was so far. You couldn't know how she was at all times, so you had to speculate. Let your mind lead itself on both hopeful and hostile paths. Most often, it followed the latter.

You'd spend hours awake worrying about her. After speaking to other mothers in Canada, you learned that you had sleepless nights in common. Many of them chased sleep even when their babies stopped being babies, quiet nights consumed with worry for a decade. Some even had to medicate themselves to get a night's rest. Your knee-jerk reaction was to think of them as weak, to see their fears as less warranted than yours had been. Than yours still were. At least they'd had their children close. Eventually, you'd realize that these things are all relative.

Almost two decades later, you still find yourself up at night. The farther away you are from her, the worse it gets. Sometimes, you try to blame it on jet lag, sometimes, you're honest with yourself. Leaving her before her nineteenth birthday eats away at a part of you. You know she's strong—she's had to make difficult decisions alone this year. But is that not precisely why she needs her mami there now? To help her begin her adulthood differently than you did? You can't exactly guide her through what you didn't experience yourself, but you can hold her hand. Be there like you wish you had when she took her first steps. You could make up for lost time.

It's upsetting to think about, still. That time apart, the pain she went through. But you don't allow yourself to spend too much time indulging in self-pity. You try to find solutions. Working overtime means that you might be able to take time off at Christmas and afford to go somewhere with your daughter. You want to give her a trip for her nineteenth birthday. You could go away, just the two of you, and spend time together that isn't interrupted by one of your shifts. Ever since December, you've made a game of distracting yourself by thinking of all the places you might go. You haven't settled on anything just yet.

You think she'd like it here in Oslo. It's summer in Norway, though years ago, you would've said it still felt like winter. It's eighteen degrees today. Not bad. Back home, they'd be layering. Last winter, you worked a flight to Tromsø, a little Norwegian island about the size of Manhattan, and you never saw the sun once. For a few hours a day, the suggestion of its existence would appear in pink clouds, a rosy hue like the inside of your cheek.

But it's sunny now. You and another attendant went into town for dinner, to a wood-panelled restaurant that served pickled herring with rye crackers. Your daughter would've loved it. It reminded you a bit of ceviche, Scandi-style.

On your way back to the hotel, you picked up a couple bags of Norwegian candy, jelly men and chocolate-covered marshmallows, from the grocery store. In a few days, you'll set them on her birthday cake like you used to do when she was a kid. You always try to bring her home a treat when you're gone for a while. A tube of fish roe from Stockholm that you ate spread over saltines. Pork rind chips from a kiosk in Copenhagen. You've yet to top the Belgian pralines.

Even though she is an adult now, you can't help but imagine the sound of her running to the door like she used to as a kid. Back then, she stayed home with a rotation of women from the airport who would help you out with her when you went away. As independent as she became, whenever you got home, all she wanted to do was lie in bed with you and catch up. For the most part, this continued even throughout the teenage years. On some days, you had to cajole her with a glass of wine or a promise to let her have a party while you were travelling, as long as she vowed nothing would happen with boys. You wanted her to have the adolescence you didn't. You didn't want her to ever resent you for leaving or for not trusting that she'd follow your rules about dating. Everything you did, you did to keep her close.

So, as tempted as you are to open one of the bags of candy to get rid of the taste of herring from dinner, you pack them away. They'll taste better shared with your daughter, between laughs and stories that only the two of you could be eager to share after a five-day separation.

When you leave Oslo, you try to picture coming back with her. For some reason, you can't. Not really. It isn't where she wants to go, as much as you know she'd like it. You know Oslo. Not well, but after a decade of visits, you feel you know it better than where Yessenia really wants to go: Honduras.

It's been over fifteen years for her. When you were in New York, you couldn't afford to take her back, and by the time you settled in Canada, even when you started making real money, it felt as though too much time had passed. You'd now spent more time away from Honduras than you had lived there. Part of you wanted your daughter to return to connect with her roots, and yet the thought of her realizing that they'd been severed beyond repair was excruciating. She had no father to tie her, no abuela anymore, either. And beyond this, another reason that would take you years to admit to yourself was that you were afraid to show Yessenia that you were a fraud, an immigrant American-Canadian who didn't really know how to be Honduran anymore.

You tried at first, when you moved to Toronto. The apartment that Mrs. Saltzman had found you was only a twenty-minute walk from Kensington Market. You made an effort to befriend women at the Emporium Latino, bonded over your quest for queso fresco and pupusas made by someone else. You'd never learned how to make them properly, and your attempts felt shameful. Most evenings, you didn't have the patience to cook Honduran food anyway. There were too many components you couldn't get right. When you'd knead the masa and try to flatten it into tortillas, slapping the yellow disc of dough on top of a moist plastic bag to keep it from sticking, your edges cracked, the surface was consistently uneven. You were overwhelmed by the number of sauces to accompany each meal, forgetting which ones were meant to be served cold, which ones to bring to a boil. There was too much frying with oil that you were nervous to use around your curious child, too many frijoles you couldn't seem to smooth out like Lita did. Instead, you stuck to easy dishes. Pastas, stir-fries, sometimes even breakfast for dinner. Every so often, though, you would bring home containers of tamales from Kensington, and you'd feel like you were participating in your culture again, doing right by your daughter, whom you'd taken away from her home.

At night, you read books to her, whatever Latino stories you could find at the library. She loved *Héroes de la Biblia* best, but she'd also sit through the short tales of Jorge Luis Borges and Elena Garro. You arrived in Toronto in February. The only way to conjure heat was through those tales. Things that could only take place in your homeland. As you held your daughter, you were brought back to that time, years ago, when you would place one hand on your belly and the other on the spine of a book, knowing that the simple act of flipping pages would provide some consolation.

You never told Yessenia exactly why you hadn't taken her back. She'd always understood that money was tight, so you let her believe it was about money. When your mami died, your daughter assumed you'd spend it to take her. But it was exam time for her, the last set of them before high school ended. You knew how important they were, how well she needed to do to keep her entrance scholarship. She offered to come with you regardless, to be there for you, to see her hometown. If she lost the scholarship, she would take on more shifts at the restaurant, work more throughout the year. You didn't want that for her. You told her how upset her abuela would be if Yessenia gave up an opportunity like that just to pack up her abuela's house. In Honduras, the body is buried the day of the death. There was no way you could've made it in time. As you wiped away her tears, you promised she would see Pespire soon. Then you rolled out your suitcase, took three days off work, and waited on standby until a seat opened up. It was always cheaper that way.

Your old neighbours insisted on feeding you when you arrived. The last time they'd seen you, you were a teenager, but they welcomed you home like you'd only left a couple weeks ago. Back then, the house had been Lita's, but after she died, your mami took over. On the rotting porch, they set up a small table and covered it in carne asada, chismol, yucca, and paper plates. You drank ice cold Salva Vidas with them and talked about your mami's final days. When the beer made you feel weepy, you changed the subject to your daughter, what she'd accomplished, what she was like now. You showed them photos.

At some point, someone turned on the stereo inside and the sound of rancheras that your mami loved made you tear up. You didn't allow yourself to fall apart in front of anyone, though, and from that night on, your neighbours barely left your side. You couldn't be sure why, but you craved solitude. You hated yourself for resenting their constant company—they were only trying to help—but all you wanted was time alone in the house to go through your mami's things.

The only time they let you be was at night. Around eight or nine, they went home to sleep, and you would go through drawers and boxes, inhale the clothes that smelled just like that jasmine perfume your mami wore in New York. Under the bed, you found a box of letters. To and from Lita, sending updates while they were apart.

Reading them felt like reliving those years through their eyes. You could feel your mami's longing subside with your arrival in the U.S., Lita's exhaustion when your daughter was left with her. Most of their letters were about the two of you, the light you offered, the grief you caused. That bittersweet blend of mourning and comfort when the two of you left for Canada. You were careful not to let your tears drop onto the letters. The paper was so thin. Your mami always bought the cheapest stuff. The No Name of No Name. Quarter-of-a-ply toilet paper. Knock-off face creams and lipsticks with misspelled brand names.

You brought the letters back to your daughter, along with a few other relics. Some photos, your mami's watch—a gift from one of her clients—and all the clothing you could fit in your suitcase. Most of it wasn't your size or Yessenia's, but you took it anyway. You hoped the smell of her would last.

Back home, you went through the photos with your daughter. Your mami had never owned a camera, so you assumed that all the photos she had were given to her by the people who took them. The sizes of the photos were all different. The one of your mami smiling in Central Park was honey-hued with scalloped edges. The one of her sandwiched between three of her roommates, Julia, Barnabela, and Isabel, at their kitchen table was long and thin.

You wished you could show Yessenia more photos of Honduras, but your mami only had three. Your daughter wasn't in any of those. In fact, you don't have a single picture of her as a baby. If North American parents heard that, they wouldn't believe you. You can just imagine the line of questioning. *Not one? From the hospital? Not a passport picture? None of the two of you? Nothing?* They'd ask if they'd been lost in a fire, if there was a backup somewhere, if family might have some. You'd explain that you didn't live with your daughter for the first three years of her life and her abuela didn't own a camera. You've never really known what your daughter looked like as a baby. At six months. At one year. At two years. You've never told anyone this. It feels like the most shameful admission you could make. You'd left her. You'd made your choices.

Still, you were grateful to have some evidence of life in Pespire that she could have, to see where she came from. The laminated photo of las tres generaciones: you, your mami, and hers nestled on Lita's vinyl-covered couch. It was a small, square print with rounded corners. The one of you, close to a year old probably, in that concrete laundry tub in the yard. You're squealing, eyes closed and nose wrinkled. You used to love those cold baths. The third photo is of your mami and your abuela. You or one of the neighbourhood kids must've taken it when you were a child. They both look so young, and the framing of the shot is crooked, thumbed in the corner. Your abuela's arm is cut out, though you can tell from her shoulder that it was raised. Whenever you look at that photograph, you wonder what, or who, she was holding on to. You know it's Sunday because they're dressed up. Your mami is wearing a black-and-white polka-dot dress. You remember her sewing it, and asking her for your own with the scraps. She cut a square from the leftovers for you to wear as a headband. You wished you had photos of that. In your mind, you looked like a princess wearing a veil.

It's hard to believe how much time has passed since that photo was taken. That your mami would have left Pespire and gone back well over a decade later. She ended up leaving New York at forty-seven, when Lita died. By that point, the winters and the labour had taken a toll on her body, and without her mother to support, there was no need to suffer through either any longer. The house was hers.

She thought she could have a simpler, warmer life. She went back to bury her mother and never left.

You couldn't make it for Lita's funeral, either, but you coordinated details in a WhatsApp group with the church members who organized it. You paid for the plot. Once your mami made it back, you would wire her money every month to help out. You tried to pay her back for the weeks she spent in the desert, the years she spent breaking her back for you and your daughter.

She didn't talk about getting to the U.S. much. But what you knew was that none of it had been painless. There had been no embassy connection, no visa like you'd had. The details, though, she kept secret. Every once in a while, you'd get a slice of it. Once, you complained about the freezing Manhattan wind tunnels, and she'd barked back an anecdote about what cold *really* was—lying in the open desert in the middle of the night, sweat from the hot day chilling her skin. When you complained about the water tasting different in the U.S., she snapped, called you spoiled. Then she told you about the bagged water that strangers had thrown to her from a train near Matamoros as she walked on the side of the tracks. That water was hot and smelled of sulphur, and she was nothing but grateful for it.

When you'd press her for more details, she'd tell you that the greatest gift she could ever give you was to not tell you anything you didn't need to know. That taught you not to ask.

By now, you've heard a little more about it from other sources. Testimonials of other Honduran and Venezuelan and Colombian and Mexican women who leave their country still. Now they have numbers to estimate how many women are raped along the way. Your mami was part of just about every other statistic—she'd had no secondary education, she'd fallen pregnant as a teen, she'd lived below the poverty line. You hoped that just this once, she had been spared.

You read the news stories. It's strange to be so attuned to the flight of your gente years later, when you weren't really before. Maybe it's because children don't really question what happens in their lives. Not at the beginning, and not when they're teenagers consumed by their own journeys. Mothers leave by crossing the desert, hiding their babies, running away. That's just life, you'd thought at the time. But now, when you look at photos of those little Catrachos, the babies with their gummy smiles, their tiny hoop earrings, you can't understand how you might've thought that this was simply how the world operated. You never had to live like them, caged, sleeping on cement floors. You never had to see your mami get hurt, or cry because someone ripped you away from her.

You know that it's images like these that make your daughter tense up, feel distanced from her heritage, because she does not see herself in them. That while she is a true Catracha who came about from a curse that only affects your people, she feels like she cannot claim to be. She got out.

It breaks your heart to know that she feels it, too. That no man's land of existence. She will reap the pain of a curse without the reward of a home, of warmth.

And it's that pain in your chest, that mucusy, tight feeling in your throat, that makes you realize, seeing those children holding on to their parents by the neck, or worse, the ones reaching out toward them as they are torn apart, that the ones you feel for the most are the mothers. They're the ones who will bruise to the bone. Who will feel the afterpains the worst. Who won't just feel fear, but also guilt, an ache that will never quite dissipate, even if they get their babies back.

The children will adapt. Especially the small ones. The journey is their reality. It'll just be. But one day, they'll sit back when they're nearing forty like you and finally realize that that was completely and utterly fucked up.

MIVI

EACH KILOMETRE TACKS ITSELF onto the odometer like a warning.

Could you make it any more obvious that you love him? Do you really think that he will die there without you intervening? How are you going to save him, anyway?

I turn up the radio to drown out my thoughts. I'm going. Clearly. I've already put 170 kilometres on the car. The word *pilgrimage* flashes in my mind like a correction. For what? I'm not sure just yet, but I pray that the gut feeling I'm following isn't just lust or envy or some other sin that's tricked me right into the curse's palms. As much as Eddie said he needed me, I woke up knowing that I needed to be with him, too. Like something irreversible would happen if I didn't go.

You already broke the curse, I tell myself, but it's like self-soothing with a sharp object—as painful as it is reassuring. Mostly because it had seemed too easy to break. If the curse was real, then the thought that I could so easily sever myself from it, from my family's history, in a matter of minutes, felt like a cruel rejection. The curse didn't fight back. It didn't beg me to stay tethered. It didn't want *me* to perpetuate it.

Pregnancy should've been easy to avoid. The way I'd seen it, Mami and Lita hadn't understood the science of it, so they blamed the cycle on a curse instead. To me, "breaking the curse" would merely consist of little pink pills, a daily alarm, and condoms, just in case. Simple as that. It wasn't even like I was having a lot of sex. Eddie was the only person I'd ever slept with.

But when my period was late back in December and the smell of Mami's toast landed me in the bathroom four mornings in a row— the shower running so she couldn't hear me retching—I wondered whether Mami had been right.

On the fifth day of morning sickness, I went to the walk-in clinic to take a test. A few minutes after I'd handed in my urine sample, the doctor led me into her office. Positive. User error was how she explained the result when I told her I was on the pill.

"Most of the time, it's because people forget to take the pills at the exact same time. Were you consistent about time? Did you miss one? Or travel recently? Sometimes, time change can be the cause. Are you taking any other medication?"

I shook my head and told her about the condoms, too.

"Just bad luck then," she said. "I'm sorry."

Strangely, I wasn't devastated. I didn't want to cry. Something closer to reassurance settled in my chest. Connection, maybe. I was Honduran. My mother's daughter. In a way, it felt like the answer to a question I'd been asking myself my entire life. Maybe I was as pure as it got after all. It's funny to think that it took me getting pregnant to realize why I'd been so upset about my classmates reducing my history to legend. I realized that when you feel so far removed from your culture, narratives—even ones as damned as ours—are what you cling to like branches. They make you feel linked to your heritage from generations and miles away. After I initially revelled in that feeling of connection, nausea returned when I remembered the second part of the curse. The one that could take him away from me. Even my abuela, who didn't believe in the curse, was sure that the second part happened no matter what. "That's what happens when you let men get what they want," she'd say. "You'll be left alone to pick up the pieces." It was unsettling to hold those feelings of solace in tandem with fear, this dark apprehension that I couldn't rid myself of.

But in that moment, I decided I would do what the women before me could not. I'd deal with two parasites in one simple procedure. Outside the lobby, I called the clinic the doctor recommended. Just in case the abortion alone didn't break the curse, I would write off any thought of being with Eddie for good.

As much as I wanted to tell my mami, as much as I wanted her to stroke my hair, as much as I wanted her to know I was Honduran, too, the thought of destroying everything she'd worked for petrified me. I could picture her crying, feeling like a failure, the carrier of a curse that would not let any of us escape it. In some of the nightmares that started when I got pregnant, I saw her running toward me, screaming, trying to warn me about something. Every time, she was swallowed into the forest floor. I could've sworn I felt my ears ringing in the morning from our blended shrieks.

VIVIAN

BY NINE IN THE MORNING, my mother has been sleeping almost twelve hours. Her body will pay for it soon.

"I need to move," she says when she wakes up. Slowly, she sits up and starts stretching out her neck. My father is used to the symphony of cracking joints. My mother plays it carefully. Section by section, in the same order every time. Neck, wrists, knees sometimes, ankles, toes. He wonders, at times, if a woman her age should sound so brittle. She's only fifty-two. Then again, he, of all people, should know that emotional pain can spread in the body.

After her stretches, my mother steps in the shower. The noise in the bathroom wakes Eddie up. My father has to ask several times, but he finally convinces my brother to get out of bed and get dressed. Though Eddie is now an adult, the process is similar to when my brother was in elementary school, my father laying out Eddie's school clothes at the foot of his bed, shaking him lightly.

"We're going to the church today," my father says, eyeing his son's tattered Devo T-shirt. "Didn't you pack something that's . . . that's more churchy?"

Eddie smirks a bit. "I think I have a plain one. Like a white Hanes one. It's not that nice. Pretty sure there's a coffee stain."

"Too bad we don't have time to buy you something before we go."

Eddie rolls his eyes but doesn't say anything. When my mother comes out of the bathroom, dressed, her dark hair made darker by the wetness of it, she announces that she is ready. My father asks if she wants to dry her hair before leaving. She shakes her head. Time to go.

As my father leads the way, snaking my family through side streets, Eddie looks at the city as if it were a film. To him, the vacant lots are poetic, the bustling areas symbolic. He tries to stare into the eight-bedroom homes with leafy sunrooms for signs of life. It's quiet on these streets, the fancy ones. They'll soon notice, though, that the buildings hemmed in by dilapidated houses are just as quiet. Boarded up and empty, like clean bones, all lined up.

Lilacs out of the Dead Land, Eddie thinks, would be a good name for his film about Detroit, the one he wants to weave out of videos captured during this trip. For the first time, he wants to stare directly at what his family has avoided, to make art out of it. He feels ready. The short would be an account of a healing city interwoven with the tale of a family confronted with their past. He plans to splice his footage together with old VHS tapes of my parents' life in Detroit.

My brother started the transfer process a couple of years ago, carefully unspooling twenty-two cassettes, digitizing a trove of memories that had, on tape, barely aged. When he'd found them, he thought he would watch them like a detective might, scan for insight on our family, on our mother, on me.

For the most part, the videos are of the early years in our parents' relationship. Picnics in the park. My mother sitting on a bench with a stack of books on her lap, concealing a miniskirt, looking particularly collegiate. My father driving the car on one of their road trips, the seat belt hanging loose beside him. In one of the clips, my mother turns the camera around to film herself adjusting her sunglasses on the ridge of her nose, then playfully sets them on my father instead. He tilts them down to strike a pose and pouts. Beers at the beach. My mother in a bikini, pulling her knees to her chest and laughing when she sees the camera pointed at her. A Christmas with friends, playing cards around the table with a silver tree glimmering in the background. Their wedding. Stained-glass windows reflecting rainbow light on my mother's veil. Rice strewn on the steps, getting caught in the lace of her neckline.

Eddie thinks that juxtaposing personal loss with a collective grief would make for a moving piece. The only problem is that as desperately as he wants to document this trip, our mother's words in the kitchen are haunting him. He didn't believe her, but it planted a seed that is growing. *What you're doing is not art.* Even if he doesn't think she was right, it seemed like she did. She apologized, sure, but that doesn't mean that she really believes in him. The other day, he wondered whether she actually dislikes him as a person, but now he suspects that the truth might be worse. Maybe she doesn't care at all. If she did, she would've asked to see his art at least once.

So no, there's no way he can film in front of her. He can't risk her saying something he won't be able to shake, or risk reacting to her words in a way they won't be able to come back from. My brother still brought his camera, because what he lacks in courage he makes up for in determination, or perhaps selfishness, or both. He's being careful not to let her see it—he buried the case at the bottom of his backpack—but he will film. Of course he will film.

It's been a few days since he picked up his camera, and he's itching to shoot again. As he lay in bed after his call with Mivi last night, he started thinking of what he might be able to capture of Detroit. Usually, shooting, editing, or even planning out his films in his head are ways to escape painful memories. But this film will be uniquely personal, not an escape as much as a deep dive into the past. As he thought of what he wanted to film in Detroit, his mind wandered back, creating a storyboard of all those difficult summers, of what had made him want to film in Detroit in the first place. The memories of past Augusts came to him vividly.

He tried to capture each August, the ones he was old enough to remember, with a mental Polaroid—a single snapshot to sum up each of my mother's failed attempts at closure. He recalled thirteen memories, composing an image out of each. There is the one where she checked herself into the hospital. The anniversary where all seemed fine until, at one of Eddie's basketball games, a newborn who looked just a little too much like me was toted in and sent my mother into a panic. That summer she kept adding liquor to her coffee. There are others he can't remember because he was too young, others he has willfully forgotten; they are too painful to absorb.

By lining each image up, he hoped he might be able to anticipate what might happen this summer, this week, to prepare himself. Instead, it triggered an unshakeable dread, undid the calm that Mivi's voice had imparted on their call. He tried to picture her in this August's snapshot to soothe his nerves, then willed himself to lower his expectations. He couldn't expect her to follow him.

As my family walks down the main strip, my father is brought back to that first drive with me in the back seat, how slowly he navigated the busy streets as he drove us home. He remembers how carefully he buckled the seat in the back, how gently my mother picked me up when they brought me inside. He can still picture the dimples in my knuckles, how much he stared at them as I lay curled up on his chest that week. My father also remembers walking down this same street days after I died, picking up a box of pads from the corner store for my mother. The store isn't there anymore.

Most of the buildings seem new, or at least refurbished, renovated, all sleek with the glow of fresh paint and signs with semi-ironic names. The General Store (a coffee shop). Death & Taxes (a restaurant and vintage store). Dave's Laundromat (a bar).

My mother points to The General Store. She wants to make the eleven o'clock service, which doesn't leave them time for a proper breakfast. A coffee and a pastry will do.

My family walks in and orders two black coffees, one flat white with rice milk, and three croissants. They carry them to a table by a window and sit on stools. Eddie remains mostly mute until my mother asks if he has heard from anyone at home.

"Well, no one knows I left," he says, "other than my boss."

My brother is suddenly embarrassed that he phoned Mivi, even feels the nausea that normally accompanies his hangovers when he replays their conversation in his head. It felt like a drunk call even though he was completely sober. He clears his throat and continues.

"My friends tend to go out on Mondays, so I'll probably hear from someone tomorrow. But I guess we won't be back?"

"Don't bet on it," my father says.

"Tomorrow's your sister's anniversary. I think the day will be long enough. We won't want to drive home after everything."

They all peer out at the street, eyes avoiding each other's, aware of the heaviness that's hanging over them. My mother knows that she's been strong so far; it's a matter of not burning out, of not letting the reminders of me, of her old life, push her over the edge. She wishes she could promise that this return to Detroit is actually going to be good for them. That *she'll* be good, like she said she would. But she can't. She can't make another promise she doesn't know she'll be able to keep, if only to comfort her son. But she has something more realistic than a promise. A plan that she will muster the courage to lay out to him soon. She hopes it'll be a step. She hopes he'll trust her.

Quietly, they finish their coffees and give up on picking at the buttery flakes scattered on their plates. My mother glances at her watch and her anxiety kicks back into gear.

"We need to hurry; we're going to be late."

"We have enough time, Rosy."

"I don't want to walk in late. Or miss anything! They might not even let us in if we're late, you know."

"It's church, not the theatre," says my father.

My mother lets out a frustrated grunt. She whips the café door open and storms out. Eddie goes after her, while my father tries to temper his own frustration with a few slow inhales before following his family.

"Mom, there's a church right across the street. Why don't we go to that one?"

"That's a Catholic church." She marches up the street, glancing down at her phone to make sure they're going in the right direction. It's been a while. "We're Anglican, Eddie."

"We're not *anything*, Mom."

That's what stops her. The pushback. She knows what they're thinking. That this will be another unsuccessful endeavour of hers, that she will be too weak to handle the consequences. They're trying to stop her before she fails.

"Your father and I were raised Anglican. We have to go to our church. Where we had planned to baptize your sister," she says, her lip stiff in an attempt not to break.

Eddie looks back at my father, a few steps behind them. My father freezes for a moment, unsure which words to pick. His eyes dart toward the backpack hanging off my brother's right shoulder, the way it makes him seem more childlike.

"Ed, I think we are done discussing it," he eventually says, wiping the film of sweat that's coated his brow. My mother turns away. She won't look at either of them.

"I'm sorry," Eddie says, his apology tinged with confusion.

My mother picks up the pace again, shaking her head and huffing. Eddie strides on beside her.

"Clearly, I don't get it. I've never heard you talk about church or God *ever*, and now it's 'We have to go to *our* church'? We're *Anglican*? I'm not even baptized. We—"

"We didn't have time, okay?" my mother yells, her palms pressed against her chest. "Vivian died before we could even organize a baptism."

She moves her hands from her heart to her face, rubbing her frown lines. My father doesn't know whether to wrap himself around her or place his hand over her mouth. He's scared to hear what she'll say next.

"After it happened, we never went back, we never prayed. Maybe we all just need to have a bit of faith for once."

There aren't many people in the street. Eddie could yell out what he wants to say to her. *Why would you want to believe in a God that gives you a healthy baby one day, then takes her away a week later? There's no way any of this is going to help. None of it will end differently. You're setting yourself up for failure, again.*

But he holds it in, reaching into his pocket for his phone like he's about to call a getaway car. Instead, he just picks at the gummy case. He still loves her enough to not tell her the truth.

———

The last time my mother was in this church, they sang some hymns, read from *The Book of Common Prayer*, listened to a sermon that did not exactly reassure my parents that I would be admitted into heaven, given that I had not been baptized. My father sat beside her, red-eyed from the days leading up to my funeral.

Not much has changed inside the church. They don't go up to the front, where their old seats were. My parents feel like they'll be caught if they get too close. The front row is for devoted worshippers.

Eddie is fidgety, thumbing for the phone in his pocket, looking down at it every few minutes. As he looks around the nave, he wonders what sitting here might've looked like had I not died. Maybe we would have snuck out together, or whispered jokes during the sermon until our parents kicked us under the pews as we snickered. Eddie wonders whether my mother is imagining me, too, picturing me beside him, riffling through my purse for my own phone.

My family sits with their heads bowed while the rest of the congregation bustles about, shaking hands and catching up before the service begins. My parents want to avoid making eye contact with anyone they used to know. The shame they feel for running from the church is particularly pronounced as they feel looks land on them. It's hard to know whether some congregants recognize them or if they're just wondering who the fresh faces are. If it's the former, maybe they're relieved to see Eddie, to know that they were blessed with another child, to think that they needn't feel so bad for them after all.

My father flips through the hymn book until my mother places her hand on his knee, a gesture that says, *Stop fidgeting*. Eddie keeps pulling out his phone, poring over his text thread with Mivi. She hasn't messaged him yet. He tells himself that she must still be sleeping. She said she'd call.

When Eddie slips his phone back in his pocket, my mother leans over and tells him not to take it out again. Bashfully, as the priest steps out onto the stage, my brother apologizes to my mother. Then, in an attempt to show that he's here to participate, he begins to clap for the priest. A sense of uneasiness fills the air and triggers hushed voices in the pews around them.

"This isn't a show, Eddie," my father says, swatting his son's hands down. A hot rush of shame consumes my father, but he knows he and my mother are to blame; it's not like they've ever taken Eddie to church.

"Let us say our opening prayer," the priest says.

For a moment, my mother considers reaching over my father and holding Eddie's hand. A small gesture, but something to show that she's not mad about the clapping, that she's happy he's trying. But she decides against it, too afraid he might recoil. *He's an adult*, she thinks. Instead, she holds on to her husband as she did twenty years ago under this very same roof. And as he did then, he embraces her back, tender as ever, stroking the back of her hand with his thumb in a pattern of three. *I. Love. You.* Their way of saying it without words.

When Mivi passes the bridge and enters the city, she feels the shift in her body. She's here. With no real plan, to meet a boy who, she suspects, doesn't have one, either. For a split second, she almost feels mortified to have come all this way. She lied at the border for him. She wonders what her mother would say if she knew what she'd done. Whether she'd call her a legacy or wonder why the hell she would do that for a boy. Mivi tries to ground herself.

Her heart was in her throat a minute ago, but she was too distracted to feel anything other than a vital necessity to not fuck up. To be young and charming and worthy of no suspicion. She's a girl and she is American, but she still has Marquez for a last name.

"Reason for entering the United States?"

"I'm visiting a friend."

The officer frowned, looked her up and down. Mivi smiled slightly as she focused on keeping her breathing regular and her heartbeat quiet.

"Where are you staying?"

She paused.

"With a friend, downtown."

"Who's the friend?"

Mivi swallowed.

"My best friend, Eddie. We grew up together, but then he moved to Detroit. Just came to see him for a bit before I head back to school in September."

For a moment, he continued to study her, vacillating between her face and her passport. And then, with a simple hand gesture, he let her in. Her mouth widened into an innocent smile until she had driven out of sight. Then the anxiety started to dissolve, and she could feel it becoming less potent with each steadying breath she took. *I made it in*, she thought.

Once she gets off the highway, she slides into the next side street she can find and picks up her phone, throws on roaming to see where Eddie is on the map. They've had each other's locations since they went to a concert last summer and got separated. Since then, she's checked it occasionally, just to know where he is, feeling intrusive and yet not enough to delete the app. Sometimes, she wonders whether he checks to see where she is, too.

Eddie's icon loads. St. John's Episcopal Church, as of one minute ago. She laughs. He got the church's Wi-Fi. She plugs the address into the GPS and then texts him for the first time since yesterday. She restarts the ignition, puts her foot on the gas, and manoeuvres her way into the city.

Mivi pulls up outside the church minutes later, while everyone in the pews is standing and singing the Introit. My father is humming, because he can't hold a tune, and my mother sings quietly, her fingers tapping her thigh to the rhythm. Eddie is focused on the vibration in his pocket. His phone vibrated once about ten minutes earlier, but he didn't pull it out. Mostly, he doesn't want to set off our mother. Beyond that, he knows that if he looks and it's not Mivi, he'll be crushed. He'll wait until they are out.

But then comes another set of vibrations. Then a third. Before he can convince himself not to, he slides his phone out of his pocket and sees Mivi's name on the lock screen. Three texts from her. The first reads: *I'm in Detroit.* The second: *I'm outside the church.* The third: *I can wait out here if you want. Let me know.*

When the hymn ends and everyone sits, Eddie stays standing. His eyes bounce around the room for escape routes. Down the aisle to the main doors seems too dramatic, and yet he doesn't have any other options. There are no side doors, that he can see at least. My father tugs at his shirt as if to say, *Sit now*, but it's like the touch grants him the courage to do it. To run out. To meet Mivi. To go with her.

He mumbles as he squeezes by them, his backpack grazing their knees as he clutches the strap. My mother looks up for a moment, though her gaze doesn't follow him down the aisle like my father's does. She just shuts her lids, settles into darkness.

Mivi's yellow dress is spread out against the beige seat, the slit up the side letting a sliver of her thigh breathe. Her window is cranked open, and a breeze rustles the fabric. She knows she looks good in yellow, that this lemony shade makes her seem fresh, not like she only slept for four hours and is running on adrenaline and gas station coffee.

She watches my brother run down the stairs of the church like a runaway bride, never looking back. The sight of her Toyota, his getaway car, makes his eyes light up. Almost cartoonishly, he rubs them to make sure he's seeing clearly, that Mivi's really there in front of him. She waves at him. Then, tunnel-visioned and in love, the most in love I've ever seen my brother, Eddie runs out onto the street without looking.

First, there's a car. Then, hot tires. The blare of a horn. Eddie's body slammed against the asphalt. Mivi's hands over her face. Screeching, an engine, and then nothing. Mivi doesn't move. She listens to the running footsteps, the steps of someone who, she assumes, will roll Eddie over to see if he's alive, who will call 911, who will place their lips on his to try to get him breathing.

"Fuck. Fuck. Fuck. I killed him," she repeats until she is breathless.

Then Mivi hears the whining of her passenger door. Hands grab hers away from her face, but she doesn't open her eyes until she feels fingers wrapped around hers. It's him. His shirt is sprinkled with gravel and he looks a bit frenzied, but he's alive. She can practically hear his heartbeat. Mivi looks as though she might throw up.

"I'm fine," he says. "He hit the brakes in time and I just tripped, okay? I'm fine."

"Fuck, Eddie!" she says, clutching on to him.

"I'm sorry, that was a bit scary," he says. "But it didn't hit me. I'm okay. Really more than okay. I'm really glad to see you."

He doesn't say anything more, too afraid that in his state of shock, he will accidentally admit to something he'll later regret. Mivi tries to steady her breath, inhaling through her nose. She pulls her hands away from him and wraps them around the wheel. They start driving. After a few minutes of silence punctuated only by the flapping of her dress, she finally says something.

"So where are we going now?"

"I'm not sure. Maybe we can just drive around a little while longer."

He reaches over and puts his hand on her thigh.

"Mi, I didn't really think you'd come."

"It wasn't that far. And this is . . . It's big, right?"

"Mivi."

He doesn't move. That was his chance to say it.

"We can go back to your parents. If your mom needs you. I can turn the car around."

His mouth opens but the words don't come out. He can't say it. He can't say anything. So he just shakes his head, then points toward the sign that leads to the highway.

ISAURA

HER BIRTHDAY IS LESS than two days away. Thirty-four hours, technically, from where you currently sit in another time zone, but you'll be back in Toronto the morning she turns nineteen. When you took off in Iceland, you thought again about where you could go with her. The fjords are so imposing, the land around the glacier water so stunning. You know she'd marvel at the stretches of green broken up by swollen rock the colour of hardened lava.

You can't compare Iceland to anything other than a darkened moon. It feels so otherworldly that it makes you question what else is out there. What formations, what shapes, what colours have you been missing? Toronto is mostly grey, right-angled. The sky around your home is clouded by light pollution and smoke from the sugar factory. People have told you that you have to get out of the city to see the stars, go to cottage country. You don't know anyone who owns a cottage.

In Iceland, you've seen the stars. No northern lights yet, though you pray for them every time you fly in. You've always wanted to see them, even though one of the locals confessed that they look better in photos. He might've been right, but you'd like to decide for yourself.

You know she'd be moved by it all. Yessenia, who has never travelled other than to move, would be in awe of the north. It would be nothing like the photos she's seen of home. Part of you would like to be the one to show her what else is out there in the world. Just how big it is. But you know that another part of you has chosen places like these because they're not like home. No connection there exists. Nothing will remind her.

If you went over Christmas, it would be cold. Not the worst, not freezing, but still the kind that settles in your bones like humidity does in your hair. You remember the feeling distinctly from last winter in Toronto. Of course, you remember the feeling from all winters, maybe your first in New York the best, but last winter imprinted itself. As though an ice cube sat in your stomach. You could feel the frost burning you from the inside out.

One of those cold-to-the bone days from December often plays back in your mind. In the days that preceded it, your instinct had you on guard. You'd heard your daughter heaving in the bathroom as the shower ran. You offered to toast her some bread when she came back to the kitchen. She declined without any explanation, looking repulsed at the sight of the loaf on the counter, and your stomach dropped. You thought of your mami, the smell of the bakery that she could not stand while she was pregnant with you. For the next four days, your daughter refused breakfast each morning.

After almost a week of noticing Yessenia's strange behaviour, you let yourself into her room when she left the apartment. Her laptop was still open on her desk, the screen unlocked, the background image of las tres generaciones staring you in the face. You had never spied on your child in this way, but your gut told you you had to. You clicked on the Messages app and scrolled through her texts. That's when you saw it. Your greatest fear, sent in a group chat to her best friends. *I'm fucking pregnant.* Sent the previous night, with no responses, just a FaceTime icon that showed she, Zadie, and Maja had talked for just under two hours.

You wanted to be more of a white mom about this. Not storm over to Zadie's or Maja's, where you thought she might be, and ask her to tell you what was going on. Not call her, crying, quoting her messages back. No. You feared that she would be too upset. She must've been terrified already, sick that you'd been right all along about the curse, furious, maybe, that you'd passed on a legacy like that. What if she left? Moved in with the boy, like you had? Like your mami had? You had been living with your daughter for almost sixteen years, yet you still worried that the foundation of the home you'd built with her wasn't sturdy enough to withstand your devastation, her fright. A baby. Her holding her child, wondering how you'd ever abandoned her. No. You couldn't even fathom it without tasting bile in your mouth, let alone talk to her about it.

So you decided to be a white mom—you'd wait until she came to you. You'd escape for a while. You'd pretend for a minute that none of this was happening, that the thing you feared the most hadn't come true, that it hadn't set off the other fears that had been building up ever since you picked her up at LaGuardia and didn't recognize her, your own child. You'd pretend for a while longer that things were all right, that you and she would be all right.

Before you could change your mind, you left. You started walking but turned around almost as soon as the air hit your face. It was blisteringly cold. Your back against the wind, you hurried to the garage, got in the car, and drove until you found yourself at the grocery store. A strange instinct, but one that you decided to follow.

You needed to restock the fridge anyway. For a moment, another thought—*Especially if you have a pregnant daughter*—slipped through, and you hated that. It was what you had worried about for so many years, and yet you almost felt like your brain had rewired itself to pragmatism. But no. No, pragmatism in this case wasn't *Buy more food*. You'd had the conversation with her before. You'd made a more pragmatic plan.

In the grocery store, you combed through each aisle carefully, attempting to distract yourself by pausing in front of items you'd never noticed before, thinking about how you might cook them. Rutabaga. Quail eggs. Plant-based tuna. You kept wandering, your basket still empty.

When you reached the canned foods, you spotted her, Eddie's mom, whose name you couldn't seem to remember. You assumed she probably didn't remember yours, either. It must've been a few years since you saw her last at that parent-teacher night. The two of you hadn't run into each other since. When you caught her eye, she smiled and walked over to you.

"Hi! Long time no see," she said, casting her eyes down quickly before reintroducing herself. "Rosy, by the way."

Of course, you remembered now. Rosy. A sweet name that reminded you of Rosita, one of the neighbourhood strays that would lie on your porch with you whenever your mami wasn't there to scare her away. You would never tell Rosy that she made you think of a stray cat, not even if she knew how enamored you'd been with Rosita.

"Isaura." You smiled as you reminded her of your name. "How are you?"

"Fine, fine. Oh, I saw Mivi the other day at our place. She told me about the clinic internship she just got. You must be so proud of her."

"Yes, thank you," you said, trying not to think of your daughter turning all of it down because of this curse you'd tried so hard to keep her from. "She . . . she's a hard worker. I'm very proud."

Rosy smiled, then tapped her fingernails against her cart.

"She also mentioned that she's saving some of the pay to go back to Honduras? Is your mother back there?"

"She actually died last year. At home."

"Oh, I'm sorry. I didn't realize . . ."

You explained that going home after sixteen years was tougher than your mami had expected. That she'd left her community in New York for one that she barely knew anymore, that the warmth didn't feel as warm without her family, chosen or real. Then she'd had the stroke.

Rosy bobbed her head, tilting it slowly as you talked. It was the reaction you always got when you told people about your dead mother.

"Sorry, that's so much information that you didn't ask for," you said, stumbling, suddenly embarrassed about oversharing. At the same time, you felt like a tap begging to be opened.

"No, please. Don't worry. I asked about her."

Rosy's face softened, and you remembered how she'd told you about losing her mother young. As she nodded, a kind of permission, you saw both the daughter and the mother in her—the person who could relate to you and the one you longed for once more. Even though you were years and miles away, you felt like you were back in the New York apartment you'd moved into when you were eighteen and still very much in need of mothering. You knew you were close to cracking. You sank your teeth into your tongue. It only helped for a matter of seconds.

"I . . . sorry. This has been a tough day," you said. "She's pregnant."

You couldn't even get her name out. Everything was rising up within you. Your panic, your mother's, Lita's. A daisy chain of women tied by men and unplanned babies and the suffering that came with them. You reached toward the shelves to steady yourself as Rosy's hand reached for yours.

"Come, do you want to go outside?"

You agreed, and Rosy pushed her cart to the side of the aisle and set your basket beside it. She placed her arm on the small of your back, and it made you miss your mother all the more. God, what would she have done if she'd known her granddaughter was pregnant, too? At only eighteen, the year she began a degree that none of the women before her had even gotten close to.

Rosy navigated you out of the store, filling the quiet with words of encouragement. She pulled you toward the parking lot and asked which car was yours.

"That one," you said, gesturing to your car while pulling out your keys. You clicked the button to unlock it, opened the door, and sat in the driver's seat. It crossed your mind for a moment to think of how bizarre this was. Sitting in a car, on the cusp of crying over a pregnancy in the same way you'd told your daughter's father about your own. He'd picked you up one day after school, and you'd broken it to him on the ride home so you didn't have to look at him. It's always easier to talk about things in cars.

"I just . . . I tried. I tried so hard. She knows how difficult it was for me. I didn't want that for her. She didn't, either. I mean, I know that much."

"Okay . . . Well, she could get . . ."

"Yes, she will." It wasn't lost on you that you'd made a contingency plan precisely for this, and yet you weren't reassured by any of it. "I mean . . . I hope she will. But I know how things can change once you actually . . ."

Rosy nodded. She kept quiet. Just listened.

"I don't even know whose it would be—she's not dating anyone. Maybe Eddie . . ." You noticed Rosy tense up. For years, you'd believed your daughter when she'd insisted he was like a brother to her. You weren't so sure anymore, but you didn't want to worry Rosy until you'd confirmed it. "Maybe he would know? I know they're good friends. He would probably know."

"Don't jump that far ahead, okay? She'll tell you. The two of you seem close. You're lucky."

The cold seeped into the car, but instead of going back into the store, you turned the engine on, idling as you continued to talk. You couldn't believe how comfortable you felt beside her, divulging secrets you'd never shared with anyone outside of your family as she nodded along, never once questioning the credibility of the curse. How close your daughter had come to escaping it. How, as it turned out, you couldn't escape curses. How they'd find you even if you left your land, changed your language, grew your hair out. How all the running was for nothing.

It dawns on you, as Iceland and its dark sweep fade into a haze of white, that you ought to remember that. About running.

You don't have much time left to decide on your daughter's birthday present. What exactly will you give her as she enters this new year? Will you take her home, show her the hospital where you broke yourself to have her, the yellow house with its terracotta roof where you took her home, the pulperia down the street, its shelves lined with fruit she's never once tasted? Will you show her the ranchita you grew up in, look for the place where you etched your name in wood, for the spot in the siding where your mami's head had been slammed when you were still inside her? Will you show her your father's grave and your mother's and Lita's? Will you show her la Ciudad Blanca?

Or will you hold her hand and keep running? Will you give her permission to look back? Will you, too?

ROSY

HE LEFT. I REPEAT THE FACT in my head to try to make sense of it, find the logic, drill it in, render his departure more palatable. *He left.* And with nothing more than a casual "Excuse me."

I don't look back. As I listen to his feet practically running down the aisle, I can feel myself sinking. Another child, gone.

My eyelids shut to hold back the flood that's coming. I hook my fingers onto the pew, bracing myself for the deluge rushing through my insides, ready to pour out. But when the church door slams shut, its echo seems to sound an epiphany.

In that nave, it hits me. I thought it had all been about you. But we were not divided by you. We were divided by my fear of losing him. The inevitability of his departure was the reason I couldn't want him.

As the priest speaks, I bow my head. For the first time in years, I pray. Your father whispers reassurances in my ear, promising that Eddie will come back. I let him believe that I am crying over you, the memories of your service, all the loss trapped in the stale air.

The sermon continues, but I cannot hear a word. It's like some-one has grasped the rusty handle of my mind and wound it. Memories ricochet like balls in a cage. The motion dusts them off. It's a rattle I can't ignore any longer.

I didn't want him. I didn't want the pregnancy or the kicks or the birth. Most of all, I didn't want another child to lose.

When I found out I was pregnant with Eddie, I was a wreck. In the weeks when it must've happened, I was finally starting to feel like a person again, closer to how I used to be and not like the shell I'd been.

We didn't have sex for months after you died. I had no desire for any of it. But once we started, that next spring, the physical intimacy helped dull the anger I had toward my body—the one I sometimes believed had deliberately cooked you with only so many days to live. That anger melted away, at least momentarily, as your father held me, kissed me, touched me. In one of those first moments of reconnection, we also made your brother.

Some days, I don't know why I kept him. I know how horrible that sounds. But I was still in the trenches of grief, in no position to grow a child. I thought that my grief might poison him, that he'd absorb too much suffering and wither inside me. Part of me even hoped for it. I know I could've had an abortion. I thought about it. A lot. But I kept waiting for something definite. For a gut feeling that I could trust. Nothing came.

Your father was so sure about having another baby. I know how agonizing my uncertainty felt to him. But still, I wasn't sure, and so I did nothing. From this state of paralysis, I fell into the deepest, loneliest pit of darkness. I felt like I'd been cursed, like Sisyphus, rolling up a boulder of your memory, watching it fall every day into a cavern so unfathomably deep. On the day when the darkness felt too vast, I decided that I couldn't live in a world that reminded me of you. A world with dates that would hold meaning to only me and your father. That's when I tried to end things.

I made four horizontal slices, lined up with an exactitude that still sometimes shocks me to see, though the scars are now faint. Almost instantly, I regretted it. I remember fashioning a tourniquet out of a tea towel and calling 911. The ambulance ride was a blur, but I'll never forget the sight of your father running into my room minutes after I was sewn up, his face pale and frantic. His heartbreak made me choke on my tears, my shame. I never wanted to feel as low as I did lying in that hospital bed, a vigilant nurse outside my door. As your father held me, insisting that we find a doctor who could help me after I left the ER, I knew I could never stand to feel so much fear pass between us. The next time we were in a hospital together, I wanted love to be passed instead. When the doctor returned to check on me, I steeled myself to tell him about the pregnancy, then asked if I'd hurt the baby. The tests they performed after that showed that everything looked normal; the baby was fine. Relief flooded my body. That was when I decided to keep the pregnancy.

Your father found a grief counsellor for us, and a meeting for bereaved mothers for me to go to. Even though I dreaded the group meetings and sessions with the counsellor, I went for him and played up how healing they were. I couldn't bear to see him worry any more than he already did.

I had no plans, no desire for another attempt. Ever since we'd left the hospital, I made it clear to your father that I didn't want to die. Still, I don't think he took his eye off me until we settled in Toronto. As I nested in our new home, with a new baby on the way, things started to feel a little hopeful again, and my attempt almost felt like it had happened to someone else. I was scared still, but no longer in that dark pit. The leaves turned red and I truly viewed that fall as a new season in my life.

At one of my obstetric appointments, my new doctor in Toronto reviewed my file and warned me about the birth. "The afterpains get worse with each child," she told me. "Prepare yourself." She was right. Although I wasn't aware of it, really, that was the day I decided I would be different with him. I would prepare for pain this time. I would not allow myself to fall for his aliveness, his perfection. I would be strong and protect myself from it all.

When Eddie was a baby, I would prepare myself to find him dead in his crib. I'd go to bed with a lump in my stomach and wake up with it in my throat. The first few days, I never wanted to put him down, but as my attachment to my baby grew, I made myself fight it. I started handing him off to your father so I couldn't fall in love with him, so that the chemicals, the oxytocin, the milky smell couldn't take over my body and force me into it. I chose not to breastfeed him for that very reason.

When Eddie was a toddler, I dreaded each milestone. Walking was a threat. Talking was torturous. The sweetness with which he said, "Mama, Mama. My mama." My only child to call me that. My only child to make me laugh when he said things like "Good boy, Mama," copying me.

When Eddie was a child, I was afraid of water, of fast balls, of other parents and teachers who were not as watchful. I remember mothers in the schoolyard talking about how much they loved watching their children turn into "real people." But it was all tainted for me. His humour. His creativity. His kindness. I couldn't handle taking any of it in. I pre-emptively mourned each new trait that he grew into.

When Eddie became a teenager and started pulling away from us, in some ways it made my feelings easier to manage. His distance helped me maintain mine. Still, there were things I had to protect myself from. I refused to look at his art. It was proof that he was growing up, that he was forming his own points of view, that he was taking the baton from his father and running with it. He was becoming a whole person, and if I took it all in, it would be the greatest thing I could ever lose.

And then, soon after Eddie turned eighteen, Isaura bore the news of the baby your brother had made with Mivi. I knew it was his. It had to be.

One night, when Eddie'd had people over in the basement, I'd overheard Mivi talking to a friend in the kitchen as they poured themselves more wine. I was lying on the couch in the living room. They must've thought I was upstairs. Her friend asked if she and Eddie were still sleeping together. Before I could move away, Mivi said no, not anymore. Lowering her voice, she said that she missed it. That it was the best she'd ever had. Then she laughed and admitted that Eddie was the only person she'd ever been with, but that as far as she was concerned, and technically only by default, it was the best. That was a couple of weeks before I ran into Isaura.

When I found out Mivi was pregnant, I did my best to stay calm, to not break down when I saw your brother. I wished I was the type of mother he could entrust with his secrets. The type who could really talk to him. Instead, I just avoided him. For a month, we barely spoke. When I'd walk past his bedroom, I'd peer inside the cracked door, looking for clues of transformation. I'd seek out hints of maturity in his face as we passed each other in the hallway, before I went to my office and studied numbers for him. I looked at the money we'd saved for Eddie's college fund. The second account your father had opened in case we'd ever wanted to have another child.

Your father had stopped depositing money into the account when it became clear that we weren't going to have another, but the savings compounded over the years. I thought I could help financially with Eddie's baby, that it might be a clean slate for everybody. I could take care of him and his child, be there for your brother in a way that I had not before—it was the most healing penance I could imagine. Sure, it might be strange at the beginning, difficult even, but babies have that magical ability to connect everyone around them. It felt poetic to be given a life at that point, almost two decades after yours was taken.

I did not tell your father any of this. I'd wait until it came from Eddie.

After Isaura and I sat in her car, talking about the baby, I wrote out a plan on my phone.

August: Detroit. Turn over a new leaf on her anniversary. Write a speech, give it over her gravestone so he knows you mean it, like swearing on the Bible. Tell him that you brought him here not just for yourself or for Vivian but for him. Apologize again and again and then tell him how you will be different. Talk about his baby. How you are not mad, you are ready, you are present, you are here. You will do better this time, you give him your word. You will mother the two of them properly.

A few weeks after I found out about Mivi, I texted Isaura. I wanted to meet with her in person, to tell her that it was Eddie's baby, too, that we would help, do what we could to be there. Two days later, her name flashed on my phone. For the first time since my teens, I found myself pacing anxiously around the living room and clearing my throat before picking up.

"Rosy! Hi, hi, how are you?" she said, her voice jittery across the line.

"Fine. How are you? You got my message?"

"I did. I would love to get together, but I'm flying for the next ten days."

"Oh," I said. I stopped pacing and leaned against the couch. "Well, no worries. Let me know when you're back in town, and we can plan something?"

"Yes, yes," she said, before letting out a shaky breath. "By the way, I'm sorry it took so long to answer you. I just . . . I've been a bit distracted with Yessenia." Isaura's voice broke. "I'm sorry. It's good news. I know I'm not making it sound good, but it's good. I found a couple of pads in her bathroom. She's not pregnant anymore."

"Oh," I managed to say one more time. There was no more baby. My heart felt as though it were being pulled down into my stomach, that sinking place, heavy with the plans I thought would buoy us. "That is good news. Very good."

Isaura cried over the line.

"She doesn't know I knew, or that I know about . . . Anyway, I'm just so happy she's not pregnant anymore."

"Of course," I said. Then I wished her a good trip, and she said she'd see me soon. After we hung up, I left the house and walked for hours until I no longer felt like weeping.

After a week or so, I edited the original plan. We'd go to Detroit, still. I'd make a different kind of speech. I'd tell Eddie that I had been so consumed by my trauma from you that I hadn't managed to work through it, but that twenty years was a turning point. He might not believe it, but I would prove him wrong. I wouldn't want to spend any more time focused on any child but him. I would catch up on what I'd missed. I'd mother him like I mothered you. And then, maybe that day, maybe further down the road, he would tell me about Mivi. We would bond. We'd be forever tied by babies that would not, could not, be.

But today, in the church pew, the oversimplification of it all hits me. My plan can't work, because the crux of it isn't true. I'm not in

Detroit to simply shift my focus from you to your brother. I'm not here to finally say goodbye to you, to "move on."

I was wrong about the loss I've been mourning, the one I've been most terrified of.

It's been Eddie. I've been waiting to lose Eddie.

MIVI

ON A BLACK-AND-WHITE SIGN by the highway, The Mansion claims to be the best discount motel in Detroit, complete with HBO, fax, and a couple other amenities that blur as we drive by. What ultimately sells it to me is the sign that mentions it's only a four-minute drive from the next exit. The tank is running low, and my hangover is kicking in. Even though we've kept the radio low and haven't said much to each other, I have to drag my thumb across my temple to soothe the pounding inside.

We walk into the lobby, and it immediately occurs to me that the name of the motel is ironic. The five-car parking lot and cramped building should've tipped me off. Inside, the smell of smoke is stifling. Then there's the carpet—a shag that blankets the entire entryway and the hallways that run out from it. It looks like it was probably once pink before turning vaguely grey and patchy from spills and bleach. Reception is like something out of a low-budget movie set, complete with laminate panelling and a painting of an eagle on the wall. As we approach the desk, the receptionist looks up from the dog-eared Harlequin novel she's reading. Her name tag says *Sue*.

For a moment, I consider suggesting to Eddie that we turn around and try another place, but my head is killing me and I need to lie down.

"Hi," I say, walking up to Sue. "Do you have any rooms with two beds available?" I avoid looking at Eddie as I kill the idea of us sleeping together.

Sue shakes her head. "The only vacancy we have is a double, actually."

I look over at Eddie, who shrugs, then mouths, *It's fine*.

I tell Sue we'll take the room. Eddie hands over a credit card. As soon as the machine beeps, Sue unhooks a comically large set of keys from the wall behind her and puts them in his hand.

"Down the hall to your left," she says. "Enjoy!"

We both smirk.

When we get to our room, Eddie heads straight to the bathroom and turns on the faucet to check that it runs clear. I set my duffle bag at the foot of the bed and lie down across the comforter—a brown garden of roses that belongs on 1980s wallpaper—my cheek pressed against the fake satin. I try not to think about when it was last washed. From the bed, I can see into the open closet. Four limp pillows stacked on top of a pilling camel-coloured throw, mismatched hangers, and a single mothball on the bottom shelf. *Seems about right*, I think, before shutting my eyes.

Eventually, the bathroom door opens, and I hear the rustle of Eddie's shoes against the carpet, getting closer and closer until the sound stops and the mattress sinks on one side. Eddie shuffles back to rest against the headboard. I can feel the springs contracting and releasing as he gets comfortable.

Lying down beside him feels too intimate, especially in this room. It's too small, too far away, too secret. No one would ever know we are here. I sit up, shoving the panic into a box in my mind. Nothing has happened yet.

As I turn my head toward him, though, I wonder whether I've made a mistake in sitting up. His face looks cool, freshly washed, stupidly kissable. For a second, I allow myself to think about what I'd do if the rules did not apply in this country. If curses knew political borders. If there was actually safety in being tucked away in this room, just the two of us. I cast my eyes to my knees.

"You know, this is my first time in a hotel," I say, to keep my mouth from doing anything else. "Or motel, I guess. Kind of different."

"This is, um, quite the introduction," Eddie says, before inching closer. He drops his head to my shoulder. His ear feels so warm, like a peach left in the sun.

"Thank you, Mi," he whispers.

We spend the afternoon in bed. Contorted in different positions, our limbs pretzelled to fit both our bodies on the double mattress without touching. Like the bed is a raft we can't risk leaving, one that requires us to move every so often to flow with the current.

We talk about everything but the reason I came. My night out with the girls, the drive, first Detroit impressions. How I'd called in sick and feel guilty about it. How Eddie feels a bit guilty, too, for having packed his camera in case he could capture some footage without his parents noticing. Also for leaving them. I ask him if he told his parents where he was going.

"Not to be all . . . you know, but they're probably worried sick," I say, a little nauseated myself as those last words roll out of my mouth. It sounds too motherly. Like playing grown-up.

"They'll be fine. I know that they're just focusing on Vivian. The usual. Planning for tomorrow, to finally see our old house and the grave and all that." I wrap a ribbon of my hair around my finger, let it go, start over again. "If anything, this is good. This way, they don't have me around to distract them from the big anniversary."

"If they really thought you were a distraction, they wouldn't have made you come."

Eddie shrugs. "Mivi . . . you really can't understand."

"Well, I definitely can't if you don't tell me any more."

"There's too much. It's twenty years of stuff. Probably even stuff in there that I think's normal, you know."

He stops there, cut off by a gurgling in his stomach so loud that it interrupts us both. *Saved by the fucking bell*, I want to say.

Eddie hasn't eaten since breakfast (neither have I, I realize), so we decide to have a late lunch and buy some snacks and drinks to bring back to the room for later. As we wind our way downtown, the sound of zipping cars puts me on edge. I can't stop thinking of Eddie's body hitting the pavement. I try to block out what I thought could happen, what I've been told the curse is capable of, and what, so far, it has never failed to do. I sneak around him so that I'm closer to the road.

Although the motel room felt charged, there's safety in its seclusion. As long as I can control myself, it seems as though nothing bad could happen in there. It's different out here. There are more variables. By the way Eddie's eyes keep ping-ponging across the street, I can tell that he feels uneasy outside, too, though for different reasons. I'm sure he's looking out for his parents.

At a crosswalk, I pull out my final Sobranie and light it. I wanted to keep it a bit longer, maybe never even smoke it, just preserve it, but now I think it might serve us better to light it. Whether it acts as a palate cleanser or just a sedative, I don't care; I'll take what I can get.

Between cigarette puffs, we make comments on the condition of the houses. The plywood windows. Toy-littered lawns. Yards sprouting only the suggestion of grass, all golden and sparse. Eddie takes out his camera a couple of times to capture the facades, and me, holding on to a shrinking pink cigarette.

Looking around, taking everything in, feels a bit like those early days in Toronto. Wondering what it would be like to be from here. To know all the shortcuts and the best and the worst of everything. To have seen things change.

As we walk past a used bookstore, Eddie swings his arm down close to my hand, his fingers grazing mine. A rush of electricity and embarrassment comes over me.

"It's too warm for hand holding," I say, regretting it immediately, even though Eddie laughs. I try to move on quickly. "You know, I read a lot of Lemony Snicket as a kid." I gesture at a box set of *A Series of Unfortunate Events* in the window. "It really freaked me out. I was afraid of my mom dying, and being pawned off to strangers, since I had no family in Toronto."

"Yeah, that's a fair concern," he says, nodding. "Good thing nothing happened. And that you're legally an adult now. Unpawnable."

"Exactly." I laugh, giving him a weak punch. "Sometimes, I do wonder, though, what would happen if my mom just died. An accident or something. I don't even have, like, a great-aunt or anything to turn to. I barely know how to fill out my taxes."

"Mrs. Saltzman was kind of like an aunt, right?"

"For sure. She would've been there for me. But she's not around anymore."

"Of course," Eddie says, before apologizing. Not for bringing her up—I like that he remembers who she was—but just in the way that people do when they don't know what else to say about dead people.

When she died, back when I was in grade nine, Eddie didn't say much, just dropped off a bouquet of white lilies with the girls. I remember Mami taking his face into her hands and telling him how much Mrs. Saltzman would've liked him. Later that night, she asked me whether anything was going on between us. It wasn't a lie to say no, because nothing had happened at that point. Sure, when he entered a room, I felt a shift. Whatever knots were in my shoulders would unspool. I could focus, I would stop looking at the door. But that wasn't anything, really. It was the opposite of butterflies. It was calm. I didn't tell my mami that. What I told her was some lie about how he was like a brother to me at that point, how it had been too long, how he was more like one of the girls. She trusted that I wouldn't date, let alone do anything else. As far as I know, she still doesn't know I've ever even been kissed.

"You also have me, by the way. I don't know how much help I'd be with taxes," he says. "But I'd cross a border for you, too, just so you know."

I smile, biting my tongue to avoid showing my teeth. Eddie slows down, takes my hand. Beads of sweat roll between our palms. It's enough to make me panic, pull my hand back, toss the cigarette on the ground.

"I should probably text my mom soon," I say, angling my body away from his as we keep walking. Another wave of sweat rushes down my back. The sun is blistering, and I can feel my skin baking, but I don't want to cross over to the shaded side before we get to the crosswalk. There are still too many cars whipping by.

"So where did you tell her you were going?" he asks.

"Nowhere," I say, picking up the pace. "I mean, I haven't talked to her since yesterday. She's away till Tuesday—"

"Till your birthday," Eddie interjects, and I can't help but smile again.

"I'll just check in when we get back, say I'm busy at the restaurant or something. Just so she doesn't worry if I'm a bit slow to text back."

Eddie dips his head down. "Part of me wants to leave right now, but I don't know."

We stop before the crosswalk. Eight seconds until it's our turn.

"We'll figure it out, okay? We will." I think about how to lure more out of him. Get him talking more about his mother, about why he had to leave this time. But I can tell he's not ready.

I take his hand back for a small squeeze, and his shoulders relax. He looks at me, at my lips, as he teeters ever so slightly on the curb. His mouth approaching mine. The countdown on the pedestrian light across the street beeping steadily. Eight seconds extending into slow, sticky time.

"It's our light," I say, turning back around when the sound of the switch cuts through the air. I twist my head toward traffic as we step out onto the crosswalk. The air feels heavy, in the way that everything does when you try to ignore the truth.

VIVIAN

ALMOST LIKE THEY ARE hunkering down for the end of the world, Eddie and Mivi stock up at the nearest corner store. Cigarettes, triangle sandwiches, pizza-flavoured Combos, kettle corn, two apples, some Jack Link's, beer, and a bottle of white wine, since Eddie's fake ID says he's legal in the U.S., too. They can't imagine that alcohol from a corner store will be any good, so they add a couple blue Gatorades to their haul for tomorrow's hangovers. "Breakfast," my brother jokes.

When they get back to the motel, Mivi places the snacks on the bed like they're a spread worthy of display and sits in front of them. Across from her, Eddie sets down his backpack on the dresser before pulling out his camera bag. As he fiddles with the lenses, imagining what he could shoot in the motel, he notices that the only sound in the room is the hum of the highway. The sound of cars and trucks whipping by. Then the light tapping of Mivi's thumbs on her phone.

Eddie watches Mivi as she crafts a message to her mother. After erasing the entirety of her text for the third time, she grabs the bottle of wine from the takeaway bag and unscrews the cap. Their mouths water at the sound. They're a bit Pavlovian like that. Mivi takes a quick swig, then puts the bottle on the side table. Eddie grabs two ceramic coffee cups, fills them up, and sits down beside her on the bed.

Mivi doesn't lift her eyes from her phone when he serves her. She's having trouble. With her mother, she doesn't usually struggle with her words, needing to edit her texts to make sure she'll be understood. With Eddie, it's sometimes like that. The process can involve measured punctuation. The careful removal of excessive emojis. The massaging of words into a message he won't misinterpret as flirting.

Lying to her mother takes more effort than Mivi anticipated. Each time she sends a text, she thinks carefully about where her mother assumes she is. As much as my brother doesn't understand their need for constant contact, he's jealous of Mivi and Isaura, their expectation to talk daily, to share news, not only personal, but also about the people they know. Eddie thinks back on that morning Mivi found out her boss's wife was pregnant with their fifth child. She texted Isaura to tell her, and it turned into an hour-long back and forth of voice notes and tangents. All of it unnerved him because he simply didn't get it. Since he ran from the church, he's been ignoring all my father's calls and only sent one simple text to tell him that he's fine, that he's still in the city and taking a breather with a friend. My father simply wrote back: *OK. Talk soon.*

Eventually, Mivi manages to conjure up a message, careful to mention that she has a couple doubles lined up today and tomorrow, so she might be a little less reachable. Other than that, she tells Isaura she's good, enjoying the sunshine, seeing the girls in the evenings. As she writes that, she prays the girls won't text her just yet. She hasn't figured out what she'll tell them and when, though she knows she'll be seeing them for her birthday dinner in a couple of days.

"I'm sorry I'm making you lie to her," Eddie says.

"You're not *making* me do anything. It's just . . . tough to explain in a text." The implication that she'll tell her mother everything once she's back hits him, and Mivi can read the alarm in his eyes. "Don't worry."

Eddie nods, then raises his cup for a sip.

"What's the plan for tomorrow?" Mivi asks, curling her lips like the words soured in her mouth. It sounded so casual. Like asking what their brunch plans were.

"They'll be going to the cemetery. My mom's never even seen her grave. So I know it's just going to be this whole big . . . thing." Eddie shakes his head before taking a swig.

"Well, yeah. I'd imagine," she says. "I'd come with you. If you wanted me there."

"No. No. Definitely not," says Eddie. Mivi's face drops, and my brother looks panicked. He shakes his head again. "I mean, not because of you, obviously, but . . . I can only imagine the scene they'd make if I just showed up at the cemetery, after I left and all. I'd ruin the whole thing for them. I just won't go."

Mivi takes a small inhale like she's about to say something, and Eddie jumps in before she can.

"And, I mean, besides, I don't even know where she's buried."

"Ed, they might be mad you left, but don't you think they'll be more upset, hurt even, if you don't go? Or if you don't even tell them you're not going?"

My brother downs the rest of his wine, then pinches the bridge of his nose.

"You're saying that because of how *your* mom would react if she was mad. She'd probably, what, just talk calmly to you about it? Not be your BFF for like five minutes? It's not like that with my mom."

Mivi rolls her eyes, though she won't say anything about it. It's hard, with my brother especially, to admit that her relationship with her mother is far from perfect. Although she may not remember their initial issues, she knows from her mami's candour that they both struggled to be mother and daughter. Given that her mother is only seventeen years older, sometimes they behave more like sisters or friends. Unlike her friends, Mivi has been treated more like an adult for years. Once Mivi turned twelve, Isaura stopped asking her colleagues to stay with her, and she was allowed to be home alone for days at a time. After relentlessly doling out lectures and cautionary tales to her as a teenager, Isaura trusted Mivi to resist temptation. She allowed her to throw parties, to drink socially, to make the right decisions with boys. The guilt of betraying her promises to her mami sometimes made Mivi feel like a bad daughter. Pressure came with wanting, needing, to be a good one. Growing up, she wished she'd had siblings whose existence would've deflected from hers at times, who would've given her mother a do-over, maybe even quelled her fear of losing her daughter to a curse, or distance, or both.

She can't really explain to Eddie that she's always craved the safety of boundaries and discipline even if she hasn't always seemed to need them. Or that she liked when Maja's or Zadie's parents got mad at them for trivial things, because she can only remember her own mother really raising her voice at her once, when they fought about the curse. She understands why he looks at their relationship with envy, yet she wishes she could tell him that there is more nuance to it.

"Look, you clearly don't get it." He pauses. "I don't think I've ever told you about this before," Eddie says, lifting his hand with the burn in front of Mivi's face. For a moment, she is free to study the uneven patches of gossamer skin that cover his knuckles and two fingers, the tiny bubble that seems to have trapped air on the edge of his index. "I'll tell you how I got this. A little context on what anniversaries look like in my family."

He refills his cup and tops Mivi's up. They both take a big gulp before he starts.

By the time Eddie makes it to the crux of the story, orange sunlight has blanketed the bed they're sitting on. He's offered context, back-pedalled, and derailed into my mother's backstory. The death of her parents, how she was supposed to be in the car with them. The cocktail of guilt and anger she continued to feed off years after the accident. The unfairness of what happened, what followed. As he talks about her, my brother pulls his knees into his chest, and Mivi can see the child that he has not outgrown. The hairs on his legs bristle even though they are bathed in warm light. Once he begins talking about the fire, Mivi wraps her pinky around Eddie's and he sighs. She is careful not to hold on too tightly as he continues.

"I was probably three at the time. I guess, yeah, I must've been if it was Vivian's five-year. Either way, that was the year my mom burned the bassinet. I remember watching her set it on fire from the kitchen window." My brother focuses on Mivi's knuckle as he talks, the small, perfect mountain of it, the hand he wishes he could kiss. "The fabric went up pretty quickly, but the bones of it just sort of turned black. They didn't crumble or melt or anything. The fire spread a bit underneath it, got the grass for sure, but it didn't go beyond that. Somehow, it was pretty contained. Anyway, when the fire died down, she came back inside and said she had to go shower."

He still does not pull away from studying her hand. He thought it'd be easier to share this story. It's not one of the worst ones, really. She didn't do anything to try to hurt him in this one. It was just an accident. That's what she kept repeating when my father came home.

Between sobs, she told him about the bassinet, an accident, the yard, Eddie being left alone for barely a minute, a terrible accident, his hand, which she'd placed in a bucket of ice water and wrapped up in gauze. The doctor did a great job, she said. He was okay, it was an accident, it was an accident.

The veins on my father's neck swelled, his eyes filled. When he scooped Eddie up in his arms, my brother began to wail. He was begging to be put down, left alone. When Eddie managed to squirm out of his arms, he locked himself in the bathroom. It took my father an entire hour to convince him to come out. He had to beg and bribe until my brother conceded.

"I must have wanted to see what she'd been doing in the yard."

Mivi is bracing herself. Even though she can guess what happened next, she's not ready to hear it, to feel Eddie's pain. She's seen photos of him at that age. A couple of them were shot in that yard, as he played in the sprinkler in little striped trunks, his belly hanging over the waistband.

"I slipped on the gasoline. The grass was just . . . soaked in it. I remember the smell. It sort of sends me back there every time we go to the gas station. Maybe that's why I remember the whole thing so well. You know how smell is linked to memory. Well, it's the smell, that or the pain. But, yeah, when I got out there, I fell on my hands, so they were covered."

As Eddie continues, he unhooks his pinky from Mivi's and begins to swirl the last drop of his wine around in his cup. Both of their cups are nearly empty now, but neither of them reaches for the bottle. That much movement feels irreverent.

"I basically just crawled toward the bassinet, and some of it was still burning. I think I was trying to feel what the burned part of it felt like, you know? Which . . . doesn't even make sense, really. I thought we were supposed to be wired to be afraid of fire."

Mivi focuses on his eyes, tries to catch them as he stares into his cup. It takes effort, but she manages not to stare at the hand she knows he's growing more and more self-conscious of as he speaks.

"My hand got too close to the actual flame, obviously, and it caught."

"I'm so sorry, Eddie," she says, her voice a half whisper. She can't think of anything big enough to say as she steals a glance at his hand. The grooves in the skin look more tender than they did a few minutes ago. "I always thought it was from an oil burn."

"Well, that's what I told you. It felt like an easier story."

Mivi wants to put her hand on his. She wonders if he can sense her hesitation. "Did your mom find you?"

Eddie pulls at the neck of his shirt, thumbs the seam.

"She heard me scream. And she froze," he says. "That's what she said happened, anyway, when I asked about it in, like, grade three or four, when I was being teased for it. Anyway, she said you freeze in moments like that. I swear I remember her looking out the window from the bathroom and not moving for a while. Meanwhile, my skin . . . I don't remember the pain, but I bet I screamed louder than I probably ever have. And that's when she came out. She ran out in a towel and threw it on me, stopped the fire. She was trying to crouch so no one would see her naked in the yard, but it made it harder for her to run back inside with me."

Mivi inhales deeply, and she can feel the sweat that's pearling under her dress.

"Sorry, it's . . . I'm not sure why I picked that story." For a moment, he looks over at her as though to say, *You asked for this, and you haven't even heard the half of it.* "There's the concussion from the bottle of Scotch. You came by to see me when I told everyone I'd fallen off my bike."

Mivi feels sick. She should've known, she thinks.

"That was because I blew up about Vivian. I wasn't . . . *nice* about it." The word peels off his tongue like it's a sticky thing. "She hit me over the head with the bottle."

"Oh." Mivi can't get more than that short breath out, feeling useless. The one thing she considers doing to help, she can't. Not that kissing it better would fix things. But it might help, if only for a moment.

"I know you probably see her as this person who defied the odds or something—who still managed to raise a kid and have a career and stay in a marriage and all despite losing her daughter." Eddie clears his throat in that way that men do to ground themselves. He reaches for the neck of his shirt again, nervously tugging on the fabric. "I see her as someone who wasn't there for me growing up. Who didn't want another kid after Vivian."

Mivi feels ashamed that she made him feel like he had to defend himself.

"Just . . . don't tell anyone this, okay?"

She assures him that, of course, she won't, and says they don't have to talk about it anymore if he doesn't want to. When he doesn't say anything, she places her hand on his chest, because to place it on his hand feels too obvious. Then again, so does trying to feel for his heart, to slow down its beating with her touch, to make them both feel better. Mivi does it anyway.

After the stories and the silence that couldn't really be filled by anything other than soft mm-hmms and broken eye-contact, my brother pulls out a deck of cards from Mivi's bag. Without saying much, they move on to games like it's a natural progression. They sit on the balcony, drinking beer, eating snacks, and playing cards for hours as the sun tucks itself away behind the high-rises in the distance. When they've exhausted their appetite for two-player hearts, they crawl into bed and talk between sleepy lulls. Mivi lies on her stomach, her skin swollen and shiny from midnight heat and alcohol sweats.

"Can I ask you something, Eddie?" Mivi whispers. "Nothing to do with your family, promise."

"By all means."

"I was just thinking about it earlier when we smoked that last one. The Sobranies. I know you're worried it would ruin the mystique, but I have to know where you found them."

Eddie pauses for a few seconds, looking hesitant. Then, with a practised self-possession, he assures her he didn't have to look that far.

"I spent at least two hours online looking for them after we saw them in *An Education*," Mivi says. "Couldn't find them anywhere. I mean, unless I wanted to buy them by the crateload."

Eddie laughs. Mivi rolls on her side to face him.

"God, please don't tell me you bought a crate," she says.

"No. But I did buy a carton."

Mivi's mouth relaxes into a smile, but she holds her gaze firmly on my brother, pressing him for more information.

"Fine. *Fine*," he said. "I did some sleuthing, and I found a wholesaler in Scarborough. And when I got there, he asked me for my business number. I'd prepared a fake number and business name, but sort of chickened out last minute. So I just told him that I couldn't find them anywhere else in Toronto and I needed them. He said that Canada stopped importing them and he was down to his last carton. Cut to him letting me buy them," Eddie says with a smirk, the memory of his I-have-to-have-these-for-this-girl speech warming his stomach. "It was just as well I bought a carton, actually, because they don't have all-pink packs, as it turns out. They're a bit of a strange mix, actually. I mean, I figured you would've been fine with the greens and yellows in there, too, but I knew you'd like the pinks the best."

Mivi pulls up the top sheet to conceal her grin, but her eyes give her away. "Really? Just like that, he let a *civilian* buy at wholesale?"

Eddie smiles and says, "I may have told him that it might be the only way to get my best friend back."

Mivi purses her lips the way she does when he's teasing her. "Thanks, Eddie. I can finally sleep easy now."

For a while, they toss in the bed, too giddy for sleep to take them right away, but eventually, and sooner than either of them expects it to, it does. Eddie wakes up a few hours later, at an hour that's not exactly night but not day, either. He looks over at Mivi. She's wearing a tank top, but her arms are dewy with sweat. A purple light from outside pours through the window, filtering through the old venetian blinds, leaving violet stripes on her skin.

Eddie picks up his camera and adjusts the aperture. He wants to capture this night. The fact that she came. In case one day he wonders whether he'd dreamt it. He'll have proof. Evidence that she loves him.

He won't tell her that he loves her. Not yet. It's not like she doesn't know it. But he's afraid that she won't say it back. Knowing is enough for now.

My brother distracts himself from those thoughts by focusing on the challenge of photographing in a dark room. He opens the aperture fully to take in the small slice of moonlight that runs across the bed, a hint of brightness that he hopes will be enough to reveal her face resting against the pillow, her purring lips.

Eddie presses the shutter-release button and captures her. No matter how it turns out, he thinks, it'll be the best photograph he'll ever take.

———

Each death day has been woven in a similar pattern. My brother shrinks himself. My father walks on eggshells. We all wait for my mother's reaction, for her inevitable break of the proverbial loom. This year, though, the day is rendered in bolder colours. The tensions are higher with the promise of a turning point that feels improbable to my family. Even my mother wonders whether she can really move on without first plucking out all the shrapnel from that morning, twenty years ago.

She's tried to forget the memory of that morning, but time has not diluted it. The images blur before her eyes in swatches of colour. The lacquered red of the ambulance. The flat greyness of my cheeks. The pale-pink blanket I was swaddled in. The firefighters came about ten minutes after my mother found me. When they reached my parents' bedroom, one of them scooped me out of my father's lap for a brief moment before setting me back. They did not attempt resuscitation. There was no use. It was too late. "You can hold her in the truck," one of the firefighters said. "She doesn't have to go in the gurney." My father cradled me in his arms as they drove us to the hospital.

An agent from Child Protective Services was waiting in the ER when my parents got to the hospital. Stoic, she explained that the police would be sent to their home to begin the investigation, that the nurse she waved over as she saw my parents walk in would take the body. As my father reluctantly handed me over, the twenty-something nurse assured my parents that the report would be back soon and that, generally, the whole process, the involvement of the police and CPS would be over soon if it really was just SIDS. My parents would never forget that verbiage. *Just SIDS.*

My parents watched as the nurse placed me in a tiny plastic bassinet and rolled me down the hallway with the agent. And then, when

I was out of sight, my father called a taxi. On the ride home, the driver looked back every so often, trying to make conversation. He asked when my mother, her hand resting on her still-swollen stomach, was due. My father shook his head, his eyes getting redder. My mother didn't say a word. She just looked out the window the whole way back, inhaling sharply every so often as though she'd forgotten to breathe. When they pulled up to the house, she didn't move. My father handed the driver a wad of bills, then walked around the car to open the door and help my mother out. She was holding her chest.

"It's my fault," she whispered, still strapped into the seat. "I didn't check to make sure the blanket was still wrapped tight when we put her down. It's my fault."

My father collected her face in his hands. "No, Rosy. It was wrapped, I promise. The first time she woke up, I checked."

My mother shook her head repeatedly. He continued. "But the second time, I didn't get up. I heard her stir, but I didn't get up to check. I didn't get up to check."

The driver's eyes widened. Slowly, he turned around and reached out to touch my mother's knee, not saying a word. That's when she finally began to cry.

It's just after midnight now. When my father sees the time glowing on the hotel's nightstand, he gets up, makes his way to the bathroom, and leans on the edge of the sink. He wipes off the sweat that's been building with the heat and his nerves. Then he picks up his phone. This will be the sixth time he has tried to call Eddie since my brother told him he needed space.

His heart beats faster and faster with each ring. He allows himself to believe that this time, Eddie will actually pick up, say, *Dad, I'm sorry. Please come get me.* But instead, a robotic voice announces that the person he is trying to reach is unavailable. My father breathes into the phone for a second, not knowing quite what to say, then hangs up. It's useless; Eddie will only be reached if he wants to be.

While my father slumps down against the bathroom counter, my mother feigns sleep in bed. She hasn't moved since this afternoon. After the church service, they walked around some more, eyes peeled for Eddie, mouths mute. When they got back to the room, they fought over my brother. My mother was adamant about just letting Eddie be for once. She would give him the space to come back to them. He wouldn't fight her plan if he felt he had chosen to hear it. Regardless, she was sure he was blowing off steam, probably getting footage for his film. She knew he'd brought his camera, and she noticed he'd brought his backpack to church. My father couldn't believe her apathy. He didn't buy the theory that Eddie had gone off to film—it seemed convenient for her to think that. It was clear to him that their son was hurting; he had run away from them for a reason she didn't want to take accountability for.

When there was nothing left to say, my mother lay down to rest, and my father went out again to look for Eddie, calling his phone every so often, only ever getting voicemail until my brother finally texted him. Lying in bed, my mother crafted two messages. Both were only a few words long, but she must've rewritten them nearly a hundred times before hitting send. She realized it was the first time in her life that she had ever really asked for help from anyone outside her family. When my father had forced her to get help after her attempt, that didn't really feel like her choice. Even when she had him take her to the clinic after she struck my brother, she didn't ask anything of her doctors. But this time, some of my father's arguments struck a chord. She heard truth in his voice, deflection in hers.

My mother knew her son was safe, but my father was right. Even if Eddie was just out filming and taking a breather, she had to take action. She had to ask for help before it was too late and Eddie pulled away from her entirely.

When my father came back alone, my mother was sitting up, facing the window, daydreaming. It isn't uncommon for her to sink back into the place she found herself twenty years ago when she came back from the hospital without me. A state of hazy fantasy.

She daydreams about me in the morning, generally, before everyone wakes or after they've left the kitchen, while she sits on the cushioned bench and looks out the window, her legs tucked under her. Her mouth curls into a sleepy half smile, and her eyes glaze over. She'll often forget to blink. If it's a particularly good one, she'll bob her head. Pull a toothy smile. Engage with this figment that she sees out the window.

She often stares at the place where my tree used to be, the one they planted in our backyard when my father suggested that my memory might go on as another living thing that could grow before their eyes. But when they planted the tree, on the seventh anniversary of my death, she began to tend to it as though it wasn't just a plant, but actually me. She spent hours in the yard, watering the tree, feeding it, speaking to it. She would bring Eddie out with her, and he would run around, kicking a ball. When it was really hot, she would turn on the sprinklers for him, and sometimes, she would run through, too, in that yellow one-piece my father used to love so much. I think some days, maybe even a couple days in August, were so full and happy that it felt like she was playing with her two children under the sun in the yard, like she was complete.

My tree survived its first two winters, but during the third, a particularly harsh and long five-month winter, it withered, and come spring, my mother could do nothing to bring it back. For months, she tried. She read books, watched videos, mulched, and pruned what she could. When my father finally called in a gardener to help, they were told that once a tree starts dying, reversal is nearly impossible. My mother was devastated; she felt that the world was not done taking from her. No matter what she tried, she thought, whatever made her feel hopeful wouldn't last.

My father thinks of that tree often. He remembers going to sit by its stump after spotting a red mark on his leg, and praying to me. *If it comes back, maybe I will see you again,* he thought. *That would make it better.* Still, he hoped for more time. For another year of remission, and then another.

In the bathroom, he takes off his shirt and checks his skin. The worry of getting sick again never goes away. He peers into the mirror, spots a mole on his shoulder that he fears is new. As his chest swells with anxiety, he picks up his phone again and opens the folder full of pictures of his torso and legs. A log of checked concerns. He finds a photo of it. The same mole, the same shape, the same colour. He won't be seeing me just yet. For the most part, this is a relief, but on my anniversary, he can't help but feel a slight disappointment.

MIVI

BACK WHEN WE USED TO sleep together, Eddie was always the first one up. He'd stir and start rubbing the dimples at the small of my back to wake me. If I didn't move, he'd dig his fingers into my ribs to pull me out of my slumber in a fit of laughter. I started staying still on purpose to see what he'd try next. Neck kisses. Thigh pinches. Slight tugs on the hoops crawling up my earlobe. As I fell asleep last night, I wondered if he'd try to wake me up at all.

This morning, though, I'm up first. The scratches on my skin are evidence that a dream woke me up. Luckily, the marks are only light pink, as though my subconscious stopped me before I woke up with clawed arms I'd have to explain. It's been a few days since the last dream, but the text I got right before bed unsettled me. I can see the grey bubble floating in my mind: *I assume you're with Eddie?*

She had signed off with her name, and the sight of it stunned me. I didn't know why she'd assumed that, and it made me wonder what else she knows. Does she think we're *together* together? Has

Eddie told her anything about us? Could she know about the pregnancy, somehow?

I look over at him sleeping. It's difficult to imagine him knowing and talking to her about it before me. No. There's no way either of them knows. Guilt washes over me when I picture him reacting to it all. Even though he never would've objected to the abortion itself, I couldn't be sure how he would feel about it later. How he would handle it, how *we* would. I don't know how I'll feel about it all in twenty years. I don't know whether I even want children. But what if she was the only one I could've made? Would I ever regret not keeping her, terminating my lineage in a clinic flanked by a chain pizza restaurant and a wax bar?

When I got there, a nurse ushered me into a waiting room lacquered with posters about safe sex and birth control. We sat across from each other at a table with brochures fanned out across it. She walked me through the procedure, swiping through an infographic on the clinic's iPad, repeatedly tucking a too-short-to-tuck piece of grey hair behind her ear. When she was done explaining everything, she opened a chart with my information on the screen.

"Okay, born August 21," she said, her fingers spreading to enlarge the font on the screen. "So you're a Virgo."

I nodded, a little confused but relieved to have moved on from images of medieval-looking clamps and speculums.

"Listen, we offer counselling. Two sessions. One before and one after the abortion. It's a new program, but it's really worth doing. It's all free."

Before I could respond, she continued.

"Don't quote me on this to the doctor, but you Virgos lead with your head, okay? All logic. Sometimes, you just have to acknowledge that the heart is part of it, too. You might underestimate how you'll feel after, even if this decision is 100 percent right for you. Does that make sense?"

I told her it did, even though I wasn't sure, and then she had me fill out some paperwork, and we scheduled dates for all three appointments. I remember thinking how strange it all was, how I'd never expected that breaking a curse would be so administrative.

The dreams started when I got pregnant. Before I even knew that I was, I'd find myself trapped in la Ciudad Blanca almost every night, the walls collapsing on me as I tried to make my way out of the jungle. Every so often, my mami or my abuela would appear in my dreams, running beside me. Though I wondered whether they'd ever felt haunted in their own way, I figured neither of them had experienced nightmares like these. My theory about the dreams was that the spirits of the curse were punishing me for carrying the legacy at such a remove. I was an intruder—I always had been an intruder. In New York. In Toronto. In Pespire. I couldn't be sure if that was why I was being haunted. I'd never even been open to believing in the curse until I'd gotten pregnant. All I knew for sure was that I needed the abortion to rid me of the pregnancy I didn't want. Maybe it would break the curse, or maybe the sessions with a therapist would disprove the existence of the curse altogether. It was hard to tell which I wanted more.

In any case, I figured that talking about dreams would be standard analysis. That some Freudian reframing might put an end to the night terrors once I understood the psychological root behind them. It would be an easy couple of sessions for the therapist. According to the degrees up on her wall (one from the University of Ghana, the other from the University of Toronto), she'd been doing this for thirty years. I wouldn't be the first to ask her what my dreams meant.

In that initial session, we briefly touched on the abortion. I explained that I wasn't ready to be someone's mom, that I had plans that a child didn't factor into. There wasn't much more to it than that. She asked me how the pregnancy itself had affected me. I told her about how I'd retraced these recurring dreams and realized that they'd started a few days after Eddie and I had sex for the last time. The therapist had me describe the dreams. I told her how the walls would cave in as I ran through, allowing parasites to crawl out of the fractured stone. How I couldn't move in the rubble as they swarmed out, gnawed their way into my skin, crawling under the surface. How I cried. How my paralysis meant that I was forced to watch my skin break. Even if I survived, my skin would scar, and I'd be marked as an outsider for everyone to see.

"All right, so you're feeling like an intruder," she said, fiddling with her pen though never actually taking notes with it. "Like you intruded on motherhood maybe? Went in too soon?"

"Maybe I'm just gravitating to places I don't belong," I said. "Because that's what I'm used to."

The therapist shrugged.

"Sorry. Armchair psychology," I said.

She asked what I thought the parasites meant. I laughed and said the pregnancy. She gave me a meek smile and I swallowed hard.

"Maybe fear."

"Can you say more about that? What's the fear?"

I sighed. If I wanted her to disprove my theory, I'd have to lay it out first. So I told her everything about the curse. I hypothesized about whether my own pregnancy had been the result of hapless coincidence or an inherited curse. I wondered if the man who had gotten me pregnant might die regardless. She didn't respond to any of these thoughts, just listened.

I asked if she'd learned anything about curses in school. If a patient fretting over one might make her press a secret button under her desk to have them taken to a padded cell.

"In university, nothing. But I grew up in Accra. I've heard of curses cast to punish people. Strange dreams can signal to people that they've been targeted."

My body suddenly felt weak. It wasn't the answer I'd hoped for. It was the nauseating opposite; it felt like a confirmation of something that I'd prayed, *prayed*, had just been lore. I needed her to reject the idea of a curse that had the potential to take Eddie. If she'd said curses weren't real, maybe I could've just moved on and blamed everything on bad luck, like the doctor at the walk-in had suggested, not some fate I couldn't ever hide from or outrun.

"With that being said, I don't think it's helpful to focus on the uncontrollable aspects of our lives. I'd rather we spend the last few minutes thinking of ways to deal with the dreams and the ways that the abortion might impact you."

As the hour wrapped up, we talked about strategies, breathing techniques, sleep hygiene. None of it felt particularly helpful, but I nodded along, nervously twisting my hair into and out of a braid. Before she let me go, she explained the procedure to me again. My follow-up with her would be in a few days, and I'd have the option of extending the counselling for a reasonable price.

When I stood to leave, I felt like a fawn, wobbly and unsure of myself. Walking down the hall, my legs felt too long, and then too weak as they fell open on the table, heels clicked into stirrups. My muscles contracted as the doctor picked up a tube of gel, then relaxed when I realized it had been warmed for me. It felt like a small offering, a reminder of safety, of care.

The doctor asked if I wanted to see the screen, and I said yes. I wanted to see proof of this tiny yoke floating inside me. She pushed the monitor toward me. I wondered if I should ask for a grainy snapshot, a talisman to hold whenever I felt disconnected from my heritage. But I didn't. Instead, I just thanked the doctor and let her pull the screen away from me.

The procedure was a blur of faint pain and cold metal, the sound of crinkling paper underneath me as I shifted on the table, a tenderness in my belly the only newfound feeling.

While I lay in the recovery room, the therapist came by to hand me some pamphlets on IUDs and shots, and a flimsy notebook to write my dreams in. I stuffed them in my bag, figuring I'd toss them on my way out. I wondered why I'd tried to find a Western cure to the curse in the first place. What if the procedure hadn't worked? What if the curse hadn't been broken? When I got home, I lay in bed and drowsily FaceTimed the girls to stop from spiralling until I fell asleep.

In the morning, I realized I'd bled through my pad. The sheets were warm and sticky, and although the sight of the blood on my thighs made me feel a bit queasy, for the first time in a while, I didn't throw up. I wrapped up my bedding in a plastic bag to toss down the garbage chute so mami wouldn't see, and then scrubbed my skin in the shower. The water ran rust red, the air was metallic. Once I got out, the bleeding subsided, and some calm returned to my body. Perhaps there was no curse, I thought.

I didn't want to go back for the follow-up appointment, but Zadie and Maja tried to convince me to when we went to IKEA to replace my sheets.

"The first session is always weird," Zadie said, pocketing a tiny pencil from the dispenser. "But you're getting *free* therapy. Worst case, you waste one hour of your life and then come vent to us about it later."

I shrugged.

Maja suggested we stop at the café for meatballs. "I'll buy you some if you just say yes," she said, hooking her arm around my waist.

I couldn't help but laugh. "Fine," I said. "But meatball bribery is not good parenting."

"Well, that's the point. No one here is ready to be a parent," Maja said, then winked. "You just let yourself be bought for a seven-dollar snack."

As we ate our meatballs, Zadie sketched Maja and me on a napkin with her IKEA pencil. She wasn't a particularly good artist, but at least you could tell who was who, and she'd captured how happy I was with them in that moment. How much I laughed even as my belly cramped and my back ached. Once we were done eating, we snaked through all the different showrooms, talking about how we wanted to move in together one day, how we should decorate, what theme nights we'd host, and I thought of how unlikely it was that we'd found each other. Three daughters of immigrants, each brought to the same city by the bravery of our parents. It was thanks to a blend of luck and the most heart-wrenching misfortune that we got to call each other best friends. When I got home, I pinned the napkin above my bed like it was a crucifix.

In the second session, the therapist asked me what I wanted to talk about. I opted for the second-most clichéd therapy topic: childhood. I talked about being sent on a plane with an escort when I was a toddler. Living in New York, spending most of my days in strangers' apartments. Seeing Mami get hit. Moving to another country in the middle of the night. Finally ending up in Toronto, the place I'd lived in the longest, the place where Mami renounced men and got a good job, and even though things were good, I never felt like it was truly home. Even after we unpacked and Mami redid the kitchen and hung pictures on the wall and promised that we'd build our lives here, just the two of us.

The therapist stayed quiet for most of the hour, though she occasionally asked some follow-up questions. At the end of the session, she said she had to ask about the abortion again.

"How do you feel about it?"

"About the abortion itself? Fine. Really. I did what I had to do, and it worked."

"You seem pretty even-keeled about it," she said, scribbling something down for the first time in both sessions. "Why did you choose to do the therapy?"

For a second, I thought to tell her about the nurse who had basically signed me up before I could get a word out, or the girls, who'd talked me into continuing. But something else, another half truth, came out instead.

"I hear the therapy at my university sucks. Figured I'd take advantage and try this out."

She didn't say anything. Just looked at me dead on. I swallowed and glanced at the clock. Two minutes left. *Fine, fuck it.*

"I want to stop having those dreams," I said. I could feel my chest tightening, my lip spasming as I bit down on the inside of it. "I want to know that I wasn't punished for being with the person I'm in love with. And that he won't be, either." The words bubbled out in spurts, the only way I could get it out without breaking down completely. I'd never said that I loved him before. "I want to know that I'm not doomed to be hurt and alone like all the women before me because I'm an intruder everywhere and nothing is for me."

The therapist nodded. She didn't say anything for a while. We just sat there, listening to the quivering in my breath.

"Yessenia, I don't think this is the answer you're looking for, but you will always be in that no man's land. That's the case for people like you and me. You should know that by now," she said. "You won't find a home in a place, and you certainly won't find a home in a person."

I bowed my head.

"He won't ever get it. No one will ever get it all, not even your mother. But what you need to remember is that the only place you are *guaranteed* to never intrude on is you. You are your home. And look at how well you've protected it. You didn't want that pregnancy and you didn't let it stay any longer. You put your home first. That's not something that lost people do. You have direction right there inside." She let that sink in for a beat. "Don't worry about finding the right place or the right person. You know that quote? 'Wherever you go, there you are.' Make sure that's a good place for you."

I reached into my bag for the notebook she'd given me last time, the one I'd forgotten to toss. She handed me her pen. I wrote that last bit she said down.

"Thank you," I said. "Glad we got to that in the nick of time."

"Me, too," she said.

I put my things in my bag and got up to leave.

"Oh, and Yessenia," she said, as I swung open the door. "If the dreams don't go away, tell him the truth. I don't just mean about the abortion."

After that last session, I was focused on rebuilding my friendship with Eddie. We were pushing through the awkwardness of resisting muscle memory and attempting to relearn what it was like to be strictly platonic. We went to the library together to study. We watched movies. We smoked. We got coffee. Slowly, we remembered how to just be together as friends.

The dreams didn't stop altogether, but they lessened. Especially after I told Maja and Zadie about the curse. And the fact that I loved Eddie. I was honest with them, and they assured me that they believed it all. Beyond the risk to his life, the girls agreed that it would be best for me, too, to keep things platonic with Eddie.

"He's gonna go away next year anyway," Maja said. "And it's not like you'd go to New York. Probably not the best idea to attempt long-distance in third year, of all years." She wasn't wrong. I wouldn't risk the grades I'd need to apply to med school for a logistically challenging romance, especially since the fear of Eddie running hadn't fully gone away. I didn't want to risk losing his friendship forever, either.

I had the sense that if I told Eddie the truth, I could rid myself of the dreams altogether. But the thought of telling him was even more terrifying than the dreams themselves.

After my last meeting with the therapist, I got into the habit of repeating what she'd told me. Now I say it to myself before bed each night. That I would always be in no man's land. That trying to find a real home that felt like my own was a futile pursuit. It was comforting in a way, to have been given an answer I'd been search-ing for my whole life, but it also made me sad. I wondered if the fallen walls in my dreams meant that my history, my ties to my homeland were crumbling.

"Hey." Eddie's voice slices through my thoughts. I pull my knees into my chest and whip my head toward him. A sliver of sun has reached our bed, the likely culprit for waking him up, but still, I wonder for a moment if I accidentally said anything aloud. He rubs his eyes to adjust to the light, and for a moment, he looks like a little kid.

"Did you sleep okay?" I ask.

"Yeah," he says as he frowns, deepening the faint line that runs between his brows. "I mean, it was on and off. Little hungover now, I think. But . . . it's nice to wake up with you."

He sits up and stretches his arms out behind his back. A heaviness settles in my mouth, makes my tongue feel strange and weighty. I wonder whether that's a sign to tell him. Maybe the anxiety, all of it, would dissipate if I could just get the words out of my mouth. Maybe the truth could live here, contained in this strange room, airtight in a capsule we wouldn't have to take home with us.

Eddie sets his eyes on mine. For a moment, we just look at each other. I bet I seem so transparent, so obviously teetering on the edge of a grand declaration. But he doesn't wait for it. He breaks contact.

"I think I'm going to shower," he says.

I roll over, tucking that bout of vulnerability under the comforter even though my body already feels hot. As Eddie gets out of bed, my phone vibrates. I reach for it on the nightstand and open the screen. Another text from Rosy, asking to call now if possible. When I hear the shower run, I press down on her name. The ringing uproots my heart once more, moving it into my ears, the beating amplifying with each ring. I count them to distract myself. On the seventh ring, she picks up.

VIVIAN

AS MY BROTHER STANDS under the shower head, he thinks of Mivi, how waking up beside her has allowed him to breathe normally again. How knowing that she is on the other side of the wall makes him feel like this day can't be as bad as he'd feared. It's hard for him to distill the feeling, but in a way, he feels she came to his rescue a bit like how doctors slash a hole into patients' throats to keep them breathing.

I know that a part of Eddie wants to tell her that she should go home, that he'll fix things with his parents somehow. That he'll step up, right all the wrongs. The other part of him just wants to stay in the shower, or crawl back into bed, and not have to deal with the size of the day, this gargantuan thing. The cooling water signals that it's time to get out, to choose soon.

He turns off the valve and steps out of the shower, wraps a frayed towel around his shoulders and hugs himself the way he did as a kid after a bath. He can hear Mivi's voice through the door. He can't hear what she's saying, but it sounds to him like she's practising a speech. He tucks the towel around his hips and turns the doorknob.

"So," he blurts out, before the door's fully open, so focused on beating her to the chase that he misses the fumble Mivi makes with the phone. He doesn't want a death-day speech from her this early, so he quickly asks, "What do you want to do today?"

She looks up at him, her brow furrowed, as he walks toward her. She hadn't thought that she'd be the one making plans today. This was his day. My day.

Eddie sits down on the bed, and Mivi's eyes swing between his damp chest and the trail of drops that followed him from the bathroom. She's surprised by how unfazed my brother seems. It's like today is just another day. For now, she decides to match his energy, pretend that things are normal.

"Coffee? Let's start with coffee."

He says sure. Mivi grabs a dress from her bag and carries it into the bathroom to change, closing the door behind her. Eddie puts on his clothes at the foot of the bed. They both feel that this separation is ridiculous, Victorian almost, given that they've seen it all before. Still, they abide by the boundaries they've agreed to.

"I saw that there's this market," my brother says, loud enough for her to hear through the door. "Probably a thirty-minute walk. Seems pretty cool."

"Do you want to let your parents know your plans for today at all or . . ." Mivi's voice trails off.

"I'll let them have their day. Tomorrow will be another story."

As she walks out of the bathroom, she just looks at him. She doesn't even raise an eyebrow or say anything, but he responds anyway.

"I'm sure," he says, then looks down to tie his sneakers. "I'm not going."

My brother grabs his backpack and heads for the door as Mivi
shoots off a text, following behind him.

Mivi and Eddie walk through the city like it's a museum. Quiet and
alert, commenting on a building or a yard every so often.

Although Detroit has always seemed to be a part of his life,
Eddie has never seen it for himself. Mivi has only ever seen photos.
Not particularly compelling ones, either—mostly, they had been of
uninhabited land still coated in the dust of torn-down buildings and
homes. She saw enough destruction in her own country. From afar,
but still. Where Eddie found captivating stories, Mivi just pictured
what never could be. He saw art; she saw severed futures. As they
pass another crumbling block, she thinks that if anything bad happens to Eddie, that will be the world she walks through. One devoid
of life. Everything would look bleak without him.

Eddie, on the other hand, is fascinated by the decrepit, the after-
math, the remnants. Finding hope in destruction feels like salvation
to him. Through making his art, he wants to show what our mother
cannot seem to understand: that the past isn't a sentence. He doesn't
want to believe that the profound grief they feel extends to Detroit, as
if haunting the entire city. He wants to prove them wrong.

They walk through a residential neighbourhood before making
their way into Midtown. Restaurants aren't open yet, but they comment on a Mexican taqueria that looks good, and they consider
coming back later. Eddie slows before a gallery and peers in. Quickly,
he jots down the name on his phone. As he walks away, he fantasizes
about his own photographs being displayed there. Detroit through
his eyes. Portraits of Mivi, of course.

When they reach Corktown, they grab two iced coffees. Mivi
sips at hers nervously, wondering what she can say to change my

brother's mind, repeatedly checking her phone for the time as they walk down the main strip. It's lined with freshly painted facades and brimming with young people like them. I see something light up in my brother. Detroit is not what he'd imagined, but it's what he hoped to find. There's destruction, sure, but there's so much beauty in the rebirth. He thinks perhaps his film won't be about collective grief, but collective strength, instead.

After winding through the weekend shoppers and stands of glossy strawberries and sourdough loaves at the market, Mivi spots a coffee shop across the street. They head inside. Mivi orders them two poppy-seed bagels with cream cheese and a couple cortados. As they wait at the counter, they crane their necks up to the chalk-board menu.

"Eight dollars for a cappuccino," Mivi whispers.

American, Eddie mouths back.

Once their order is ready, they grab their drinks and paper bags and sit on the bench outside. They sip at their cortados, stopping only when a dog passes them. "Iver," my brother names a blue bull-dog. Mivi dubs a Pomeranian the size of a teacup "Stephen," making Eddie's smile widen when she specifies that it's with a *ph*. Within a few minutes, Mivi has polished off her bagel. My brother just picks at his food.

"You should eat," Mivi says. "Grieving people forget to some-times, but it's going to make you feel better. That's why you always bring casseroles to mourners."

"I'm not mourning," he says dryly.

"Doesn't mean you're not still grieving *something*— "

"I'm not— " Eddie starts to say. He clicks his tongue and utters a pissed-off sigh. He's already explained this to her. "My mom is the one grieving, okay? And no amount of food fixed her. *I'm* not. I'm just . . . trying to escape that for a while."

Mivi picks at her cuticles. She feels he's not being fair to her.

"I'm sorry," he says a few seconds later.

Mivi ignores him. After one too many beats of silence, Eddie stands up and says he wants to go back to the room. Mivi opens her mouth to object—she doesn't want him to regress, to go back to hiding in there—but she can tell by the way he announced he wants to go, not posing it as a question to her, that she's not going to be able to convince him right now. She gets up to follow him. It's only ten o'clock.

As they get back to the motel, Sue, the receptionist, looks up from a book of sudoku and asks if they'll be staying another night. Mivi looks at Eddie.

"Yes," he says.

Mivi lets out a huff. If she's not home by tomorrow morning, she'll have to tell her mother where she is. She has to keep trying before he decides to keep them captive all day in this vacuum of a room—where he can pretend that nothing is going on. There's only so much time left to turn this situation around. Mivi knows how much this day means to our mother.

As Eddie slides the key in the door, she grabs his hand to stop him from unlocking it, as though she has to warn him about something inside.

"Look, I know I have no real sense of what this day is really like for you . . ." A rush of sweat comes over her as the words roll off her tongue. "But . . ."

She pauses to gather her thoughts. He says nothing, braces for an ultimatum, or a threat, imagining what she might be about to say. *But*

I can't stay any longer. But it sounds like you're making it out to be a bigger deal than it is. But you need to grow up. Eddie looks at her as if to say, *Go ahead. Show me exactly how little you understand me.*

"I know what it's like to feel like an outsider. And I'm sorry that you feel that, too, with your own family."

His shoulders drop, and he pulls her into his chest. She is careful not to breathe him in too much. To linger on his smell or look up at any point, in case he takes her eye contact as a sign to kiss her. But he doesn't move. He just holds her. The key hangs in the door. Those were the last words he thought she'd say. My brother often expects the worst, but to be proven wrong by Mivi, yet again, feels like a gift.

ROSY

TWENTY YEARS AGO TODAY, I woke up in pain. You hadn't
cried out in the night to feed, and my breasts felt so full that *engorged*
doesn't feel like a strong-enough descriptor. I remember thinking
that no one had warned me that this portion of motherhood would
be more painful than childbirth. Then I went to pick you up.

You weren't exactly cold yet, because the room had been so
stuffy and you'd been tucked under a wool blanket. You even had
mitts on because you'd been scratching your cheeks the night before.
But it was when I slid my arms under your back to pick you up that
I realized how stiff you were.

I try to forget what happened next. How hard your body felt,
how I placed you back down right after I initially tried to pick you
up. How disgusted I was by my own instinct to be so scared.
Revolted by my reaction to your body.

Two decades later, I can still hear my voice on the call with the
911 operator, telling her my baby wasn't breathing. I can still see your
father covering your ears as a fire truck's siren rang out. I can still

feel the pull of your pallid face as I watched you being taken away.

I remember coming home in tears, going to our bedroom, and grabbing the breast pump because I could no longer handle the pain inside me, like razor blades were slashing me from within. It was the last thing I'd imagined doing, but I had no choice but to pump.

That morning was my first time using it. Your father helped set it up and held me once he got me hooked up to the machine. I wept as it let down my milk, my sobs drowning out the whirring of the suction that felt both like alleviation and the most painful thing I'd ever subjected my body to. It felt like the most unfair, cruel thing, having to pump for weeks after you died. Every day, your father poured the milk down the drain.

On the first night without you, after the police finished examining your cot and interviewing us, your father and I sobbed onto each other while lying on the couch. I remember telling him how much I regretted setting you down after I'd picked you up that morning. I hated that I hadn't held you in my arms, drank in the weight that you'd never surpass, studied the feeling of your edges, even though they were harder, more pronounced. I wished we'd had more time with you before they took you away at the hospital, wished I'd accepted that we wouldn't get any more. But I wasn't brave enough to hold on. It is still one of my biggest regrets.

No one would allow me to hold you again, even after the coroner's office filed the preliminary report four days later that suggested it was SIDS. We wouldn't have the final confirmation until the winter. Once they had gotten what they needed from you, they arranged for your body to be placed in a casket the size of a breadbox and transferred you to the funeral home.

The funeral director suggested it be a closed casket. You would've been blue and swollen, sliced down the middle. I didn't see you, but I remembered the autopsies done on my parents (whose car accident was then explained by my father's defective heart), how gruesome they'd been, how they'd left stitches running across their bodies when it was all over. Makeup could've helped make you look more peaceful, but we felt it was wrong to do that to you. To make up a baby, fill the little scratch lines of your own making with powder and blush so that you looked more doll-like, coat your blueness in goopy foundation. In any case, the home called and said that infant funerals generally did not show the body. It was too disturbing, they said, which we found strange to hear from a funeral director. He was right, though. I couldn't open the casket to hold you one last time.

I never saw your headstone in person, either. I've only ever seen it in a photograph I made your father take after the funeral. He'd picked it out. A little marble slab with a butterfly etched over the inscription.

VIVIAN MARGARET POWELL
AUGUST 14, 1998–AUGUST 20, 1998
Forever in our hearts.

After the church service, I sat in the car. I refused to get out, because I knew I'd barely be able to walk and see how small your plot was. I would've let out a horrible sound when they lowered you. I didn't want that. I wanted to keep my suffering apart from my love.

So I just sat there, waiting for it to end. All of it.

On our drive home, I wished we would crash. I wanted us to take the highway so that the speed would increase our chances of dying on impact like my parents had. I wasn't at the wheel, though. Realistically, I probably wouldn't have done it anyway. I never told your father about that. Only our priest, one night when he called to see how we were.

"I think it took guts not to," he said, and it made me feel so naked. "You'll see, one day. One day, you'll wake up and it won't feel as heavy. You'll be able to do things without thinking of her, and then, eventually, stop feeling guilty about it. God will never give you more than what you can handle."

He'd meant to be comforting, but those were the words that shook my faith. It had been tested by you, nearly lost, but it wasn't until I heard the emptiness in his words that I questioned whether I could ever find comfort in faith again. It was all hollow. This idea that I'd been given your death was an insult. The concept that I was expected to handle it, even more so. I didn't. I couldn't.

Instead, I stayed in that state of shock. I coddled it, fed it, adopted it. Excused it by the fact that I'd been so wronged so out of the blue. Your loss wasn't a gradual one. There was no reason for it. Not one that doctors can understand, not even now, really, twenty years later.

I went through the conversation with dozens of specialists. Ran through countless hypotheses. Had you overheated? Suffocated? Had it been my fault for not swaddling you properly? Had some damage occurred during birth? Was there something wrong with me? Most doctors told me to stop asking myself questions. That no amount of torture would lead to an answer. There was none. You died because you stopped living.

But I couldn't just accept a loss like that. And so I kept you like a stone in my belly. A foreign object that weighed everything down, that I could not properly expel. Each August, I failed to get you out. *This is who Vivian's mom is,* I'd think.

The stone felt particularly heavy last night. Eddie gone on the eve of when you'd gone, too. And while I was alone, while your father was out, something compelled me to pick up my phone. I texted them. First Mivi, then Isaura. For hours, neither of them answered, and regret started to set in like a hangover. I especially wished I hadn't sent the second message. As I tossed around, trying to fall asleep, I thought of how I could've phrased it less pathetically.

This might be a bit strange but I'm having some issues with Eddie. I'll spare you the long story but I could use another mom's advice.

If I couldn't unsend it, I wished I could at least edit it. Said hello first, asked how she'd been, not written so cryptically. I could've pretended to be more adept as a mother, as a potential friend. When I woke up, though, I saw that she'd answered. I clicked on the unread message before my nausea could worsen.

I'm so sorry to hear that, Rosy. They're getting to an age where it feels like you have to learn how to parent them in a new way. Or at least I think we have to. I don't know how much advice I can give, but I can definitely listen. Currently in Stockholm but back in Toronto on the 21st. Should we meet up for that coffee? Here for you in the meantime if you ever want to call.

Her words washed away the sick feeling in my chest, leaving something I hadn't felt in a long time: relief. Something close to hope. Listening as a substitute for advice. In that moment, I thought of my mother, her pale pink nails as she squeezed lemon juice into a bowl of milk when we were out of buttermilk, telling me, "It's fine, Rosy, it's fine, we have this." She was right.

I text Isaura back. We set a date to meet up, and I realize it's the first time I've done something like this in decades: initiate a plan with the intention of sharing. Of talking about Eddie, about you, with someone who has not been paid to listen, whom I haven't been forced to see, whom I won't be meeting with the intention of getting out of there as quickly as possible.

As I put my phone away, I imagine myself speaking your name at a café with Isaura. I wonder if she would understand the metaphor of you as a stone. How I won't ever be able to excise you completely. It's not as simple as cutting you out and stitching myself back together, I know that. But maybe it would help if I could pass the stone to her for a moment. I imagine your name on her tongue, maybe on Mivi's. Maybe in this way, we won't feel the need to carry you always. Maybe our whole family can feel a little lighter. Maybe I can move without feeling like doing so is an affront to your death. I have to trust that, just like your loss didn't make me any less your mother, I do not need to feel you in each movement to honour you.

As I lie in bed, I start to twist my extremities. My wrists and ankles crack. Fingers and toes writhe. I will start slowly, like this. One joint at a time. I pray that when I see your brother, he'll see even the slightest difference in me. A glimmer of light. A rebirth through the smallest of acts.

VIVIAN

AS THEY NEAR OUR OLD HOME, my parents carry out one of their annual rituals. They recount the milestones they've missed out on this year, guessing what I might've been like by now. The tradition helps to mitigate the anxiety that's been building about their homecoming. Neither of them knows what to expect when they see our old house, only that it's time to face whatever awaits them there before going to my grave tonight. Treating today like any other anniversary grounds them as they walk through a minefield of memories, their tired eyes tucked behind sunglasses.

As they pass by a sign for the old General Motors plant where he worked before starting his corporate climb, my father talks about how I'd be trying to figure out what I wanted to do with my life. That they don't have a clue what I would've liked or disliked. What would've really lit me up. They venture a few guesses—maybe I would've wanted to become an architect or a social worker. It makes my mother smile a bit to think of me, a tiny baby, being interested in either of those professions. When they walk by the old pub that they spent countless nights in, my mother sighs.

"She probably would take Eddie out for his first legal drink later this year," she says. The thought breaks my father's heart. He feels the pang he often feels when he looks at Eddie sitting alone on the couch or having a beer in the kitchen, his head bent to his phone. He wishes they could have given him siblings, even though Eddie never asked for any. As a child, he knew that he did not want his mother's attention to be split any more.

For a while, they don't speak, and the silence thickens with everything they're still afraid to say aloud. When it becomes unbearable, my mother slices through it. They are close to their home now, and she doesn't want to get there still holding things in.

"I know what you're thinking, Desmond."

Moments from yesterday appear in her mind like a slide show. She imagines what her husband saw that day. How she placed her hand on his knee to keep him seated after Eddie got up to leave the church. Her stillness after the service. Her crossed arms as he accused her of not caring for her son. Her red face as she spat that she was giving him what he needed, for once.

My father shakes his head. He doesn't want to fight on my anniversary, not again, not when this year is supposed to be different. She presses on.

"I know I act like all I am is Vivian's grieving mom. Some days, it feels like it's all I can be." She turns to him as she keeps walking. "I will always be sad on the day she died. And I will think about her every single day. But . . . I'm tired, Desmond." My mother wipes her tears, smearing remnants of the makeup she didn't take off last night. "I thought we could go see her and close that chapter in a way. I could open myself up to something new. Show Eddie that I was done. I wanted him to see me at the cemetery. See how strong I could be. See me change. Maybe he'd feel a little something, too, standing in front of his sister's headstone. Do you know how much I've thought of this? God, I had plans to take his hand when we walked away and tell him how much he means to me, how I want to make up for lost time. I know that most mothers don't make plans like that. They just do stuff like that all the time. But I haven't acted like most mothers for most of his life. And I want to take action—I can't just *think* it anymore."

My father pauses, looks down, rubs the scar on his thigh. It hurts in the heat of the summer sometimes and seems to worsen with stress. He shakes his head again when my mother pauses too, before she can fuss over whether he's okay. He assures her he's fine, then starts walking again to prove it. My mother follows, quiet only for a moment before continuing with her thoughts.

"I know how it all sounds. It's so embarrassingly . . . simplistic. I wanted to take Eddie to the gallery he told us about. He probably doesn't think I remember him suggesting it. But I figured that it would be a good place to just talk about him and only him for once. I could ask to see what he was filming, maybe see more of his photos. I know I haven't been focused on his plans. But I want to hear what he wants to do this year and next, if he goes to film school, ask him what he wants to learn there. I know it won't make up for everything, but it would show him that I care. That I'm trying to change."

My father removes his sunglasses, pinches his nose for a moment.

"Why now?" he asks. His voice is spiked with frustration. "Seriously, Rosy. Is it really the twenty years?"

She shakes her head, then inhales deeply.

"I ran into Mivi's mom last December at the grocery store. I'd only met her once, years ago, at their school. She'd told me how she was planning on going to visit her mom, who she hadn't seen in years, so when I saw her again, I asked her about her mom.

And she just split open in the middle of the aisle, talking about how her mom had died before she ever made it back to see her. It just dawned on me that that could be us. Eddie and me. I've already missed so much, but I could miss it *all*, time could run out for me, too."

"Rosy . . . Eddie isn't gone."

"He's not far off. I don't just mean now . . . here . . . But he's just so removed from us. From me, really. That's my doing. I never let myself feel like he wasn't already gone. And I know that I don't have infinite time to right my wrongs."

My parents' pace slows as they start to realize how close they are, only a block away from where I died.

"So you're telling me her story shifted something enough for you to want to change everything?"

"It wasn't just that."

My mother takes another sharp inhale before she can divulge Mivi's secret, how that day in the car yoked her to Isaura, how it drove everything. Then her body freezes at the sight of their past.

The picket fence is still there, wrapping around the lot. The red mailbox is now dented and dull. The swing set has been taken apart, its components piled on the lawn. But the house, the place I was loved in and where I died, is gone. In its place is a dirt-filled pit and yellow machinery.

My father brushes his fingers on the fence as though he has to touch it to make sure it's real. He can still picture the sage brick of their house that he and my mother painted together. He can almost smell the smoke that would drift over when Lorraine was sitting out in her yard.

"Of course," he says. "Of course it's gone."

"I can't believe it," my mother replies.

And yet they can. They don't double-check the map on their phone or even twist their heads to look at the neighbours' houses. Instead, they stand in front of what had once been theirs, hands pulled together. As my mother strokes his palm, my father admits that he's spent a lot of time imagining what it might look like all these years later.

"It was never like this, though, in my head. I always pictured it being vibrant. The porch full of kids' bikes. A van in the driveway."

"An alternate reality," my mother says.

He shrugs, then slumps down to sit and lean his back against the fence. "I suppose. Isn't that what we do? Escape into fantasies to feel better about real life for a while?"

My mother bends down to join him on the grass. As she settles against the chipping brown fence, she wonders how many coats of paint or stain have covered the white strokes she once made. Quickly, as though she has to get it out before she changes her mind, she goes back to what she'd been on the verge of confessing.

"That's what I did after that day with Isaura," she confesses. "She told me that Mivi was pregnant. I knew it had to be Eddie's. And I just couldn't stop thinking about what it would be like to have a second chance. One I was ready for."

My father's face drops. He asks how she could keep the news of a grandchild from him. Tears form in her eyes, and my mother cowers, making herself small as she plucks the dry blades of grass around her legs. She doesn't apologize yet.

"She didn't keep it, Desmond," she croaks. "And it sort of broke my heart on top of shattering the whole . . . fantasy. Not just because she wasn't going to have the baby, but because Eddie didn't tell us. But then I felt even worse when I realized that *of course* he wouldn't tell us."

My father lays his hand on my mother's to stop her from picking at the grass. He is so frustrated, it's all he can manage. He wants her to stop—the picking, the secrets, the deflecting.

"Desmond," she says, releasing a clump of grass from her fingers. "That's who he's with right now. He's with her. She came for him. I've been messaging with her."

"How come you didn't tell me all of this?" he asks, throwing his hands up.

"I wanted *Eddie* to tell us. I thought if we tried to get him to talk about how he was, what was going on in his life . . . on this trip, especially. I thought he might even try to relate with us. Two lost babies. I thought maybe Mivi's experience might enlighten him. Show him that it's not easy, even if you don't want the baby. Maybe he'd imagine how much harder it would be if—"

"You could've said something."

"You know that's not easy. Not with me and him. He'd get defensive if it came from me. Ask where I got the information. Probably warn me off the bat that it wasn't going to be some way of relating to Vivian."

"To *me*, you could've."

My mother admits that he's right. But this is the only thing she thought she shared with Eddie. They've never had secrets, inside jokes, code words. She wanted that for a moment. To know the most about her son. To feel the way most mothers do. She tells my father she's sorry, and when he doesn't answer her plea for forgiveness, she continues.

"Look, my plans for this trip kept shifting as everything else changed. But the one constant has been wanting to find a way to mend things with the child we still have with us before it's too late."

She takes a deep breath to steady her voice. The street is quiet, and each shaky word seems to fill it. My father reaches for her hand,

and she shifts so that they are facing each other, their knees grazing each other as they centre themselves. Suddenly, they are back at their church, warm under the stained-glass windows, making promises about moments like these.

"It's about being unafraid of my love for them." Her words come out slowly as she looks back at the space where our house once was. "Trusting that I don't have to hold on so tightly to Vivian to honour my love for her and her siblings. Trusting that my love for Eddie won't end in pain. And hopefully, getting him to trust me enough so that I can try again. So that he doesn't have to go on feeling so alone, either."

My mother sets her palm on his thigh, and as she presses down, he strokes her hand with his thumb. One, two, three times. It's all he can say right now.

MIVI

THE KEY IS STILL HANGING in the lock as Eddie and I stand outside our room. His hand has travelled from the small of my back up to my neck. I don't move. I'm holding still in an attempt to numb the feeling of his heartbeat in my ear. For a beat or two longer, I allow myself to indulge in it like it's a consolation prize. When I step back, I blurt out something about being hungry, even though we just ate breakfast. The bubble pops, and we are back in the hallway of a cigarette-smelling, faded-wallpapered motel off the side of the highway, the shininess of our moment fading into sweating palms and silence.

Eddie drops his hand from my neck and reaches back for the key in the door. We walk inside, and I head right to the mini fridge. I take out an apple, then reach toward a Gatorade bottle to round off my hangover meal. But before I grab it, Eddie reaches in to hook his fingers around a beer.

"Hair of the dog? Want to take them to the balcony?" he asks.

I look down at my watch. "It's just after ten," I say. I'm worried about not being sober enough to drive to the cemetery, and Eddie not being sober enough to meet his parents. Then again, there aren't that many beers and we still have a few hours. Maybe the alcohol will make him feel more sentimental, more open to seeing his family. "Sure. Why not."

I grab a bottle and take it out onto the balcony. Eddie follows, and we set up the plastic chairs side by side to face the parking lot. We both joke that it's quite the view. Vacant asphalt peppered with potholes, a steep ramp toward the highway like a mountain in the background. I raise my feet up to rest on the railing. The metal is shaded by the roof, and it feels cool.

I sink my teeth into the apple and grab the bottle opener that has been out on the patio overnight. Beer and fruit don't exactly pair well, but I'm too hot to care. I suspect the alcohol will quiet my internal clock, the one that keeps warning me that time is running out.

"I know I haven't made a decision yet," Eddie says with a sigh, looking out onto the parking lot. "But I just don't know what the right one is. If it's the one I have to make for them or for myself. I'm not sure they're the same."

A slight sinking feeling kicks in, and I raise the bottle to my lips. It's a bit early for beer, but the first taste of it seems to settle the tension in my stomach. I take another sip, and Eddie continues.

"I know this sounds awful, but I don't get how she hasn't been able to compartmentalize at least a little bit so that it doesn't just ooze out on everything, you know. For the longest time, she couldn't even say *Detroit* without breaking down. I know that they can't think of this city without being reminded of Vivian's death. But what happened could've happened anywhere, it wasn't about the city itself."

Sitting there, I think of my session with the therapist. How she didn't need to say much to get me to realize some big things, even if I hadn't really wanted to go there. So I continue sipping as he talks about how his father has an archive of their time in Detroit, photo albums and slide decks sitting in the basement. He says that over the years, his dad rarely brought them upstairs, but sometimes, he'd go through them down there with Eddie, the projector casting onto the blank wall of the laundry room. They'd spend hours together just talking about the mechanics of photography, lighting, lenses. How important it is to capture memories, how in the end, we photograph what we fear losing most.

"Do you think that you and your mom could ever have something like that?" I ask. "Anything that could make you two . . . connect a bit more? Not necessarily a hobby like with your dad, but maybe a shared experience?"

His gaze shifts as he looks at me, eyes sharpening, like he suspects I'm up to something.

"The only thing she's interested in trying to connect over is Vivian," he says. I shrug back. "Listen, Mi, I don't think that me holding her hand through one anniversary will suddenly bond us." Eddie stands up and grabs the door handle.

"I didn't say that, Ed."

"I know what you meant, though. Give me a minute." He steps inside, sliding the glass door shut behind him.

Fuck. I have to text her. It's not going to happen today.

I failed. I let myself believe that I could reunite a family whose dynamics I barely understand. I knew I shouldn't have, but I got invested. I wanted to try for Rosy. It was the least I could do for her.

When she figured out that I was here and texted me to ask if I could get Eddie to the cemetery, I didn't want to let her down. The truth is, I am still horribly afraid that the curse will take Eddie and leave her childless. This could've been their opportunity to fix something that has been broken for too long. To get closure before it's too late. Instead, they've strayed even farther. I don't know why I thought I could help them.

I'm no hero. I'm too selfish, too afraid for that. Half a curse hangs over my head because I can't stop myself from loving him, following him, constantly orbiting him like I'm his moon.

The tears I held back in the hallway start to build again. As I look out onto the parking lot, all blurry and vacant, I think of the girls. What they'd say if they knew what's happening, what kind of advice they would give me. What I can tell them when I see them at Zadie's without betraying Eddie's confidence. I wonder what he and I will do back home. What will his mother do? Will she hurt him again? Will she end up heartbroken? Would she blame me if something happened to Eddie before I could get him to her? I shut my eyes again, try to focus on keeping my tears restrained.

A few minutes later, I hear the sound of the door sliding open, and I jerk my head up to find Eddie standing in the doorway with a new beer and our pack of cigarettes in hand. I don't say a thing, just blink away the gloss that has built up and lean over to grab the opener on the ground. I toss it to him. Eddie opens the bottle and I hear that tiny hiss. He tilts the frothy neck toward me to clink it against my bottle.

"I'm sorry," he says, and it feels like I've been given one last chance.

After Eddie settles into his second bottle, he seems to want to talk again, but not about his mother. He turns the questions on me, asking me about work, and I can't help but indulge him. There's no use in pushing him farther away. So I tell Eddie about how some days I hate serving rich people, but can't afford not to. He asks about the clinic I hope to open one day, the kind of studies I want to do on women's kidneys, what I'd do with all the doctor money. I tell him I could help Mami, get my groceries at farmers' markets, always leave the change in the coffee shop's tip jar. I ask Eddie what's inspiring him lately, and he tells me about a new Scandinavian director who's blowing his mind. He tells me how much he wants to challenge people with his own work and have his audience see things like loss in a new light. We talk about what we want to do when we get back to Toronto before school starts up for me. (He says go dancing; I say get Korean barbecue.) We talk about how he'll fill his year off, how I'll have to sneak him into the university library so he can work on applications, and how he wants to film a short in the grocery store. We talk about him moving away next summer, about the long drives we'll take to visit each other, the beds we'll share, pretending a while longer that getaways like these are just the kind of thing good friends plan.

We play backstories as people enter or emerge from the motel. I point out an old man in short shorts and decide he's staying at the motel to escape a loveless marriage he entered into at twenty-one. He stuck around for decades because it was easier than leaving. He's road-tripping across the U.S. in pursuit of true love, but all he's finding are dingy rooms and a dwindling faith in the whole concept of love. When a couple holding a leash runs through the parking lot and then down an alleyway, we suspect they are going to meet an exotic animal dealer who will sell them a fully grown Arctic wolf.

We laugh at how terrible our stories are. But when a woman opens her trunk to pull out cleaning equipment, my focus shifts. Eddie begins a story about a maid-for-hire who specializes in crime scenes. While he details her origin story, my mind jumps to Mami.

I wish I could talk to her. Hear her voice telling me it's all going to be okay. I want to hear her say that the curse isn't real, that it didn't follow us from Pespire to New York to Toronto. That it won't follow me in Detroit, too.

As I think of her, it occurs to me that what Eddie said about Vivian earlier, how it could've happened anywhere, is true, and that perhaps it applies to me and Mami, too. That maybe it wasn't

New York after all; maybe it was just a bad time, a bad man. I want to talk to Mami about that. Ask her how she feels about it all now. We haven't brought up the city in ages, and for the first time, I see a piece of us in Eddie and Rosy. In the unspoken. I hope I'll have the strength to bring it up with Mami at home.

By the time we both reach our third beer, Eddie and I start talking about what our friends would think of us day drinking in Detroit, sharing a room with one bed. I can imagine the sarcastic, drawn-out *Suuuures* we'd get if we said that nothing happened.

I down the rest of my beer before harnessing the courage to ask him why he's never shared anything about Vivian with our friends. Even knowing what I know, I find it hard to understand why he can't tell even one other person.

He slides a cigarette out of the pack and lights it. "Sometimes, I feel like I don't tell people because it's not mine to share, right?" he says. "They've just made me feel like I could never be a part of it, in some weird way. Like the *real* family is Vivian, my mom, and my dad. I'm just the intruder who came along after."

"I get that," I say. I feel a wave of sadness come over me like a shiver. "I mean, I know how you feel about . . . intruding."

Eddie passes the cigarette. I take it between my fingers and study it for a second as though it has my next line written on it.

"There's this really small moment that I think about a lot," I say eventually. "My mom and I had just gotten to our apartment in Toronto, maybe a few months in. And we were having fruit in the afternoon. She'd sliced up some mangoes, and on hers, she was pouring salt. It's a thing in Honduras. In a lot of warm countries, probably, to retain water. And for some reason, up until then, I'd never asked for salt on my fruit before, but I did then." I shrug. I've never told this story before. I didn't think anyone would get it. "But she said no. Not in a mean way, but she just sort of brushed it off and said it was a bad habit and it wasn't very healthy, and it was really only helpful if you were in a warm climate. I remember feeling like I'd tried to connect with my culture, and my own mother had denied that connection. I know it sounds a bit crazy, but that was the moment I was sure I'd never feel like I'd fully belong anywhere. All because of a mango and some salt."

I pick up the apple I'd forgotten about. The flesh inside had turned a light shade of brown since my first bite. I bite it and return it to white.

"And here I am, enjoying an apple. The whitest, most boring fruit."

Eddie reaches out to set his hand on my knee.

"I'm sorry, Mivi," he says.

"I get some of it. I don't get it all, but I get some," I say.

He lets go of my leg and looks me in the eye, his gaze shifting into something serious. "Whether or not you feel like you belong, I promise you that any place you walk into is better for having you in it," he says. "I wouldn't lie to you."

I pull a smile to stop the quiver in my lip.

"You okay?" he asks.

"Mm-hmm," I manage to say before turning away from Eddie and setting my face in my hands like a child. "Just tired. Too much beer too early."

"Do you want to take a nap?"

I tell him I do. As I stand up, I can feel the beer. My body feels both heavy with carbonation and light with the kind of optimism only alcohol can instill. A nap will be good. We'll wake up fresh and try again. I'll help close this loop for Eddie's family, and then I'll leave. And maybe, just maybe, helping his family end their own haunting might end ours. Some form of karmic balancing act.

I lie down on the bed and shut my eyes. The springs squeal as he settles in beside me. Our shoulders touch. Neither of us moves.

As we lie beside each other, I focus on the sound of Eddie's breathing. I pray it will slow and morph into that slight snore he seems to only emit when he naps. I just want him to sleep so I can feel his skin and absorb him in a way I never get to anymore. I know what will happen if neither of us falls asleep. We'll slowly inch toward each other. I'll thumb the dew off his lip. He'll peel the hair off my neck. We'll look at each other and see how badly we both want the same thing, and then it'll just be unstoppable.

I take a shallow breath, and as I do, Eddie rolls over and rests his hand on my stomach. The weight of his palm sends another heat wave across my body. *It's happening*, I think. *It can't be. But maybe.* No.

I lift my lids a crack and watch as his hand rises and falls against my dress with each breath I take. The warmth of it makes me want to cry. I wish I could place his hand under my dress so that he's touching me, touching everything. But I can't. I am frozen. I shut my eyes in the hope that the darkness will recentre me.

Then I twist my body to the side slowly, his hand moving to my hip as I contort myself to face him. I move gently, tentatively, like I am feeling for a ledge. Soon, his breath is on my cheek. I nuzzle my face in closer.

And then the soft snore begins.

He is asleep.

My chest tightens at the thought of what I almost did. The trap I walked into, the one that Eddie's fatigue has miraculously saved me from. The weight of it makes me breathless. I roll over and face myself in the window's reflection. *You've come this far. Do not fuck this up now.* There are only a few hours left to fix things on her anniversary. I will set an alarm. I will close my eyes, sober up, pull myself together. I will do what I came here to do.

ISAURA

THE DAY BEFORE YOUR daughter's birthday, Rosy texts you. Asks for another mother's perspective. It's the first time anyone other than Yessenia has sought you for counsel. Even your daughter, you realize, hasn't done so in a while. You try not to feel the twist of the blade that sank in when she didn't tell you about the pregnancy.

When she was younger, she'd always defer to you. Her questions made you feel so important. They made you forget you never finished high school, that perhaps it didn't matter.

"Mami, what should you do if your tooth is wiggling but there's still a string attached to your mouth?" "Mami, what is the best way to get someone to like you?" "Mami, do you think I'm Canadian, American, or Honduran?" "Mami, what should I do if the girls are fighting but I don't want to pick a side?" "Mami, why are most songs about love?" "Mami, what would you say if I told you I wanted to study medicine? Is it too expensive? Can we do it?" "Mami, what should I wear tonight?" "Mami, can you quiz me on this later?"

"Mami, what kind of Spanish accent do I have?" "Mami, how do you know if it's worth risking a friendship for something more?"

That last one stumped you. It came a year after you had forbidden her to date. She hadn't forgotten, quickly following it up by saying the question was really for Maja, who was torn. You didn't believe her, naturally, but you advised her, nonetheless. You told her that love is always a risk, that her gut was the best compass. Yours ached as you told her that. You hoped her gut knew better than to risk three lives for puppy love.

As she got older, the questions changed. When she stopped crawling into your bed at night, you started going into hers, determined not to lose her to teenagehood. Determined, also, to keep her from straying too far. Some nights, she fought you—the questions turning into accusations: "Can't you just let me have a little privacy?" "Don't you get that I don't want to talk every second?" "That's TMI, Mami. Isn't there anyone else you can talk to?"

Whenever she snapped, you'd pull away, and the next morning, you'd find a note on the kitchen table that she'd scrawled before school: *Perdoname, mami. Te quiero mucho.* Always in Spanish, which she knew you loved, since she rarely spoke to you in your mother tongue after she started school. The nights after her blow-ups, she'd leave her door wide open like an invitation. You would tiptoe in, and she would regale you with stories. Schoolyard dramas that you ate up like candy, not because they were good pieces of gossip, but because she was confiding in you. Nothing could be sweeter.

When she started grade ten, you decided to join a book club. She was right, you needed other people to talk to. One of the women in your building, Louise, had invited you a couple years back, but you'd told her that whatever time you had in Toronto was precious; it was to be spent with your daughter.

Louise had smiled. "Feel free to come when she hits her real teen years and you want an escape."

You'd shrugged. She wasn't even a mother; how could she know. Somehow, she'd been right. Contrary to what you'd assumed, you weren't spared the growing pains. Louise didn't dole out any I-told-you-sos. She just texted you the name of the book and details of their next meeting.

You inhaled the book in two days, highlighting passages you liked, placing your daughter's sticky notes on pages that seemed important.

The first night you went to the book club, you brought a bottle of orange wine that Yessenia had helped you pick out because you weren't sure what to bring. You felt intimidated. Louise taught French literature at the University of Toronto. You didn't know much about the other women, only that her best friend, Xiomara, was a Guatemalan diplomat. According to Louise, you'd hit it off with her. If you'd told Mivi that, she probably would've retorted, *What, she's pairing you based off your geographic proximity? Skin tone?* You didn't care at that point. You needed friends, and you certainly weren't going to deny any before giving them a chance.

As it turned out, you did hit it off with Xiomara. And with Joni. And with a woman whose name you still weren't sure was LC or Elsie. And with the other women, too. They were happy to welcome a younger member—"a fresh perspective," Louise said. No one asked you the questions you wanted to avoid: *Where did you go to school? Why did you leave Honduras? What about your daughter's father, was he in the picture? Do you really want to be a flight attendant forever?*

Instead, they asked you what was the most exciting place you'd gone for work. Where you'd gotten the idea for orange wine. What you thought of the book. If you had any favourite authors.

Those were questions you could answer, questions you wanted to answer. They put you at ease.

Over wine and canapés, you unpacked the novel. The bubbles must've gone to your head, because an hour into the discussion, you found yourself challenging your host about her take on the protagonist.

"I like her," Xiomara said to Louise, raising her glass to you.

"Me, too," Louise said with a laugh. "And point taken."

You were invited back. You hosted. You started to feel seen as a woman with opinions, with ideas.

Book club was not, as your daughter would sometimes tease you when she counted the empty bottles in the morning, just an excuse to get drunk with other moms. It was a community for you to matter in.

"How old-school of you to assume that all women my age are mothers, mi vi."

"Fair. Although I'm pretty sure none of the women are your age, Mami. Didn't you guys just read a book about menopause a couple months ago?"

You had, and that night, you'd happily assumed the role of student. Some of the women teased you, thanked you for being a good sport as you quietly listened to them trade notes on hot flashes and libido crashes. You explained that you'd never learned any of this in school, that you were glad to be learning with them before going through it. You admitted that you weren't in school very long, that most of what you knew came from books you read after you left, and from the wisdom that came with age, of course—you winked, knowing you'd be met with jokes about how you were still a baby.

"En todo caso, don't you think it's good that I have some friends to get a bit drunk with? What would you do without your girls?"

Your daughter paused, her eyes searching the ceiling. "I don't know. I can't even imagine it."

"Aha, sin vergüenza," you said. "Go put the bottles on the sidewalk, and then I'll tell you all about last night."

You wonder if you'll ever be able to tell those women about what's happened this year. You wonder if it's wrong to not want to be seen as a mother first in their eyes. To protect this space that has become so special to you, one where you are not the anxious bearer of a curse, you are not penitent, you are not a victim, you are not trying to prove yourself as a "good mom." You have been that for more than half your life now. And maybe it's because your daughter is outgrowing the nest, and you are nearing your late thirties, which, according to your book club friends, is a time of redefinition.

As you hold your phone, you think about how things are different with Rosy than with your book club friends. You are connected to her by your children, by the fact that you are both mothers. Initially, by your feelings of failure as a mother. But here she is now, turning to you for help. With her, you think you might be able to share more of the darkness from your life. The growing pains that mothers experience, too. The shame and the moments you have to laugh at because they're so upsetting. Whether or not she believed it, she hadn't shied away when you told her about the curse. A new friendship could be a sacred space.

You tell Rosy that you're away but that you would love to talk in person, that you will be back soon. In time for your daughter's birthday, though you're still unsure about what you will gift her, where you will go. The questions you asked yourself yesterday rush back.

Will you keep running? Will you look back?

You don't want to jinx it; there's still some time for something to go wrong. You don't yet feel comfortable declaring the curse broken. But you suspect it has been. You aren't sure, still, if she aborted the pregnancy or if, by some breaking of the curse or pure luck, she miscarried. Or perhaps your daughter and your mami were right after all. Perhaps there never was a curse.

You wonder what Yessenia thinks of the curse now. But you won't ask; you will wait for her to share with you in her own time. You trust that eventually, one day, she will.

When you think hard about it, you suspect that despite her age, she knows what she's doing. What she wants. How to get it. She is resourceful. She is the progeny of your mami and your abuela. Women who made mistakes but didn't dwell on them. They are the pillars that have made Yessenia the strongest out of all of you.

That's when it comes to you: you will give her the choice. It will be up to her to decide where the two of you will go. The prospect of her picking your home terrifies you, and yet you know that running from it doesn't feel that much safer. The fear is clanging in your brain, but your gut is settled. You know it's the only thing you can give her now.

You trust that she will make the right decision for her. That will be the gift you give to your daughter.

VIVIAN

IT'S ALMOST SIX P.M. Mivi and Eddie have been in bed for nearly three hours. The day drinking put them out initially, but they've continued their nap, even after the alarm went off, to stay side by side in the bed just a little while longer. They haven't said a word, but their legs are stuck together and their pinkies intertwined. They both know that things will change when they get up. They'll have to talk. A decision will have to be made.

They can't know what will happen once they get back to Toronto, but it will be different. The secrecy could bond them or curdle into something toxic. Eddie might retreat back into himself like he did last summer. Mivi might not get him back a second time.

When my brother wiggles his fingers to clasp all five around hers, she rolls over, unhooking them altogether. Her eyes open wide, then set on the bottle of Advil on the nightstand. As she rattles out a couple tablets, Eddie sits up against the headboard.

"I think I need one of those," he says, before coughing out the sleep in his throat.

She exhales out of her nose with a bit of dramatic flair to show that she's somewhat amused at their situation, not mad at him. Then she pinches two tablets out and drops them in my brother's palm. Her eyes are puffy from sleep, and she shuts them briefly as she swallows the rust-coloured pills.

"I don't know why I thought drinking would cure the hangover," she says, her head lolled back against the headboard. "It's only prolonging it."

"I think I could use a cup of coffee," Eddie says. "Want to go grab one around the corner? Come back here? Recover a bit."

"Look, Eddie . . ." Mivi drops her hands to her lap. She squeezes her shoulders together and lets out a groan. "I need to shower. Rinse the smell of beer and . . . *boy* out of my hair."

"I just . . ." He scratches at his curls. "I can't think about much right now. I'm all fuzzy."

"I know," she exhales, in a way that says, *You're not wrong.* "But it's getting late. And I didn't come all the way here to just lie in bed with you and not do anything. I came here because I thought you needed me to help with your family. I thought I'd be your buffer at the cemetery or—"

Mivi's phone buzzes. She reaches for it on the nightstand and unlocks it. For a moment, the defensiveness mounting inside my brother keeps him quiet. She doesn't say anything as she reads my mother's latest message: *We'll stay an hour after we get there. Just in case.*

"Is that really why you came?" he shoots back.

"Eddie," she says, setting the phone back down casually as though the message had nothing to do with him, "you're not going to get this day back. There are no do-overs. Just regrets."

Before he can tell her that she hasn't answered the question, Mivi heads to the bathroom and closes the door. She knows that the feverishness she's feeling stems from everything that she and my brother aren't saying. Anxiety is rising through her like heat. She twists the handle and steps into the cold shower, hoping to steady herself. As the water pummels down on her, she breathes through the discomfort until it feels like she's no longer fighting it; she's given in. She's accepted it. Then she steps out and faces herself in the mirror.

Just tell the truth, she mouths to her reflection, her lips trembling.

Through the door, she can hear Eddie saying something, too, though the bathroom fan muffles the sound, and she can't tell whether he's on the phone or speaking to her. Before she can find out, the door to the room slams. Mivi's stomach drops. *He wouldn't just leave*, she thinks. But he's done it before. He's left his parents and he's left her. *Fuck*, she thinks. *What the fuck do I do now?*

She wraps a towel around herself and steps out of the bathroom. The first thing she notices is that his backpack and camera are gone. The dresser is bare, without a trace of him being there. With no proof of my brother in the room, she is sure he has run away again. Done what he said he wouldn't and left her to feel like she'd imagined things.

Her damp toes sinking into the carpet, she strides toward the nightstand and reaches for her phone. She opens her favourites and clicks on the first contact: *Mami*. Immediately, the call goes to voicemail. Her mother is working. She can't help her.

Maybe it's a sign, Mivi thinks. That she shouldn't tell her mother where she is and why. The real why. She can hear her abuela telling her what she already knows: *This is what happens when you let men get what they want. You'll be left alone to pick up the pieces.*

Once again, she's been abandoned by the person she loves, with no explanation.

Panic surges through Mivi, and she needs distraction. She hopes a cigarette will do the trick. She throws her phone on the bed and pulls out a dress she'd stuffed in her duffle bag, tugs it on as the fabric sticks uncomfortably to her skin. It won't matter when she slides a cigarette out of the pack and puts the filter to her lips.

Out on the balcony, Mivi momentarily blocks out all her thoughts. Her sole focus is taking the smoke into her lungs and watching the cigarette disappear as it burns away. She is almost proud that she can self-soothe so easily. As Mivi's eyes follow the tail lights going up the highway entry ramp in the distance, she decides she will take that same route after her smoke. No use in putting it off any longer. She won't be passive this time.

She'll go get her phone again and call my mother. She'll tell her she tried, but that Eddie left her, too. Then she'll pack up her things and maybe keep a bottle cap as a memento of these last two days. She'll leave and it'll be like last August with Eddie, only this time she won't allow a rekindling. They'll just burn out.

With her cigarette still in hand, she steps inside to get her phone. On the home screen, another text has appeared. This one is from her mother. Before she can open it, ash falls onto the comforter, burning a hole in one of the roses. Mivi pats it down, then returns to the balcony. She slides open Isaura's message.

Hola mi vi. Can't call back right now but I wanted to write you a little something since I was thinking of you when you called. This time nineteen years ago I was going into labour with you and somehow, I blinked and you became a fully formed adult. When you were born, I wanted to protect you from every bad thing that could happen on your way to becoming a woman. But what I've realized is that mi hija was born strong enough to meet each challenge. You have proven yourself so capable of doing hard things. You have inspired your mami more than you'll ever know.

Then a second text:

Start thinking about where you'd like to go for your birthday. It's up to you and only you. Happy early birthday, mi vi. Te quiero.

Mivi's throat tightens as she reads and rereads the messages. They make her feel like her mother knows, like she can see her, like telepathy might be possible after all. She types out the only response she can manage—an *I love you*—and sends it off. Until that moment, Mivi had forgotten that her birthday is just a sleep away. Isaura's message reframed it, in a way, appeased some of the dread she's had about the milestone, the disappointment in how she's fared this past year, these past few days. Maybe she shouldn't spend her adulthood pretending that this year never happened, that it hasn't made her who she is. Maybe.

Mivi puts her phone on the chair and leans over the railing to take a final puff before getting on the road. And then, as she looks out, she sees him. My brother, walking across the parking lot with two cups of coffee. Coming back.

He didn't leave, Mivi thinks. *He didn't leave me.*

Mivi does her best to pretend that she knew he was only stepping out for those coffees he'd mentioned earlier, realizing that's what he must've said when she heard his muffled voice through the bathroom door.

"I managed to get a shot of that building across the street with the sun backlighting it," he says, lifting the camera strap from his neck after he hands the coffees to Mivi. She takes them and leans against the frame of the balcony door. He places the camera on the dresser and takes off his backpack. Mivi's body feels weakened from the roller coaster she set herself on. *He's back*, she tells herself. *Calm down.*

Eddie grabs one of the paper cups and slides to the floor against the wall. He zips open his backpack and places a couple packs of candy in front of him. Mivi sinks down to rest her back on the foot of the bed, just across from my brother, her wet hair slowly dripping onto the carpet.

Once they've drunk their coffee, Mivi asks him, once again, what he wants to do. It's almost seven. They have an hour before our parents will be at the cemetery. My mother wanted to go for sunset. He has to make a choice: go to the cemetery or go home to Toronto.

"Mi . . . I don't know," he says, picking at the lip of his cup.

"I think that you just don't want to make the decision."

He shakes his head. "If I don't go to the cemetery, she won't understand why I didn't go. She'll never get over it. If I do, she'll find a way to say I tarnished it somehow by leaving earlier, creating all this drama just to show up in the end. It'll be more confirmation, that I was the one she shouldn't have had, the one she regrets."

Mivi can feel herself breaking. Eddie's comments about our mother eat away at her restraint. "You can't know what it's like for them," she says, interrupting my brother.

"Mi, I've seen it all. I've seen exactly what it's like for the past two decades."

"People do the best they can."

"Look, I know what you're saying, but she didn't fucking try. She could have at least pretended that she didn't love her dead daughter *that* much more than me."

"Eddie."

"You know, she's actually said that I was an accident."

"I was, too. It happens."

"That's not the same and you know it," Eddie says in a calm voice. The evenness of his tone is more unsettling to Mivi than if he'd yelled. "She tried to kill herself when she was pregnant with me. You heard her say it. I see the scars all the time. That's how much she didn't want me, okay?"

Mivi can feel the blood rushing to her head. She is overwhelmed by all that she wants to say and do. The real reason she's fighting for my mother so much, the love she has for him, how sorry she is that he really believes that his mother hates him. She wants to hug him and shake him at once. She wants to be honest.

"I don't need you to be like . . . another parent, trying to convince me that everyone just handles things in their own way, and that's all we can ask of people . . . They're just platitudes."

"You called me here, Eddie."

"Not for this."

Mivi inhales sharply. Here we go, she thinks.

"For what then? To try to fuck? Or just to get cool motel footage of me for your movie? When I help my friends out, I don't just sit there quietly and listen to them lick their wounds over and over."

"That's not fair," he says, the volume of his voice building. "You don't even know. You don't know everything that she's done or the ways she's neglected me. But also, why are you so . . . You say I don't know what it's like, like somehow you do? We don't come from the same kind of family. You're all your mother had. You literally are her whole life—it's your fucking name! It's what she calls you every single day! I was just born into this impossible void. You can't get that."

"Eddie." Mivi can feel herself teetering. She can't tell if she's about to faint or yell. It's all bubbling up. She feels like she's back at her first day of school in New York, when no one talked to her because she barely spoke English. How they'd made fun of her accent, her name. She feels the way she did years later, when she called her abuela to vent about her classmates making fun of la Ciudad Blanca, and she'd said, gently, "Well, I can see why they wouldn't believe it, coming from a gringa."

She is excluded again, and it's even more painful because this time, she thought she was a part of it. She really thought she was on the inside. Now she looks at Eddie like something else she'll never fully be able to know, no matter how badly she tries.

"I called you because I just needed someone to be with. Maybe to just *listen* to me instead of telling me why I'm wrong to feel the way I'm feeling."

"Eddie, stop. Please. I wasn't—"

"I'll stop when you stop trying to explain everything away."

"I had an abortion, okay!" Mivi yells out. Her arms shake.

My brother's face crumples as he tries to piece it all together. The when, the who. Why she's kept it to herself and for how long. Mivi's face is stony, fixed that way by the bite she's sunk into her tongue. Eddie's frown lines deepen. He plants his eyes on hers, his vision blurry with shock. She can read his question in his gaze. *Was it mine?* She nods.

"Look, I know it's not the same as your mom losing her baby. It's different in a million ways. I know I don't want a kid now, and still, it's overwhelming to think of how different life would be if I did. Maybe one day it won't be, maybe I won't wonder what if. But right now, I sometimes do."

What if? blooms in Mivi's mind again. It's not the picture of a child, but the prospect of continuing a lineage whose women she loved so much. As Eddie stares at her, Mivi bites down again, harder, though now on the inside of her cheek.

"I may not know what your mom and your family have gone through, but I know that wanting your mom to just forget and move on is not logical. It's not possible. I didn't want a baby, and I'm still probably going to think about it every year. I mean, I don't know for sure, but I imagine I will. And your mom, she actually had the baby. She *wanted* her and she got her, and then she was taken away."

"I'm sorry, Mi," he says.

They look at each other briefly—holding eye contact feels like a threshold of intimacy they can't quite bear to cross just yet. Instead, Mivi reaches for the Sour Straws Eddie bought. The crinkling of the plastic helps to fill the silence. Mivi bites into the piece of candy. My brother smiles weakly, his eyes fixed on the lips he loves so much, the lines that smooth out on Mivi's face as the sourness turns sweet.

"Does it make you sad?" Eddie asks eventually. "When you think about it?"

"No. I mean, sometimes it makes me feel . . . I don't know. I was relieved when the due date passed, but it was strange. I don't know how I'll feel next year."

"When . . ."

"August 7." She looks at her feet as she says it, aware that the date has just passed, and also that August is difficult enough for him.

Eddie picks up a Sour Straw. He studies it between his fingers before taking a bite.

"I mean, I just calculated it online, based off, you know, that night. Might not be accurate."

"Right," my brother says. He can't help but think of me as the date imprints itself in his mind. "Either way, August is kinda the worst for birthday parties and stuff when you're a kid. Everyone's away."

Mivi lets out a smile at Eddie worrying about their child having a bad birthday party. They sit in the stillness of imagining for a while.

"Do you know what . . . kind of kid?"

The way Eddie stumbles over it makes Mivi laugh. A real laugh that releases some of the tears that had been pooling.

"A green one. Four legs. Very unusual kind of kid. Probably would've been born with the ability to walk right out of the hospital."

"Mi."

"I'm sorry," she says, wiping her eyes with the backs of her hands. "But no. No. I don't even think it was any *kind* yet. It was just a ball of cells."

"Okay," he says, the word washed in slight defeat.

"What?" she snaps back. "It was."

"I know, Mivi. I understand that. It's just, this is the first I'm hearing about it. That's all."

She inhales sharply, then looks down to see that her right hand has reached instinctively toward her belly. When she'd been pregnant, placing her palms over her stomach had been a comfort, even after she'd made her decision. What her body had been capable of scared her, and yet a sense of power emerged as she took control. Through her skin, she'd try to absorb the feeling of newfound safety. This time, though, she's not alone with the feeling.

"This is why I didn't want to tell you. It's not helpful. I've dealt with it. And now you . . . Now there's another dead baby to burden you with."

"I thought it was a ball of cells?"

"I thought *you* thought it was a baby."

"It could've been."

"Maybe."

"Maybe," he echoes, earnestly. He fiddles with the Sour Straw in his hand, pressing into the small ridges of the candy. When it feels like it's melting in his palm, he eats it.

"I respect your choice, Mi. Fully. And I would've been there to show you that."

"I just—"

"You don't have to wonder what if for that," he says. "I wouldn't have wanted you to worry about anyone other than yourself that day. From what it sounds like, you probably would've, so I'm glad you made the decision for you."

Although there's nothing to defend, Mivi can't help but try stringing something together. My brother has seen that face before, the furrowed brow, the slight shake of her head, the clenched jaw as she bites down on a tongue readying itself to speak but not yet. It's the one she made at school when she wanted to push back against an argument, the one she made when she carefully told Eddie that they should just be friends. It's what her face looks like when she doesn't want to say something but feels she has to.

"It would've been my whole life," she says finally.

"I know."

They're inching their hands toward each other, and it's all so obvious. Eddie grabs her hands, and their bodies relax as they touch. There are tiny sugar crystals between their palms, but they don't break to wipe them off.

"Did you . . ." Eddie steadies himself, then rubs the back of her hand with his thumb. "Did you ever think of keeping it?"

She sighs, loosens her grip on him. He squeezes harder, letting her know he's got her.

"No," she says, and it's the truth.

Eddie looks at her, tries not to let his face show his heartbreak. It's a pain he's metabolizing like another rejection, even if he knows it's not about him. He knows why she didn't tell him, and he can't blame her for wondering whether it would've made him run again. My brother also knows that Mivi isn't someone who *needs* him. Still, it's painful to not be wanted. His reaction might be different if he understood the full scope of the truth. She can't help but tiptoe around it, nervously thumbing at Eddie's hand as she tries to steady her breath.

"Look, I know this will sound crazy or superstitious to you, but getting pregnant was something I knew might happen, no matter what precautions I took. It happened to all the women in my family. That's why I had you wear a condom even though I was on the pill. But . . . it still happened. Defied the odds. And I couldn't keep it. I couldn't. I had to be the first to make it out of my teens without a baby."

She can't say any more, but it's enough. Eddie thinks she's talking about an unfortunate cycle, a generational pattern in her family, and she has no reason to correct him. He knows she made the right decision. And yet he can't help but wonder if this odds-defying thing had happened for a reason, one they were supposed to figure out together.

"I'm sorry I didn't tell you," she says.

Eddie thinks, *I would've done it with you. Maybe we could've done it right.* He doesn't say a thing, just shakes his head before scooting himself even closer to her. They look down at their hands.

"I think I want to go," he says, squeezing his finger tighter around hers. "To the cemetery. To see them. Maybe they're still there."

Mivi studies their clasped hands, apprehensive still. She knows he's going for her, at least in part, but she also heard a surrendering, an acceptance, when he said *them.* He, too, has to let go in order to move forward. My brother lifts his head, and so does she. They lock eyes. Mivi feels it then, the truth is all there, more evident than ever in those green pools. He is good. He is not like any of the men that the women in her family have loved before. He has never tried to hurt her. He has loved her. He loves her, still.

If the curse was real, then maybe this was how she'd broken it. The women in her family hadn't had choices, but they spent their lives making sure that Mivi would. Their sacrifices made way for different conditions, for a different outcome for their girl, who not only had options but faith in them. They gave her choice, and she chose what was right for her.

As she considers this, she allows her tears to roll out, full and sweeter this time. Mivi leans in and drops her head on his shoulder. He cups it gently, cradling her into him as they sit on the floor a moment longer, together.

The cemetery is a two-hour trek from my parents' hotel. They returned to their room for a much-needed rest after seeing what was left of our old home, then set out on their pilgrimage, each step dedicated to their children, all four of them. My parents talk about what it would've been like to have raised us here, to have Eddie be the baby of the family, not the only child. They reach their hands out to each other to hold them until the heat slithers between their palms and forces them back apart. Once they've dried off, they return to each other's grasp once again.

After the hypotheticals, memories of the past twenty years file in like a procession. The August of walks. The August of the burn. The August of drinking. The August in the hospital. The August of broken frames. The August of smashed dishes. Then this August—a slate ready to be inscribed upon, though my parents are still unsure with what. I know they wish Eddie was here with them, but they're calmed by the assurance that he's safe where he is, with Mivi. She hasn't texted again, but my mother still has hope.

My father returns to that first August. He does on every anniversary, of course, but as they walk toward my grave, he makes a confession he's never been able to verbalize to my mother. Now that they're back in Detroit, en route to the plot they buried me in, he's flooded with a feeling that's impossible to ignore, and now he has the words.

"I know that the hardest part for you is that we can't get her back," he says, his eyes focused on the sidewalk. "And of course, that eats me up, too. But I think what's worse for me is that two decades later, I still don't understand it."

My mother unclenches her hand from his. Gently, she wraps her arm around his waist.

"I don't understand what happened with Vivian. After she died, we never found out where she went. Every once in a while, I still think of that. I think okay, our Vivian had SIDS. We may never understand why, and we have to accept that. But where is she now? Where is she with her SIDS? Sometimes, I look and I look, but I don't know where she went."

With her arm around him, my mother guides him to the edge of the sidewalk, stands in front of him like she did at the altar. She bites her lip, and my father's heart begins to speed up. He tries to envision how they will make the rest of the trek if she collapses into a fit of tears. She takes a shallow breath.

"Thank you," she says, her voice quivering but calm. "For telling me. And for looking."

My mother rises on her toes to kiss my father. He closes his eyes as he inhales the smell of coconut shampoo in her hair. Once she lowers herself, she places her hand back in his palm and pulls him forward gently. They continue to walk, quietly, as they try to collect themselves.

After all that, my father is at a loss for words. It's the most honest he's been in a while. Sometimes, he holds back when he feels his grief and doesn't talk about it with her because he's afraid his pain will just give her more to fret about. But what he doesn't always realize is that his moments of weakness make her feel needed, like a wife, like a mother. It gives her purpose to feel like she might be able to care for him. It's what happened when he got sick, and when their first baby died. When he broke down, she knew she had no choice but to carry them both. My mother may not be the one to predict a looming burnout, to step in right before it's too late, but she will do right by him when he needs her. She will carry what he cannot. And so, when she sees my father in pain, when she sees him heartbroken over me, she is brought back to the image of him holding me on the couch, that feeling of wanting to protect her family. She could not protect me. But she can protect him. She will.

When my parents finally arrive at the cemetery, it takes them a while to find my plot. They wind through the path, breathing in the air filtered by the poplars. It's fresh here. It is a beautiful place to be buried, they both admit. The sun has turned orange and dropped low. They follow it as they look out for me.

The cemetery is big, and the decades away have atrophied my father's memory of it. He shakes his head each time they recalibrate their path, but my mother remains calm. She even pulls him to a bench to rest for a moment. There is no rush anymore. They're so close. They rehydrate from the water bottle my mother accidentally packed—it's my brother's and looks the same as hers. The metal has retained a slight spice from the rum Eddie poured into it a few days earlier, and it makes them both cough and laugh. Later, they'll say it's what helped them find me. A secret potion of sorts.

The overgrowth around my grave almost makes them miss it. But it's the butterfly that catches my mother's eye. The one she'd never seen in person, etched in the marble. Above it is the hint of my name, the letters blanketed in grass and weeds.

"There," she says, pointing to a patch on the lawn. They walk over to my grave.

My father bends down to clear the headstone. He digs his fingers into the overgrowth, ripping through the layers that have spread over the past twenty years, blowing on the dirt that settled into my name. He is winded by the effort. My mother kneels beside him. She pulls his hands away and encloses them in hers. Bits of dirt and white clover pass between them.

"I don't know where she is, either, Desmond," she says. "She's not here."

My mother takes her husband into her arms.

I thought I could only let go when my mother did. But as I look down at my parents, I see strength. Enough to share with my brother. Enough to refuel my mother, at least for today. That's all that I need to see. The promise of one day, one step, before I let go.

Behind the row of poplar trees, I can see Eddie and Mivi stepping out of her car in the parking lot. He takes her hand, and she holds on tight as he reaches for his phone to call our mother. I can see her face as my brother's name appears on her screen. It goes from surprise to relief as he tells her where he is, that he is looking for her.

I can see them walking toward each other without quite knowing it as they try, almost laughably, to describe their surroundings—trees, headstones—so that they can reunite.

I can see my parents' bodies soften when, finally, Eddie and Mivi appear in the distance like a mirage. I can see my family moving toward each other as though they are magnets.

But I can also close my eyes.

I can rest.

They will be all right.

ROSY

THAT LAST DAY IN DETROIT, I took your brother to the sculpture gallery. We spent the afternoon walking around quietly, looking at art together. I asked him questions. What he thought of a certain piece, whether he liked it. Mostly, he answered in one-word whispers. It wasn't until we were faced with a bassinet rendered in scrap metal that he said much more. Not in words, but with the simple squeeze of my hand. It was more affection from him than I could ever have expected. Afterward, we called your father, and he met us at the brewery around the corner. When the server asked Eddie for a piece of ID and he got away with using his fake one, we bit down on our laughter until the server was out of earshot. It was the first time we'd laughed together in a long time. Neither your father nor I could be upset with him for having a fake ID after that.

I stuck to sparkling water, but they got flights of IPAs. First, we talked about the different flavours and which they preferred. By the third flight, Eddie told us a bit more about Mivi. She had left after the cemetery, driven back so she could wake up at home on her birthday, welcome her mami back in the morning. We talked about her for a while, promised we'd make sure he got back in time to celebrate with her that night.

That fall, the idea of moving to Detroit started percolating. One afternoon at home, I overheard Eddie talking to Mivi about it, and later watched them scroll through websites of potential colleges together. I think we were all surprised that he'd want anything to do with Detroit. But the more he talked about the schools and the programs and the art scene, the clearer it became that he'd given it serious thought. "It's not New York, but maybe that's a good thing," he said.

It has been almost three years since then. Eddie is twenty-one now. He's in film school in Detroit, working on the short he started on our trip. It was difficult for us to watch him choose a city that we'd broken apart in, but ultimately, it made sense. Another loop closed with a new beginning.

We couldn't make it down before the land border closed, but Mivi went a few times. Sometimes I swipe through her posts, the snapshots of their weekends in "the city of love." The first time I saw her refer to Detroit as that my stomach dropped, but I've since softened to the term, their inside joke. Now I look at her photos whenever I wish I could drive down and bring Eddie home. When I see the community he is building, the memories they are creating in Detroit, I am reminded of the tenderness that exists there, too. I hope he gets to create more with Mivi before she starts med school in the fall.

Over the past few years, I have become good friends with Isaura. Before we had to deal with lockdowns, we tried to see each other at least every other week. Dinner, coffee, sometimes just a walk. Eddie was tentative about it at the outset. He and Mivi were taking it slow at the beginning. To him, having their mothers bond was a bit much.

"But she's fun, and I'm a lot more fun with her," I told him. "I promise I won't call her my in-law or anything. Just let me be her friend."

Eddie acquiesced. Isaura is good for me, and I think your brother knew that. She gets me out, shucks me open. I'd like to think that I'm not bad for Isaura, either. I give her good financial advice and act a bit like an older sister, the person whose mistakes you try to learn from. Even though we haven't been able to see each other as often during the last year, we chat nearly every day. Our phone calls make me feel like a teen again—for the first time in forever, I find myself talking for hours, laughing into the night.

Although our family is trying to be more open with one another, I still have not brought up the pregnancy with your brother. The timing has never felt quite right. I'm waiting for Eddie to deem me trustworthy enough. Isaura is waiting, too, though I'm sure Mivi has her own reasons. Neither of us cares to rush them. And so we, the mothers, have made it our secret, too, something to only bring up when we are sure our children will not overhear.

It's just as well that Mivi and Eddie don't know that we know. They don't read any of our shared glances as pained. They still get to feel like they have something to themselves.

I don't know how much Mivi and Eddie talk about it. Perhaps not a lot. Not because they can't, but because they are looking to the future. They're in their early twenties, pursuing dreams that they each want so badly. Sometimes, I look at them, see the passion seeping out of their pores, and wonder what will happen. What tragedies will test them, whether their paths will diverge or merge into one.

But I try not to burden myself with worries like that. Things I have no control over. I've taken baby steps in that area. In others,

I've taken some bigger ones. I have confided in Isaura. We have bonded over our afterpains. Swapped war stories of motherhood. The tales of you and your siblings. The tragedy of Isaura leaving her baby before she was even weaned, the guilt that settled in her bones and still aches every time she boards a flight.

Before we had our babies, we thought that the toughest part of it all would be giving birth. We had no idea that our recovery would be a lifelong project, and that the physical tests would be far less taxing than the rest. Even now, we are discovering new pain points and learning how to soothe them.

It's strange to think that people say it's not the natural order for parents to mourn their children, when the mothers I know best are connected by just that. We think of our lost babies, the ones we missed years with, the ones who grew out of childhood, and the ones who didn't grow at all, and we think of each other. It's the struggle that tethers us. It's the tightrope that we walk along, that reminds us that motherhood is not just a solitary role; it requires bravery, trust. And when you slip, I've come to realize, the best thing to do is reach out for a hand. It will not make the pain or the fear disappear, but it will wrap itself around your head and press you into its chest and say, *Shh, I know, I know, I know.*

ACKNOWLEDGMENTS

I AM INDEBTED TO MY incredible agents Amanda Orozco and Samantha Haywood for championing my first baby and to Random House Canada publisher, Sue Kuruvilla, and the team at RHC for loving it as their own. I could not have asked for a better editor than Sarah Jackson, who shared my passion for these families from the beginning and worked tirelessly to help me tell their story in the truest way. She made me realize that the adage is true: to write is human, but to edit is divine.

This novel would not have been possible without my family's trust. I am deeply grateful to my tía Yocelyn, who opened her soul to me when she knew I wanted to write about motherhood and remittance, and to my abuela, my mami Nolvia, who encouraged me to write. Thanks to her, I got the strongest mother in the world, to whom I owe most of the best things in my life. The others I owe to my papa, who, among other things, instilled in me a love of reading and the confidence to follow my own path. I miss him, and I am so glad that he got to read this story before he left us.

Thank you to the teachers who believed in me—Sofia Mostaghimi and Carolyn Smart, who encouraged me even after I'd left their classrooms, and my mentor, Camilla Gibb, who helped me shape the first draft of this novel during my master's, meeting me outside on her porch with blankets and hot coffee so we could workshop it in person during the first winter of the pandemic. Thank you also to Richard Greene and my wonderful, challenging, cohort for your invaluable feedback.

Completing a book requires both time and money, and I am grateful to have received financial support from the Social Sciences and Humanities Research Council as well as the Toronto Arts Council to pursue this novel pre- and post-graduation.

I cannot begin to thank all the friends and family who have supported every single one of my many (many) projects—please know how much your love and encouragement have fuelled me. Thank you especially to my soulmates, Gab and Irena, for being lighthouses even when we're oceans apart. Thank you to my brother, Michael, who always gifts me with comic relief when I need it most. I am so grateful that neither of us are "lonely" children.

Finally, to my Marcus, whose faith in me, in this book, never once wavered—thank you, I love you.

ANNA JULIA STAINSBY is a Honduran-Canadian writer from Toronto. *The Afterpains* is her first novel.